DARK TOMORROW

BO BLACKMAN
BOOK SIX

HELEN HARPER

DARK TOMORROW

By Helen Harper

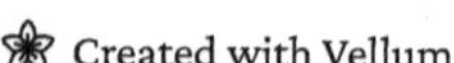 Created with Vellum

CHAPTER I
SMOKING RUINS

The smart thing to do would be to hightail it out of London before the Kakos daemons decide to finish what they started. As I slink from one shadowy street corner to another, I know I'm not the only person who's keeping their head down. The city is in virtual lockdown and everyone, humans and tribers included, is running scared. I imagine that the only ones who are sitting with their feet up and looking happy are the daemons themselves. The others, even those who hated the vampire Families with a passion, are terrified about what's coming next.

Television screens all over the country are running an endless loop of the screaming bloodguzzlers and piles of rubble left smoking at each Family's stronghold. Drops of rain from the overcast grey sky plop heavily onto a discarded copy of *The Metro* near my feet. Out of the corner of my eye I catch the word 'genocide' and hastily look away. I'm having a hard enough time keeping my angry darkness damped down as it is. I don't need all these constant reminders.

Of course, not all of us are dead. Bombs are indiscriminate. While the majority of the vampires were taken out in one fell swoop, some have been pulled out from the mess. Some were not even present, busy attending to other pressing matters which even Medici's now-vanquished threat couldn't supersede. But those lucky survivors are on their way out; they've been granted asylum by friendly factions in the States and in Europe, and they're in a rush to leave. It doesn't help that there are rumours of death squads taking advantage of the chaos to stalk the streets and settle old feuds by killing any remaining vampires. Whether those rumours are true, it seems that nobody wants to stick around. Nobody apart from me.

A black witch, identifiable by his tattooed cheek, trudges towards me. I pull up the collar of my leather jacket and angle my face away. The last thing I need right now is the world knowing where I am, let alone the black witches. It's no secret that I survived – plenty of voyeuristic Instagrammers and Tweeters caught me screaming at O'Shea on my way to the destroyed remains of the Monstserrat mansion. If I had the wherewithal, I'd track down every damn one of them and smash their stupid smartphones into oblivion but I don't have time for such pettiness.

I only slow my steps when the grim façade of the police station comes into view. Weak sunlight, filtering through the heavy clouds and seemingly undisturbed by the continuous drizzle, bounces off the dirty windows. There was a time when all I could think about was being strong enough to withstand UV rays. Now that I've achieved that milestone, I couldn't give a flying fuck. It makes life easier in terms of getting around but it doesn't make me happy. Right now, very little could.

The police station is busy. I lean against a wall on the opposite side of the street, using the awning above as shelter and a crumpled pack of cigarettes to make it look as if I'm nothing more than a desperate smoker stopping for a puff. I keep an eye on the door as I cup my hands against the wind and light up.

Two humans and an Agathos daemon leave the station; three humans and a white witch enter. They're giving witness statements, I suppose. Or stating their worries and seeking police protection. I could tell them that they don't have to be afraid but they're not my concern.

I inhale smoke, filling my lungs and almost choking. It's been a long time and the taste of nicotine in my mouth is foul. The glowing tip of the cigarette reminds me of me the fires flickering across the Montserrat ruins. I scowl and hunch my shoulders.

I've just about finished the cigarette when a familiar figure appears, her clothes well starched and her hair in a severe bun that Miss Jean Brodie herself would envy. She's followed by another detective who is rather more rumpled. Even from this distance I can see that they are both tired and drawn and I wonder how much sleep they've had recently. Then I shrug. At least they'll be getting overtime. At least their lives haven't been obliterated.

Foxworthy and Nicholls ignore the police cars parked out front and walk along the pavement. I check my watch; it's only just gone ten. It won't make much difference, though: the Altered Trout, a police hangout, is open twenty-four hours a day to accommodate all shifts. They'll be planning on having a swift pint before heading home. Unfortunately, not all plans come to fruition.

I wait just long enough to confirm their destination then toss the cigarette butt aside. There's a soft sizzle as it hits the wet pavement. Litterbug that I am, I leave it where it is and walk swiftly to overtake the two police officers. Their heads are bowed in conversation so neither of them even glance in my direction. I beat the lights and cross the road just ahead of them, push open the pub door and slide inside. Warmth hits me, along with the yeasty smell of beer. I scan the room, spot a recently-vacated table in the far corner and hastily shuffle over. I grab a grubby pint glass with a few dregs left inside as a prop to make it appear that I'm nothing more than another punter who's been here for hours. Nobody pays me any attention.

I let out a silent sigh of relief and hunker down in the seat. My view of the bar is unobstructed. As Foxworthy and Nicholls enter, I count the other customers and carefully assess them. There's a bullish-looking man perched on a stool, his arse too large to fit it comfortably. Despite his thick neck and the tell-tale reddened complexion of an alcoholic, he has that air of law enforcement about him. If it wasn't for the fact that he's wearing comedy socks, barely visible under the hem of his trousers, I'd consider him a threat. Instead I know that he's the sort who's little more than bluster, regardless of his rank.

A group of younger policemen and women are sitting at another table, occasionally laughing nervously. I frown slightly. It's youth that is dangerous. Youth encourages passion, a willingness to succeed and a strong sense of right and wrong. It's only when we get older that we tend not to get so passionately involved in every little matter. Experience encourages cynicism, and cynicism encourages apathy.

I reckon that, in a pinch, I can take on the group. I can't see any anti-vamp gear on them. I suppose every cloud has a silver lining. There was a rumour that Magix, the vast conglomerate with a stranglehold on the magical market, had recently signed a deal to supply every police force with specially adapted tasers and handcuffs designed to bring down and restrain bloodguzzlers. It was one of many signs of changing sentiment towards us; after all, vampires are supposed to be above the law but Magix seemed to be banking on the law changing. I allow myself a brief smile. All that money they must have spent on research and production, not to mention political lobbying, and now there aren't any vampires to use their equipment on.

I return my focus to my target. I don't give a shit about Nicholls; she wouldn't help me if I were the last vampire in the world. Foxworthy, however, is a different matter. Relations have become rather strained between us of late but he did let me hide out in his house a while back. I'd have waited for him there – with his invitation to enter, I can go in whenever I please – but I want him on my side. I won't use the intimidation card unless I absolutely have to.

He pays for the drinks – a white wine soda and a pint of ale – and the pair of them find a table out of earshot of everyone else. The younger police officers nod respectfully in their direction but, other than that, they're left alone. I note with amusement that Foxworthy is the wine drinker. The big man doesn't feel the need to look butch and obviously doesn't care what others think. He takes a delicate sip, his large fingers incongruous around the slender stem of the wine glass. In contrast, Nicholls gulps at her ale. A beat later, before I can stand up and head over, Foxworthy stands up again and walks to the loo. Perfect.

Without looking at Nicholls, I veer round the tables and chairs and make a beeline after him. Everyone is focused on themselves and no one clocks my entry into the Gents. The door thuds shut behind me and I walk up to the urinal next to Foxworthy. Good grief, men's toilets are truly disgusting.

He grunts as I approach, no doubt expecting a fellow male. A pale yellow stream of urine is hitting the stained ceramic with perfect aim but, when I murmur a soft hello, he jerks in shock and sends an arc spinning out towards me. I only just manage to jump backwards to avoid it.

'Sodding hell!' I exclaim. 'Watch it!'

He hisses but, together with annoyance, there's something like relief in his eyes. Aw, Foxy. He returns to his ablutions, finishing up before zipping his trousers. Then he turns to me.

'Wash your hands first,' I advise.

'You shouldn't be here, Bo.'

I cross my arms. 'I'm serious. Germs can be dangerous.'

'I don't think I'm the one in danger.' All the same, he turns and goes to the sink. 'This isn't the place for you,' he tells me above the sound of the tap. 'You know the government is offering safe houses for all remaining bloodguzzlers.'

I snort. 'Yeah, they're all heart.'

'You should take them up on it.'

I think of Vince Hale, the slimy politician who worked with Medici to try and gain prominence over us – and worked with Tov V'ra to kill us all. I wouldn't trust anyone in power. 'Have any vampires taken them up on the offer?'

Foxworthy dries his hands and doesn't answer. Yeah, that's what I thought. 'Do you have numbers?' I ask him. 'Of survivors?'

'It's not like your lot are beating down our door to tell us they're alright.' I wait. He sighs. 'Best guess is around sixty, fairly evenly spread across the five Families. Most of them have already left the country. Some have been killed since the bombs.'

I swallow. So those rumours are true. No one would have dared kill a vampire if the Families were still around.

Foxworthy turns to face me while I struggle to keep a rein on my rage. This isn't the place. 'Who was it really?' he asks.

There's no point playing dumb and pretending I don't know what he's asking. I like that he knows there's more to this than Tov V'ra, a nutty group of fake believers. And there's no point hiding from the truth any longer. 'The Kakos daemons.'

The only sign that Foxworthy hears me is his sudden blanching. I continue, 'They were pissed off that the Families were growing. They thought we were getting uppity and decided that the best way to deal with us was to slaughter us like pigs.'

'Do you have proof?'

No. 'I can get it. What exactly do you need?'

Foxworthy's jaw clenches as he meets my gaze. 'That's why you're here.' It's not a question. 'You want us to round up the daemons and punish them.'

I lift a shoulder. 'It'll take multiple life sentences of rehabilitation.'

He exhales. 'It's not going to happen.'

'They're not vampires. They're not above the law.'

A sad smile traces across his mouth. 'You know that doesn't matter.'

'I can get proof.'

'It won't make any difference.'

He's absolutely right, of course. I knew it before coming here to find him even crossed my mind. All the same, I feel compelled to make my case. 'The Kakos daemons are responsible for thousands of deaths. They're criminals. They could strike anyone else at any time.' I tilt my face upwards and lean in. 'Are you really going to let that hang over the heads of every living person in this country?'

Foxworthy looks away. We both know that the Kakos daemons are too strong. If the entire Metropolitan police force went after just one of them, there would be a bloodbath and the daemon would be the one still grinning at the end.

'I can pass your allegation on to my superiors,' he says finally.

Allegation? Ha. I'm speaking the truth and Foxworthy knows it. He knew it as soon as I opened my mouth. 'You didn't like it when I was a vigilante.'

He tenses. 'No one should be able to take the law into their own hands.'

'The Kakos daemons have,' I respond softly. 'They've acted as judge, jury and goddamned executioner. And they're going to get off scot-free because everyone's too bloody scared of them.'

The flicker in Foxworthy's eyes acknowledges what I'm saying. 'Are you asking for permission to go after them, Bo? Because I'm not in a position to give it. And neither will anyone else, no matter what proof you get.'

'Yeah,' I say, bitterness colouring my voice. 'They've got too much power and they're too good at what they do, so all this will be swept under the carpet until the Families are nothing more than a footnote in history.'

Foxworthy runs a hand through his hair. What he doesn't say is that the Families are already that.

I take off my baseball cap and gaze at him, openly pleading. 'All I need is the location of one daemon.'

'I can't...'

I hold up my palm. 'You don't go near him,' I say. 'You don't do anything more than follow the paper trail. Rogu3 has been trying but he's got other things to do; also, this particular daemon already knows of his existence and has taken measures against him. You have access to files which we don't. The daemon has a human face and he works in senior management at Streets of Fire.' Well, technically he owns the bloody company but at this point that's unnecessary information. I hand over a slip of paper with my old address on it, the flat which X had lent me for my own use. 'This is one of his properties. All I want is another address where he might be located.'

'You can't go up against a Kakos daemon. I know you killed one before, Bo, but you got lucky.' He's referring to X's little game where he pretended to attack me live on television. X permitted me to 'kill' him. It was, like everything X has done, nothing more than a ruse.

'I didn't actually kill that one, it was set up for the cameras,'

I say absently. Foxworthy blinks. I dismiss his surprise. 'And he's the one I'm after. He was with me in front of the Montserrat building right after it...' I swallow, my words disappearing.

'He's alive?'

I barely manage a nod. If I think too much about X, the darkness inside me begins to take over. I'll do almost anything to see him dead – but I can't give in my baser impulses. Not again.

Foxworthy rubs his chin, his rough stubble hinting at how long it's been since he was last home. 'There were some vague eyewitness reports of a Kakos daemon in the area. I think a team started to look into him but they were called off onto other matters.'

I hiss in irritation. I know the police have to prioritise but sometimes they can't see the damned wood for the trees.

Foxworthy reaches forward and touches my arm. 'I'm sorry about Michael Montserrat. I didn't know him personally but I knew he meant a lot to you.'

He doesn't know that Michael's still alive, doesn't know that he's been turned into a human by X, every vestige of his vampirism stripped away. I don't tell him; the fewer people who know right now, the better. Michael's safety depends upon it.

'Thanks,' I say gruffly.

Foxworthy isn't finished. 'But you can't do this, Bo. You can't start a vendetta against the Kakos daemons. They'll eat you for breakfast. You need to leave London, get as far away from here as possible. There's nothing left for you now and it really isn't safe.'

'I appreciate your concern,' I tell him. I mean it. But this is my city and I'm not leaving. Not for anyone.

There's a loud knock on the door and Nicholl's voice drifts through. 'You fallen in, Foxworthy?'

'You should go.'

I nod and reach into my pocket, pulling out a burner phone. 'Find an address for the daemon,' I urge. 'You can contact me with this.'

His fingers brush against mine as he takes it. 'Okay,' he says simply and I know from the way he looks at me that he will do his very best. It's all I can ask for. I force a smile and step back, letting him go. One down.

THE AGATHOS COURT seems much less busy than the police station. It's hardly surprising; I think all but the most urgent of cases have been postponed, given the events of this week. All the same, I'm glad that Harry is actually doing some work for a change. His office building has some stringent anti-vampire security in place and, while I can easily circumnavigate it, I've already threatened the building's owner once before. I have enough people gunning for me; there's no need to add to the tally unnecessarily.

I stride in through the plate-glass front doors, restored and reinforced since the court was attacked last year. Fortunately, the personnel hasn't changed. The frowning face of the woman at the front desk is one that I recognise. There's only one person in front of her, an irate Agathos daemon who is blithely unconcerned about what's been going on in the city and who is only worried about his own predicament.

'I demand that my trial goes ahead today!' he shrieks. 'I've been waiting six months! You can't expect me to wait longer just because a bunch of guzzlers have corked it. It's completely unreasonable!' With each word, his voice gets higher and higher. I wince. Extra reinforcement or not, if he manages much more of this then all that pretty new glass will be shattered again.

Meg, the stern receptionist with eyebrows that have a life of their own and a personality as charming as a python's, glares at him icily. 'Do you see my badge?' she enquires. 'Are you literate? What does it say?'

'I don't give a rat's arse what it says! I...'

She reaches over and slaps him round the face with considerable force. I'm impressed. The daemon is stunned into silence. 'I am a receptionist.' She points again. 'See? Re-cep-tion-ist.' She enunciates each syllable as if the daemon in front of her is stupid. Which he probably is. 'I am not a lawyer. I am not a judge, although you can bet your soul that I'm judging you right now and finding you wanting. I cannot affect court dates. I cannot run trials.' She leans across her desk again and the hapless daemon shrinks backwards. 'Now get the hell out of here before I decide to stop being so nice.'

He doesn't need telling twice. Spinning round and almost colliding with me, he hurtles off, skidding on the floor before slamming open the door so that it judders. He's not completely cowed, however; he glances over his shoulder and throws Meg such a look of hatred that lesser mortals would flinch from. Not her. She reaches calmly under the desk as if she's about to draw out a weapon. The daemon drops his gaze and departs abruptly.

I clap. Meg's eyes snap to me. 'What do you want?'

'What? Are you going to be mean to me too? I saved your life, Margaret.'

The expression on her face is one that a sullen teenager would be proud of. 'I don't care.'

My eyebrows fly up. 'You don't care that you're alive?'

'Don't be ridiculous. I don't care that you saved me. I'm not going to bend the rules just because once upon a time you hauled me out of a burning building.'

I stand my ground. '*This* burning building.'

She shrugs. 'You can't corrupt me. I'm sorry all your pointy-fanged friends are dead.' She doesn't look sorry at all and I like that she's not changing her tune. She's a woman of conviction, if nothing else. 'But there's not a damn thing I can do about it. If you had any sense, you'd have left London by now.'

'I'm here for Harry D'Argneau,' I explain.

'He's in court,' she snaps. 'It's an important case and can't be interrupted. It's one of only three still going ahead today.'

I remain patient. 'I know. I'll wait quietly at the back of the room until he's done.'

Her malevolence increases. She actually hates me more now for having saved her life. Then I consider the daemon who just skedaddled out of here; maybe she hates just about everyone. She's an equal opportunities kinda person.

'I'll be good. Scout's promise.'

She regards me silently before heaving a sigh as if all this is a great imposition. 'Fine,' she says. 'Sign in here.'

I scribble my name, making sure it's illegible so that it could belong to just about anyone. There's no point in making life easy for anyone who might be tracking me. Then I bow my head respectfully and stroll off in the direction of courtroom number two.

There's a single guard stationed outside. Without glancing at my face, he gestures at me to wait so I rock back on my heels and try to be good. After a couple of minutes, at some invisible signal, he steps aside and lets me to enter. Frankly, I think he just wants to look important. Pleased that part is over, I head inside. There are plenty of empty seats; most people are choosing to stay home this week and even the usual court tourists are absent. I sit towards the back and then I wait.

Back in my PI days, I spent a fair bit of time in courtrooms. It's not as exciting as it sounds; usually there's just a lot of hanging around. Plus the legalese, which I'm sure is designed to be incomprehensible, makes the proceedings seem far longer than they need to be. I have a reasonable respect for the legal system – both Agathos and human – but surely they could spice things up sometimes? *A Few Good Men* this is not.

D'Argneau is at the front, head bowed as he pretends to take copious notes. The barrister for the prosecution appears equally bored. I'm not surprised; there's a witchy witness with astonishingly frizzy hair droning on about accounts up at the front. Less than a minute in and I already want to shoot myself in the head.

The defendant seems to be a youngish daemon wearing a sharp suit. It's difficult to tell for sure, as I can only see the back of his head. I recognise the tailoring, however; I've not spent years hanging around my grandfather for nothing. Whoever this character is, he has a fair bit of money. He's wearing Savile Row's finest but, despite his apparent wealth and his proud posture, the tips of his pointed ears are flushed red. He's as guilty as sin.

My own ears prickle and I realise that the judge's attention has been diverted from the proceedings. He's noticed me sitting quietly and is gaping at me as if he's never seen a vampire before. He swallows hard, his Adam's apple bobbing in his throat, then he starts to tug at his collar and twitch. I give him a little wave in return. It does just what I hope and makes him even more uncomfortable.

'So, as you can tell from the dividends arrived at through calculation of Mr Aaron's assets, the taxation requirements are substantially...'

The judge coughs. 'Let's take a break.'

Everyone jerks in surprise. D'Argneau's head turns, his eyes suspicious, but comprehension dawns when he catches sight of me. He immediately stands. 'Excellent idea, Your Honour.'

The guilt-ridden Mr Aaron isn't particularly thrilled. He tugs at D'Argneau's sleeve. The lawyer soothes him expertly. I slip back out again.

When D'Argneau emerges, he jerks his head to the right. I nod imperceptibly and follow. For once, he's being discreet; who knew he was capable of such a thing? I suppose it's testament to just how dire the situation is. I run my tongue across my teeth, pausing at each fang. The feeling is strangely comforting.

D'Argneau opens a door and gestures inside but I wait for him to enter first. I want him in front of me and visible at all times. As soon as the door closes behind us, he stretches out his arms and envelops me in a hug. He squeezes tightly. 'I'm so sorry. I'm so sorry.'

I wait until he's done and then step back. 'I thought only important trials were running today,' I say, to avoid hearing any more sympathy. Platitudes don't make me feel any better.

He frowns. 'Oh, you mean the Aaron thing?' He waves a hand dismissively. 'There's not much the government takes more seriously than tax evasion.'

'Unless,' I say expressionlessly, 'they're the ones evading tax.'

He looks blank for a moment then laughs. It sounds forced. 'Oh, they take avoiding their own tax quite seriously, too.' He pauses. 'Has Michael's body been found yet?'

I tell a version of the truth. 'No.'

D'Argneau's lips tighten; I can almost imagine he cares. I examine him more closely. There are heavy shadows under his eyes and his hair isn't as perfectly coiffured as usual. He looks almost as haggard as Foxworthy. I have a sudden flash of insight. 'You've lost a lot of clients, haven't you?'

He winces. 'Yes.' His nose wrinkles and he balls up his fists. 'Just as I was getting somewhere. No human lawyer had ever got so close to a Family as I did. I was earning respect and. I was gaining their trust. And now,' he exhales heavily, 'now all that's gone to shit.' He glares at me. 'Before you castigate me for thinking only of myself and money, a lot of people at my firm are going to lose their jobs because of what's happened.'

'It's early days. The Families might regroup yet.'

D'Argneau snorts. 'You and I both know it's too late for that.' He lifts his chin. 'They're saying it's this religious group. Tov V'ra?'

'They were just the puppets.'

He leans towards me. 'Then tell me. Who were the masters? Because I swear to God, Bo, I will hunt them down and...'

'Kakos daemons.'

D'Argneau shrinks. 'Oh.'

'You're going to hunt them down and what?'

He sits down heavily on the nearest chair. 'Shit.'

I don't pretend to be surprised by his sudden volte-face. 'Listen, this isn't a social call. If you want to help bring down the people who did this, I need a favour.'

His shoulders slump. 'I didn't think it was the Kakos daemons. They stay hidden. They stay out of things.'

If I thought that he would swing his allegiance towards them, always in pursuit of the next big thing or next quick buck, I was mistaken. Harry D'Argneau is well and truly terrified. 'They're not interested in you,' I tell him.

He raises his head. 'You don't know that! I worked for one of the Families!' He gets to his feet. 'I need to leave. If I can get out of the city, out of the country, then...'

'Harry, they got what they wanted. They wanted the Families destroyed. You're small fry.'

There's enough of his arrogance left for him to manage another glare. 'No, I'm bloody not! I'm well respected! I'm...'

I hold up my hand. Maybe this wasn't such a good idea after all. 'You know what I mean. If they wanted you dead, you already would be.'

He's only slightly comforted. 'I should still leave. Maybe I could come back in a few years when things have quietened down.'

I shrug. 'If you want to leave, then leave. You can still do me that favour from abroad.'

He shakes his head violently. 'I'm not going near any Kakos daemons. I'm just not.'

'You don't have to. I only need some information.'

'No! Didn't you hear me? I'm not touching them!'

I gaze up to the heavens. There's an odd damp spot on the ceiling in the shape of Italy. Huh. 'I'm not asking you to.'

'It's alright for you,' he complains. 'You've already killed one. They're probably terrified of you. That's why you're still alive.'

'I didn't kill one.' It seems like I'll be repeating this story for a bloody long time.

'Yes, you did. It was on TV.'

I run a hand through my hair. 'So it must be true? Because it was in glorious technicolour?'

He's still confused. 'But...'

'Look. Half the reason the daemons are going to get away with this is because of reactions like yours. People are too scared of them, they're too afraid to act. It's a ridiculous way to behave.'

D'Argneau is momentarily silent then he angles his face stubbornly towards me. 'Is it? Because that's how the vampires have been behaving for centuries. They've used people's fear to get what they want.'

I'd argue if I didn't agree with him. 'You're right.'

Slightly mollified, he nods. 'What is it you want me to do?' Before I can tell him, he rushes in with, 'Not that I'm promising I will, mind. I'll need to consider all the ramifications.'

'I need a detailed report of the legal status of the vampires now that the Families don't exist.'

D'Argneau's face clears immediately. 'That's it?'

'You don't get off that easily. I also require information about any legal proceedings during the last hundred years that have been brought against Kakos daemons. If any of them got so much as a fine for avoiding the congestion charge, I want to know about it. Also, dig around Streets of Fire.'

'The internet company?'

'Yep. Find out who really owns it and whether there have been any under-the-table deals.'

'I don't understand.'

'It's probably better that way.'

D'Argneau's expression is troubled. 'I can do those things, even though that's three favours, not one. But Bo, what exactly are you planning here? Because if you're thinking of taking on the Kakos daemons...'

I soften my tone. 'Wouldn't you?'

He grimaces. 'No. I'd run away from this city as fast as I possibly could. As I think I've already made clear.'

'You don't give yourself enough credit, Harry,' I tell him. 'I think you'd probably stay and fight.'

'I can't fight a Kakos daemon.'

I smile, although there's no humour in it. 'Oh, you'd be surprised. There's more than one way to skin a daemon.'

My words ring hollow, even to my own ears.

CHAPTER 2
SAFE HOUSE

I wait at the back door. It's difficult to put in security features when you're dealing with a bunch of tribers who can read your mind; as a result, we have been forced to resort to the most basic identification techniques – I see you, I know you, there's no daemon with you, you can enter. It's hardly ideal but it's the best we've got right now.

I think O'Shea is hoping that Kimchi will alert us if X shows up but Kimchi is no attack dog. Even if he weren't chubby, with more drool than fang, he loves X. He's more likely to roll over and beg for a belly scratch than to warn us that we're all about to be murdered because X has changed his mind.

Maria lets me in. Of all of us, she's managed to remain the most cheerful. Then again, she's the one who has the least connection to all this. Part of me wonders, though, if her cheerfulness is a mask. I found her a few weeks ago in a seedy sex club where she was being trafficked and I can't begin to imagine what she's been through. Even so, her spirit has most definitely not been cowed. I keep trying to persuade her to move on. I can give her money, contacts, whatever she wants, and I know of at least two women's shelters which would do her a damn sight more good than I can. She insists she's staying. A teenager's veneer is harder to break through than I'd expected – especially one who's had such a godawful time of it up till now.

I raise my eyebrows at her.

'Is okay,' she tells me. 'No change.'

I sigh; I suppose that's the most I can hope for right now. I step across the threshold and head upstairs.

The house, which Rogu3 found for us, is in a small, well-kept street in Hounslow. It was lying vacant – a result of the many bank repossessions in the area. There's no furniture or running water but there's a roof and it's relatively safe. Once upon a time we could have used virtually any property but my vampire status has made that considerably more difficult. If a person owns it, whether they're on holiday or not, I need a damned invitation to enter. Even this place has time limitations because we've decided never to stay anywhere for more than two nights. We have to keep moving and we have to keep Michael safe. X has let us go for now but he might change his mind. He told me that he's petty like that. Besides, the other Kakos daemons are an unknown quantity – and there are others we need to worry about. I'm not going to take unnecessary risks, not with my friends and most definitely not with Michael.

O'Shea appears in the hallway. I pretend not to notice his relief that I'm back. 'Good. I've just been up to see him. He woke up long enough to take a few mouthfuls of soup and now he's back down again.'

'Did he say anything?'

O'Shea shakes his head. I wait for the normally cheery Agathos daemon to comment on my absence but he remains silent. I can tell from the way he's acting that he thinks I'm making a mistake by going after X and his buddies. Whether he's not saying anything because he knows he won't change my mind or because he's afraid that I'll do something scary to him for speaking up, I'm not sure.

I lick my lips and fill the void. 'You shouldn't have left him alone.'

'Rogu3 is there.'

I curse. 'He's supposed to be investigating Vince Hale.' X might have tightened his security but Hale is another matter. An adept hacker like Rogu3 should find it easy to break into his systems – *should* being the operative word, of course.

O'Shea steps back. 'I'll let him explain.' I nod tersely then start up the stairs. 'Bo?'

'Yeah?'

'We need to leave as soon as night falls. You've got an hour or two at best.'

I nod in acknowledgment. 'Okay.'

The room where Michael is sleeping is dark. The first thing we did when we got here was block the windows with cardboard. He seems to find light painful, together with moving, talking, breathing and anything else involved in staying alive. I check his chest; it's rising and falling with his shallow, ragged breaths and there's a wheezing sound. That's my man, fighting to the last.

Kimchi, who is curled up at Michael's feet, wags his tail. I scratch his ears and eye Rogu3. The teenager has had to do a lot of growing up recently. He gives me a crooked smile. 'He's doing okay,' he tells me quietly.

Another okay. I don't like okay, in fact I'm starting to bloody well hate okay, but I force a smile in return. 'Have you got through to Hale?' I ask.

He grimaces. 'I don't have the right equipment, Bo. He's a Member of Parliament and the firewalls surrounding those systems are stringent. If I can get home, I have some software that...'

'It's too dangerous. Tell me what you need and I'll go out and buy it.'

He rolls his eyes in exasperation. 'This isn't the sort of stuff you can buy off the high street. It took months to build those programmes.'

'Can't you access them remotely?'

'My parents made me uninstall it all after...' His voice trails off. Bugger it. He runs a hand through his hair. 'I kept copies but they're hidden away. Only I can access them. I splashed out on some biometric protection, thinking I was being clever.' His shoulders slump. 'I have to go home.'

I'm adamant. 'No way.'

He draws himself up. 'So it's alright for you to go waltzing out on the streets but not for me? You're the famous one. You're the one people are likely to recognise.'

'They'll recognise you too.'

'Not if I...'

Michael groans and we both freeze. He coughs weakly. 'Go and get some rest,' I whisper to Rogu3. 'We have to move soon and we'll need to be alert.'

He blinks in affirmation. I pat him on the shoulder and turn my attention to the former Lord of the Montserrat Family. His face remains pale, as if all the colour has been leached out of it. Even when he's asleep there's evidence of pain around his eyes and his mouth and his dark hair hang limply. His visible wounds are superficial but what's going on internally is anyone's guess. We have little tomformation to go by.

Rogu3 was turned before returning to human using the same blood from X that has affected Michael, but Rogu3's stint as a bloodguzzler was only momentary. Michael is recovering from decades of being a vampire. If I thought a hospital could help, I'd take him there and stand guard over him for every minute of every day until he recovered. But not only will that mean the whole world knows what's happened to him, it could place him in greater danger. And there's only one of me.

Trying to be gentle, I wipe away spittle from his chin. He stirs, his eyes fluttering open. Every time it's the same: there's a cloud of confusion, followed by pain. And fear.

'Hey,' I soothe. 'It's alright. You're safe.'

'Bo,' he whispers.

'I'm here.' I find his hand and grip it. He tries to squeeze my fingers but the pressure is barely noticeable. He's as weak as a damned kitten.

'Turn me,' he begs. 'You can turn me.'

I bite down hard on the inside of my cheek and shake my head. 'I can't. I don't know how. And even if it was possible to be turned twice, you're too weak. You'll die.'

His lips move but I can't hear what he's saying. I dip my head to listen. 'Anything's better than this.'

I squeeze my eyes shut. 'You'll recover.'

He stares at me, the unspoken question hanging between us. What if he doesn't? I press my cheek against his and lie down beside him, taking care not to hurt him any further.

'We'll get through this,' I say. '*You'll* get through this. Just wait and see.'

MOVING HIM IS NOT EASY. We have a stretcher, helpfully purloined by O'Shea. Twenty minutes before we go, he also boosts a van from a window cleaner living nearby. We hustle out with Michael between us. While Maria and Rogu3 stay with him in the back, O'Shea and I sit upfront, ready for any evasive – or retaliatory – action.

We travel less than five miles before switching to a pre-booked rental car from a small outfit that is too cheap to buy CCTV or to check IDs. Then we set off again, doubling back several times and looking for any tails. Only when we're absolutely sure that we're in the clear do we head for the next safe house. It might seem like over-kill but no one's complaining. Our biggest concern is that the constant upheaval is merely delaying the inevitable and damaging Michael's health further.

I bang on the partition when we arrive to let Maria and Rogu3 know, then I glance up at our new home – an abandoned warehouse by the look of things.

'I think you'll be pleasantly surprised,' O'Shea tells me. His eyes crinkle suddenly. 'I don't know about you, darling, but all this cloak-and-dagger crap is playing havoc with my complexion.'

I frown at him, not understanding what's so wonderful about our latest digs. The location is good: we're central enough to make it easy to get out and about if need be. There's also excellent visibility and only one road leading in, so there's no worry about getting surrounded without realising. It's just a shed, though. There are probably rats.

We hop out. This is our fourth move and we're starting to get into a rhythm. Kimchi and I check out the perimeter, skulking around to satisfy ourselves that we've not been followed before moving in on the property itself. The others stay with Michael until I give them the all clear.

Rounding the first corner, I'm assailed by a reek of rotting food so powerful that I almost gag. Kimchi, who will eat pretty much anything whether it's green and furry or not, whines. The back of my neck twitches. I don't like this. Something doesn't feel right. The path round the warehouse is covered with weeds, sprinkled with the odd crushed fizzy drinks can or discarded crisps wrapper. It doesn't look as if anyone has been here in months. Possibly years. And yet...

All of a sudden, Kimchi jerks at the lead. For all his rounded stomach and gentle, soulful eyes, he can exert power when he wants to. It doesn't help that I wasn't expecting the sharp tug. I'm yanked forward, more from surprise than anything else. His paws skitter cartoon-like along the ground and he yelps loudly. I feel my fangs lengthen in preparation. This place is a mistake. But Kimchi is determined to pelt forward.

I take out my phone, ready to send my SOS text. It's not that I'll need saving, of course; it's the signal for O'Shea and the others to get Michael out of here. My thumb hovers over the button as I yank Kimchi backwards and make a vain attempt to calm him down while keeping my voice low.

Without warning, Kimchi's tail drops between his legs and he wheels round, now trying to bolt in the opposite direction away from whatever is waiting for us up ahead. I let go of his lead and he careens away at a gallop as I hunker down and snarl softly. Come on, then.

A tiny shape appears from out of the darkness. It hisses, its eyes flashing at me in disgust. My shoulders drop as a voice booms. 'For pity's sake, Bo. Aren't you training that vile creature?'

I curse under my breath and straighten up. The voice is coming from above my head. I crane upwards, scanning until I spot a small speaker nestled next to the drain, almost obscured from vision by a lump of ancient moss. As I grit my teeth, the cat saunters towards me, stopping less than a foot away. It starts to wash its face but one slitted eye remains on me at all times. Bloody creature.

'Everything alright?' O'Shea enquires from behind.

'You could have told me the old man was out of hospital.'

He shrugs amiably. 'He was released on his own cognisance.'

The ornery idiot. The voice booms once more. 'And that, my dear, is why I didn't tell you first. Your thoughts are written all over your face. You really should learn to maintain more of a façade, you know. You'll never make a spy.'

I ignore the words and remain fixed on O'Shea. 'I take it he's inside?'

He grins at me. 'Yep.'

'What is this place?'

O'Shea holds out his hand. 'Let's find out.'

'Don't use the front entrance,' my grandfather's voice says cheerfully. 'It's booby-trapped. There's a hidden door round the other corner.'

Of course there is. I roll my eyes. Secretly I'm beyond relieved. The pressure of trying to keep everyone safe has been bearing down on me; at least now there will be someone to help, even if that someone spends hours telling me off for not speaking properly or for wearing form-fitting leather clothes.

O'Shea and I return to the others, who have managed to grab hold of Kimchi after his escape from my grandfather's cat. We haul the stretcher with Michael's prone body towards the small door concealed round the side. There's no doorknob and no apparent way to gain entry. I wait half a beat but, when it doesn't open from the inside, I exhale in irritation. I fumble round until I spot a small knot of wood. When I touch it, it slides open revealing a smooth rectangle of black plastic with a blinking light on the bottom.

'No way,' Rogu3 breathes. 'That's a state-of-the-art optical scanner. I read about them last month. They cost the earth because, unlike previous versions, they can't be fooled. You can't just rip out someone's eyeball and hold it up. It's a work of art. And the technology is supposed to be limited to the...'

'Government?' I ask.

Rogu3 nods, awe still reflected in his expression. I tighten my mouth. My grandfather is one thing; MI7 is quite another.

I angle my head so I'm looking directly at the rectangle. Is something supposed to happen? The little light momentarily flashes green, there's a faint whoosh and, just like that, the wooden door slides open, revealing a small entrance area. Unlike the exterior of the warehouse, which is made of what looks like rotting timber, this is shiny chrome.

Maria squeaks. 'I no want go.'

Her and me both. There's another whooshing sound and another metal door glides open, this time revealing my grandfather. He has a walking stick in one hand and there's no denying his frailty but the intelligence in his eyes is as sharp as ever.

'How wonderful to see you all,' he says.

I'm tempted to curse him for escaping from the hospital and forcing me to go through with this stupid charade but it would be pointless; he'd only make me feel bad about myself. It's his special gift. Perhaps I'm also learning something about self-control.

Nah.

I step forward and kiss his cheek. It feels delicate and papery under my lips but when I draw back, concerned, he ignores me.

'Devlin. Thank you for bringing Bo. I know she can be … difficult.'

'Buthy baby! It was my pleasure!'

My grandfather's lip curls and he nods at Rogu3. 'And thank you for your collusion, Alistair.'

Rogu3 coughs and shuffles his feet. 'Wasn't much.'

Feeling put out, I fold my arms. 'You could have told me,' I say accusingly to them both.

My grandfather doesn't let them speak. 'If they had you wouldn't have come.'

'This all belongs to MI7, right?'

'Naturally.'

I hiss. 'Well, then. I've already had one bloody Member of Parliament trying to kill me. I don't need to knock on the government's door and present myself for the taking. Michael...'

'Lord Montserrat is too weak to keep being moved,' my grandfather interrupts. 'And there is a world of difference between the elected officials at Westminster and MI7. They are temporary; *we* are not.'

'You're retired. One leak and...'

'No one is going leak anything about you being here, Bo, because no one *knows* you're here.' His eyes gleam. 'Besides, I didn't yield all of my power, knowledge or abilities when I retired from MI7. Only a handful of people are aware of the existence of this facility. You have no need to worry.'

From the back of our small group, Maria spits. 'Here,' she says. 'Take stretcher. I no stay here.'

'Maria,' my grandfather says gently, 'you are in more danger than everyone else. As you well know.' She stiffens and I narrow my gaze. They've never met each other before so what is going on? There's always been more to the damaged girl than is visible to the world, and my grandfather has an uncanny knack for picking out triber elements in all manner of people.

Before I can say anything, he steps to the side. 'Why don't I show you around first? Then you can all make up your minds.'

I look at O'Shea and Rogu3. They both nod. Maria's bottom lip juts out but she shrugs reluctantly. Kimchi's tail wags. Michael doesn't say anything. He's dropped back into unconsciousness and it's that alone which makes me decide. 'Lead the way.'

'You can leave the mutt outside.'

Aware that he's suddenly the topic of conversation, Kimchi nudges his way forward before rising onto his back paws and angling upwards for a slobbery lick. I beam. 'I can't. He's missed you too much.'

My grandfather scowls.

I EXPECTED the interior to be large and cavernous but it is remarkably compact. 'The walls are three feet thick,' my grandfather says. 'They're capable of withstanding almost any attack.'

I wonder whether any building, regardless of its high-tech equipment, is capable of holding off an attack by a Kakos daemon. For now, I hold my tongue.

We trail through numerous corridors. Leading off them are bedrooms, each one very simple but with real beds and real en-suite bathrooms. This will be better for Michael; he'll have a real chance of recuperation here. But I'm still afraid.

'You can leave Lord Montserrat in one of these rooms.'

'He's staying with us,' I say firmly. I need to know the lay of the land first.

A trace of a smile crosses my grandfather's lips but he doesn't argue.

We continue to a larger room. There are camera displays at the front, each one showing a different angle of the warehouse's exterior. Something flashes in the corner of one of the screens and I immediately stiffen before realising it is heat-sensing imagery picking up the bloody cat.

'This is so cool,' Rogu3 breathes.

I glance at him. 'Maybe you'll be able to get that software you need here.'

He looks excited and darts over to a desk with a computer.

He runs a worshipping hand over it. 'I'd be surprised if even Streets of Fire has this model.' He sits down on the swivel chair and beckons to Maria. She and O'Shea lay Michael's stretcher down on a long leather sofa and she joins Rogu3.

My grandfather raises his eyebrows at me. I shrug and look away.

'This place was designed for visiting dignitaries,' he says. 'In case of attack upon their person.'

'Oooh, I like having my person attacked,' O'Shea remarks.

My mouth quirks up slightly. I appreciate his attempt to keep the atmosphere light but we need to know more about this place before we break out the champagne. 'What if someone gets inside with a bomb?' I ask.

My grandfather smiles sympathetically. 'The attacks on the Families weren't your fault.'

'I know,' I snap, before regretting it.

He pats my arm. 'Each door can be sealed off with the press of a button.' He points towards a console. 'Every eventuality has been thought of.'

'Magic attacks?'

'There are spells and wards across every access point. Even the most concerted attack would be foiled. There are also mechanisms in place to ward off any squatters or hapless passers-by. Perhaps you noticed the smell?'

I wrinkle my nose but I'm not yielding just yet. 'Supplies?'

'Enough for three months. Electricity runs from a separate generator. Water is recycled and completely bypasses the London mains system.' He points to the left. 'Take that door and you'll find a lift going underground to a bunker built to withstand nuclear attacks.' He points to the right. 'Go in that direction and you'll reach a viral decontamination area. Everything has been considered.' He pauses and looks at Michael. 'Straight ahead, there is a fully equipped medical facility with every drug and medicine you can think of. He'll have what he needs, Bo.'

'I don't know what he needs,' I whisper. Then I straighten my back. 'This place seems too good to be true. How long before one of your MI7 buddies comes wandering by?'

'It's highly unlikely that they will. And I'm sure your boy there can do something to lock them out beforehand.'

Rogu3 looks at me. 'I can manage that,' he allows.

I sigh and go back to Michael. I brush my fingers against his forehead. His skin is clammy and he seems even paler than before. 'We'll stay,' I say softly. 'For now.' My grandfather nods as if he always knew I'd agree.

'What did you mean about Maria?' I ask. She bites her lip and stares at me. 'Why is she in more danger?' I meet her eyes and address her directly. 'It was you he wanted to meet,' I say, referring to our recent joint encounter with X before my world exploded. 'At La Boheme. X wanted to have dinner with us not because of Rogu3 but because of you.'

'He wanted to confirm what she really is,' my grandfather answers for her.

'Which is?'

'It's up to her to tell you.'

I draw in a breath. 'I'm getting a little tired of all these secrets and evasions.'

Maria stands up. 'I am Romany.' She glares at me, challenge lighting up her face as if she expects me to throw her out on her ear.

Er... 'So?'

'Honestly, Bo,' my grandfather says scornfully. 'This is why I wanted you to have a decent education. Your understanding and knowledge is severely lacking in so many areas that it's a wonder you can even add up.'

'Look,' I say, with a flash of anger, 'I...'

'Guys,' Rogu3 interrupts, 'take a look at this.'

The tone in his voice makes us all turn. Maria takes in the computer screen and blanches.

I hurry over. 'What is it?' Then my stomach drops. 'Oh.'

It's a live feed from Covent Garden, barely a stone's throw away from the New Order offices. A figure is pressed up against the wall and he's surrounded by a group of witches, many of them with twin black and white tattoos on their cheeks. Something flies towards him and, as he ducks, the flash of his fangs is suddenly visible. It's a vampire – one of the few still alive and in the city. And there are at least a dozen hybrid witches after his blood.

CHAPTER 3

PREDATORS AND PREY

The damned van is determined to not go above sixty. My foot is pressed right down and I'm gunning the engine for all its worth. No matter what I do, it's not going to go any faster. It swerves round the corners, almost coming onto two wheels. I knew I should have taken the time to go back for my bike but, after all the explosions at the Family mansions, it seemed too much of a risk.

I'm certain that by the time I get to the vampire, he'll be dead. I park illegally, getting as close as I can, and then sprint towards him. The sound of jeers fires my blood. I realise the witches are stretching out this moment, enjoying taking down the hapless bloodguzzler as slowly as possible. There's no fear of retaliation; there are no Families left to go after them. I smile grimly as I push myself faster. They've forgotten about me.

Since I left the warehouse, the group of witches has grown. Where there were only around a dozen, now there seem to be about thirty. The night sky is lit up by their flashes of foul magic. Cameras held by quivering journalists are recording the action. I'm not going to get into an ethical debate about whether the press is there merely to record events, but damn those parasitical vultures for not lifting a finger to help.

Ignoring them, I reach into the crowd and grab the nearest two witches by the scruffs of their necks then haul them backwards and smack their heads together. They collapse onto the ground with a heavy thud. The others are so intent on their victim that they don't even notice. They're all taller than me and they're crowded too closely together for me to peek through them, so I can't see what state the vampire is in. I'm betting it's not good. I can't take on this many witches at once and, sooner or later, they're going to notice I'm here. I need to be smarter.

When you think about it, fear really is the ultimate weapon. The Kakos daemons have had to do very little for generations because everyone's so bloody scared of them. With their actions against the Families, they've just cemented their reputation for the next century. It can be tricky, though; there's a fine balance between intimidating someone and riling them to the point where they come at you like a rabid dog. Or in this case, a pack of rabid dogs with black magic at their fingertips and blood already on their hands.

I reach down inside myself for the iciness I know lingers there. It's dangerous but it's going to be worth it. Then I select my target: the younger and more vulnerable the better.

I quickly find who I need. Towards the far end of the scrum, there's a scrawny kid with a sickeningly proud smile pasted across his thin face. My mouth flattens into a grim line. He should be at home. No doubt his parents have decided that he can get a better education by beating a bloodguzzler to death at the witching hour than by going to school in the daylight like someone normal. Sucks to be him. I crick my neck from one side to the other as a light from one of the watching cameras swings in my direction. I guess the paps have spotted me, at least.

Wasting no further time, I spring round and curl an arm round the kid's chest. He yells loudly in surprise as I drag him backwards. It's enough to draw the attention of the other witches. One by one they elbow each other, spinning round and falling into silence when they see me. I keep the kid close, his thrumming heartbeat singing to mine. This could almost be fun.

One of the mob – who surprises me by his human appearance – steps forward. His features are ugly and twisted, despite the sudden panic in his face, which suggests he feels kinship with the kid. I guess he's here with the witches because a shared antipathy for vampires proves that the enemy of your enemy is a friend. So much for sympathy for what's happened to us, then.

'Let him go.'

I smile disarmingly. 'Sure. I'll do that right now.' I pause. 'No, wait. Maybe I won't.'

'Might have known she'd survive,' someone spits from the crowd. 'She's like a bleedin' cockroach.'

'Got that right,' I coo. 'There's no getting rid of me.' Using my free hand, I trail my index finger down the kid's cheek. He flinches and tries to jerk away but I hold him fast. 'Now, what do cockroaches eat, I wonder?' I cock my head as if trying to think while I deliberately let my fangs grow. 'They probably like their meat young and succulent.'

'Get your filthy hands off him!'

I allow my teeth to scrape the skin of the boy's neck. Right now, he's nothing more than a plain, normal-looking kid; he doesn't even have a faint tattoo of either white or black magic across his cheek. If he is a witch, the tattoo won't reach prominence until he comes of age when, no doubt, he'll undergo the same procedure as the others in order to become a hybrid. I'm starting to think, however, that he's human. Even without the human man jumping in to attempt a rescue, the faint scent emanating from the kid's skin suggests it.

His eyes are throbbing with hatred. I sniff once more and glance down. The boy's knuckles are bruised and bleeding. He's not all that innocent. Despite the situation, I feel hunger stirring inside me. It's not been easy to feed myself the last few days and this boy does smell good.

One of the witches lunges towards me. I pull back just in time. 'Now, now, now,' I tut. 'That's just not polite.' I dip my head further and nick the boy's skin, just above his jugular. As blood trickles down, I use the tip of my tongue to lap it up. 'Mmm. AB. I don't get that very often. How yummy.'

A tall woman strides out from the back of the crowd. She's dressed from head to toe in black. It's almost like we're matching. 'What do you want?'

I meet her cold gaze. 'I should have thought that was obvious.'

'You'd kill a child for this?'

I smile sympathetically. 'Children are the future, aren't they? And this child has been involved in beating a vampire to death.' I gesture at the dazzled journalists. 'Look at his hands. Is this boy an innocent? Is thirty against one a fair fight?' My smile grows. 'Is a bunch of cameras filming the action – and therefore silently condoning it – something this country should be proud of?'

I'm pleased to note that several of them flinch. Good: it means I'm being scary enough. Bring on the fear, ladies and gentlemen. Bring. It. On.

'He's a Medici bloodguzzler. You hate them as much as we do.'

'You might have missed it,' I say softly, 'but Medici are no more. The guzzler is mine.' I stroke the boy's cheek. 'Or this boy is mine. You choose.'

Several of them mutter amongst themselves. Another man extricates himself, walks up to the self-appointed leader and whispers in her ear. I watch his mouth and the anger inside me solidifies. I was pissed off before; now I'm incandescent. I don't let it show, though. Screw what my grandfather says; I can keep my emotions hidden when I need to.

Indecision crosses the woman's face. 'A life for a life,' I remind her. 'It's up to you.'

'Scarlet,' the man, who is probably the boy's father, begins.

'Scarlet?' I beam. 'And I'm the Red Angel. It's like we could be sisters.' I look down at the boy and let my pupils dilate. 'Blood is scarlet too,' I purr.

Scarlet pushes the man away. 'Fine,' she snarls. 'Release the boy and you can have the vampire.'

'I think not. Vampire first. Then I will give you the boy.'

She hisses and spits but she does what I ask. She snaps her fingers at two of her henchmen who growl and retrieve the beaten body, dragging him forward through the crowd. They drop him at my feet. His face is a bloody pulp.

I tilt my head and listen. He's close enough for me to ascertain the truth. Fuck. 'He's dying.' I say it calmly and without inflection.

'You don't know that.'

I sigh. 'I do. And I did say a life for a life.' Still holding the boy, I reach down and grab the vampire's limp body, tossing him over my shoulder in a fireman's lift. Then I start backing up. Between the vampire and the boy, movement is awkward. The kid starts writhing and jerking; he's going to try almost anything to save his sorry skin. He opens his mouth and bites down hard on my arm. In response I cuff him hard on the side of his head and it lolls to the side. Huh. I'd have thought a teenager would have a harder skull than that.

'Let him go!' the father shrieks. 'Let him go!'

Any second now, the crowd will decide enough is enough and come after me like some amorphous angry monster. I take in a deep breath. This isn't going to be easy with my two burdens but I'll do my best.

I spin round and start running. Admittedly it's more like a lopsided shuffle than a run but I do what I can. There's a sudden roar from behind. I've probably only got a three-second head-start. Damn it, that's not enough time to get back to the van.

I drop the kid. I'd hoped to use him as collateral to get further but his weight is holding me back. Of course, now that he's no longer with me, the witches have no reason to hold back. I zigzag, trying to avoid the bursts of magic streaming towards me but there's a limit to what I can do. I'm struck at least three times and my right arm goes completely limp.

Something tightens around my shin. I glance down as I run and realise it's a bloody snake. Now it's my turn to experience fear. The snake opens its jaws, ready to sink its fangs into my skin. I don't have time to reach down and shake it off. Stabbing pain shoots upwards. I'll just have to hope that MI7 includes snakebite antidote in its medical room otherwise I'm going to be seriously sick. I limp a few more metres, fling open the van door, toss in the Medici vamp and extricate myself from the snake, throwing it onto the road. Then I put the pedal to the metal.

'He's dead,' my grandfather informs me.

I push back my hair and sit up. My leg is still throbbing painfully. Apparently, I'm now strong enough as a vampire to avoid death from even the nastiest of snakes, with or without an antidote. Yippee – but it still bloody hurts. And vampiric strength isn't enough to keep you alive when there are thirty magically endowed people beating you up at the same time.

'They murdered him. Sodding witches.' To survive the bombs, only to be ripped apart by a baying crowd of idiots who are being dangled on a string by someone far, far smarter than them, makes the now-dead Medici vampire's situation seem even shittier than it already is.

My grandfather sits on the edge of my bed. 'Most people are on your side, Bo. Yes, there are factions taking advantage of the situation but, by and large, there's been a lot of sympathy for the vampires since the attacks. We British don't like to think of ourselves as homicidal maniacs.'

'Even if we are.'

'Yes,' he agrees quietly. 'Even if we are.' He waits a beat before continuing. 'You have to be careful. You looked like you were going to kill that child. That kind of action is not going to endear you to anybody.'

'I wouldn't have really hurt him. Not much.' I might have taken a good long drink from him to make sure he spent the rest of his life looking over his shoulder for the next pair of fangs but I wouldn't have killed him.

'I know.'

I look up at his careworn face. 'Do you? I've done some pretty bad things. I *have* killed.'

He sighs. 'The vampire part of you has taken root. It's in your soul. There will be bloodlust, Bo. There will be less ... conscience inside you. It doesn't mean you're not you, though. It doesn't mean you can't still make right and moral decisions.'

'Moral?' I scoff. 'Is there any part of this world where morality still exists?'

He brushes away a lock of hair from my cheek in a familiar gesture that I remember from when I was a child. 'You know there is.' He looks away. 'And if you are going to stay in this country and not get yourself killed, you need to present a better image to the world. You're the public face of the vampires now, whether there are five of you, or fifty, or five thousand.'

I reach up and turn his head, forcing him to look at me. 'What if there's only one?' He doesn't answer. I shake my head and swing my legs round. 'How's Michael doing?'

'His pulse is weak and thready. He's running a temperature. There's no internal bleeding that I'm aware of but I've started him on intravenous antibiotics to beat any internal infection.'

That's a better answer than 'okay'. 'Should I have taken him to a hospital?'

'I don't think it would make a difference and it would have been incredibly dangerous. There will be others besides the Kakos daemons who want to see him dead now that he's so vulnerable. However, we can still try that if you...'

I hold up a hand. 'No. He's safer here.'

My grandfather regards me steadily. 'It's not going to work, you know.'

'What?'

'If he makes it. If Michael pulls through.'

I notice that he's stopped calling him Lord Montserrat. I ignore the chill. 'He's going to make it,' I say through gritted teeth.

'Maybe he will. But you and him? A vampire and a human?' He shakes his head. 'It's not going to happen.'

I stand up. 'Let's just concentrate on getting him better first.'

Rogu3 appears in the doorway, saving me from further conversation. 'I've got the clip you wanted.'

'Perfect.' I don't smile.

'What's this about?' my grandfather enquires.

I tighten my jaw. 'Come and see.'

We troop through to the main room. O'Shea is lying on the

sofa and covering his face with his hands as Kimchi tries to find a spot he can lick. I have to give it to the dog, he's certainly determined.

'Mmmmph!'

Maria, her arms crossed and her posture stiff, eyes both of them warily. She is more relaxed around Kimchi in the sense that she doesn't loosen her bowels in terror whenever he's there, but she still doesn't like him. I have the feeling that Kimchi's merely biding his time before he begins his all-out doggy cuteness assault.

'O'Shea!'

'Mmmmph.'

'Stop messing around. I need you to see this.'

With some effort he heaves Kimchi off his chest and sits up. 'Your dog is a beast.'

Maria and my grandfather nod in fervent agreement. I'd like to give them a demonstration of Kimchi's prowess in the art of slobbery but there are more important matters to deal with. I pass a hand across my forehead. 'Just get over here. I need you to tell me what you can see.'

O'Shea bounds over, Kimchi trotting at his heels. I nod to Rogu3, he taps a key and the video starts playing.

O'Shea scratches his head. 'I don't get it. We've seen this. We were watching the whole time you were there.'

I keep my eyes on the screen, trying not to notice my frozen features and the terror of so many of the witches staring at me. I really do look like a thug. Scarlet steps forward and starts speaking. There's no sound. We watch as the silent conversation plays out once more and I pretend not to see Rogu3 shudder when I stroke the boy's cheek. Then the second man pushes forward and whispers in Scarlet's ear, his thin lips forming the words that almost sent me over the edge.

'There.'

'What?'

My grandfather sucks in a breath through his teeth and turns away. The others haven't caught it yet. I tell Rogu3 to go back and play it again. This time O'Shea's breath quickens. 'Oh. The slimy politician strikes again, I see.'

So I didn't imagine it. Rogu3 stares at the screen, mouthing to himself as he works it out. His lip curls. '"Hale won't like this."' He turns his head to me. 'That's what he's saying, right?'

I keep my arms loose at my sides but my fists are tightly curled, anger bunching every sinew. 'Yeah. I think so.'

'So he planned with Medici to bring down all the Families. When Medici was destroyed too, he shifted gear and is making sure there are no more vampires left. I wonder what he's offered the witches for their compliance.'

I snort. 'They probably jumped at the chance and did it for free. And there are humans there too.'

'Hale wants to ensure that the Families don't regroup,' O'Shea says. 'He wants to exterminate every last trace of the bloodguzzlers for good.' He glances at me. 'And I thought you were the psycho one, Bo.'

Without turning round, my grandfather speaks up. 'That dead guzzler is Medici. Perhaps Vincent Hale was attempting to get rid of any last witnesses who might know his role in all this.'

'Whatever his motives,' I say coldly, 'we can't let him get away with it.'

'Bo, he's a Member of Parliament, a democratically elected official. It's one thing going after petty thieves or black witches but a human MP? The consequences could be devastating.'

'MI7, yes?' Maria asks.

I jerk. 'Pardon?'

'MI7.' She waves a thin, pale hand. 'This MI7. You tell them. They take care this ... man.'

The annoying, insistent voice in my head pipes up in angry

reflex. No, I want to do this myself, just like I want to find X and destroy him myself. I know I'm being a stubborn fool but that's not going to change how I feel. I focus on the ache in the centre of my chest. I try to remind myself that this isn't about my feelings, there's much more at stake. I have to look at the bigger picture.

'As much as I hate to say it,' my grandfather says, 'MI7 won't involve themselves in this. Without incontrovertible proof, they can't.'

'We've got proof!' O'Shea gesticulates wildly. 'There! That bloody video is proof!'

'It's nothing more than hearsay.'

'Bo...' Rogu3 begins.

I hold up my hand. 'I know, I know.' I curse under my breath. I didn't want it to come to this but Hale has forced my hand. 'We'll go to your place and get that damn software you need. That wanker needs to be stopped.'

CHAPTER 4
PHOTO BOMB

Rogu3 doesn't call ahead. It would make life a damned sight easier if his parents knew we were coming but we can't risk their phones being tapped. Rogu3's association with me is well-known; anyone could be watching his house. Whether it's hybrid witches, vulture-like journalists, Kakos daemons or Vincent bloody Hale, there are more than enough groups that we need to avoid if we want to keep everyone safe. That means sneaking in under cover of darkness and in full-blown stealth mode. In this scenario, less is more and Rogu3 and I would have managed it fairly easily. Unfortunately Maria has other ideas.

'I come,' she insists. She hooks her arm through Rogu3's.

I can see the shiver of delight in his eyes at her touch. I don't care. 'No.' My tone is meant to brook no argument. If only.

'I come,' she repeats.

'It's too risky. It's bad enough the two of us going. We don't know who's waiting out there for us. Someone might have staked out the place.'

O'Shea sniggers. 'Staked.'

I glare at him. He's not helping. I look at my grandfather for suggestions but he simply appears amused; in fact, his expression is actually quite smug, as if he's saying that now I know what it's like to have to deal with a stubborn idiot. He's had the monopoly on that for years with me.

I sigh. 'You have to stay here.'

For Maria, the answer is simple. 'No.'

'Why?'

She shrugs. 'I want see Alistair home.'

I glare at Rogu3. He smiles innocently as if it's nothing to do with him. Bloody teenagers. 'You are not coming,' I tell her.

She releases Rogu3 and steps up to me, her long hair swinging. She flips it behind her back in a practised move and meets my eyes. There's something vaguely degrading about having to crane my neck to look up at a teenager. Damn my height. 'You no want me come because of danger.' She cocks her head. 'Who you think I am? Years I spend in danger. Years I spend as plaything of ... men.' Her voice lowers and she speaks without any inflection. 'They hit me. They refuse me food. I am...' she struggles for the right word '...slave. You think I afraid of daemons? Of witches? Of you?'

The amusement has vanished from both my grandfather's and O'Shea's eyes. Floored, I swallow hard. 'Okay,' I say eventually. What else am I supposed to do? 'You can come. But you do everything I tell you to do.'

'Yes, Bo,' Maria replies serenely.

'Like that's going to happen,' O'Shea mutters. 'And if she's going, why do I have to stay behind? You might need back up.'

'You need to stay with Michael.' My grandfather is strong mentally but he's going to be no good in a fight. MI7 safe house or not, I need to know that someone is protecting the man I love. I harden my voice in case my own vulnerability is showing. 'Don't leave his side.'

I'm not fooling O'Shea. He reaches out and pulls me into a

massive bear hug, squeezing me tightly against his chest. Tears prick my eyes. I'm not going to cry though, I won't let myself. 'I won't, Bo. Besides,' he whispers, 'I've always wanted to have that hunk of gorgeousness in bed beside me.'

I manage a smile. 'I can always count on you.'

He grins back. He knows what I mean. Sometimes I forget that I'm not the only one who's suffering. Maria has known more pain than I could possibly imagine. O'Shea lost the love of his life only a few months ago. We all have our demons.

'There's an MI7 car out back,' my grandfather says. 'You won't find it on any database. It's completely secure and untrackable.'

We all turn and stare at him. 'Does it have an ejector seat?' O'Shea enquires. 'Because if it does, Michael Montserrat can drown in his own blood for all I care. I'm coming.'

'Rocket launcher?' Rogu3 says. 'Go on, tell me it has a rocket launcher.'

My grandfather folds his arms. 'It has outstanding manoeuvrability.'

'It turns into a boat when it hits water?'

He exhales in disgust. 'I don't know why I bother. Take the car and get out of here. You've only got a couple of hours before dawn.'

I glance at the others. 'Let's do this.'

As it turns out, the MI7 car is an unremarkable sedan of indeterminate age. Everything about it screams bland; I guess when discreet is your byword, it pays to have a vehicle that wouldn't draw the attention of a gnat. I note the tinted windows approvingly then hastily get into the driver's seat before Rogu3 can volunteer to drive. He's still under age but that hasn't stopped him so far.

There's something oddly comforting about driving through the quiet streets of London at this hour. I suppose I've been conditioned to enjoy darkness. I was sure that as soon as I was strong enough to withstand the UV rays during daylight I'd never return to stalking the streets at night but it actually feels good. Perhaps, once all is said and done, I really am a creature of the night.

We whip through the city centre. Even those areas with nightclubs and twenty-four-hour drinking establishments are almost completely dead. I spot a few homeless people shuffling along, the orange hue from the street lights lighting them up in such a way that anyone who didn't know better would view them as almost romantic figures. Some prostitutes are out and about but their bored expressions tell of a night with little passing trade. I'm tempted to stop the car and pay one for a drink to make sure I keep my strength up but, with the kids in tow, I feel uneasy about being so transparent. Although, as Maria has already pointed out, to view either her or Rogu3 as children is to ignore what they really are and what they've already experienced.

The things we do to innocents.

The car pulls almost silently into Rogu3's leafy street. It might look like your typical family cruiser but a lot of money has gone into making it as stealthy as possible. I kill the lights to aid our approach. Apart from a cat sauntering along a wall, everything is still. We roll to a stop and wait.

The house looks the same as ever. So does the street. 'It's fine, Bo,' Rogu3 insists quietly.

'It's not paranoia if they're really after you,' I tell him in return.

He leans forward. 'That car belongs to the Goodsons at

number twenty-three. That ancient Rover is the old bloke's who shouts at passers-by. The one next to it is the Lairds' pride and joy.' I flick him a look. He shrugs expansively. 'What? I engaged in criminal activity too. You don't think I didn't know how to cover my tracks and pay attention?'

I don't answer. Instead I step out and activate the child-lock, securing both Rogu3 and Maria inside. Ignoring his yelp of protest, I stroll across the road. I'm not letting either of them out until I'm sure we're safe.

I circle, keeping every sense alert. He's right about the cars: no one is hunkered down in any of them. None of the houses display flickering shadows or twitchy curtains. So far so good. Next, I move up to his parents' house.

The garage door is firmly closed. I wonder idly whether they've turned it into a typical suburban depository for lawn-mowers and wheelie bins now that Rogu3's equipment has been turfed out. I inch towards it and listen. Nothing. Satisfied that it's empty – of people at least – I walk over to the house. The curtains are closed but there's a gap at the side of the living-room window which I peer through. The room looks the same as ever.

I skirt round the back way and check the garden. There's a scrap of lawn edged with newly turned earth and a spinning clothes dryer. I crouch down and count to a hundred in my head. Nothing changes. Nothing moves. There is, however, a single footprint in the earth to my right.

I stare at it. The toe is pointing away from the house towards the fence that divides this house from its neighbour. Someone was here very recently and, judging by the imprint, it was a woman. A stiletto-heeled woman. Hope flares briefly inside me but I quash it. There's no time for this right now. I gnaw my bottom lip. Whoever she was, she's not here now. It's time to get on with the matter in hand.

I release Maria and Rogu3 from the confines of the car. Both of them scowl at me. Maria opens her mouth but I gesture at her to keep quiet. 'Do you have a key?' I whisper.

Rogu3 nods. We steal back to the front door and, with the merest clank as it turns in the lock, he opens up. Before he can step into the porch, I bar his way with my arm. 'Bo,' he hisses. 'It's fine. No one's here. No one's after me.'

I don't remind him that the last time I was here it was because X himself was hanging around in the street outside. Or that there might be any number of surviving Tov V'ra members who realise Rogu3 double-crossed them and have come looking for vengeance. I just wait, cocking my ear and listening. There's the faint rumble of a snore from upstairs. I exhale silently and pad forward, gesturing to Maria and Rogu3 to follow.

The interior of the house is as I remember it. I've never been up to Rogu3's room before but I have a good idea where it is. I place a foot on the first step, then the second. A heartbeat later, Rogu3 grabs my arm and squeezes it hard. I glance back at him in alarm. He points down at the third step and I understand: squeaky floorboards. I nod and skip up to the fourth step. The snoring continues.

At the top of the staircase, it's obvious which way to turn. To the right, there's a closed door emblazoned with a huge sign written in binary. Underneath are the words: 'This means keep out!!!' I throw Rogu3 a look and he shrugs, the tips of his ears turning pink.

Maria is enchanted. She beams at him. 'Very cute,' she mouths.

His eyebrows snap together in a glower. He sniffs and pushes past, opening the door and beckoning us inside.

If I expect the room to smell like teenage boy, I'm sorely mistaken. Rogu3's mum obviously takes cleaning seriously. There's been a considerable amount of air freshener dispensed within these four walls. There's a bunk bed, with neatly laundered sheets, a desk stacked high with computer manuals, school books and a few photos, and a large wardrobe. There's also a life-size poster of some Z-list celebrity wearing very little clothing. Rogu3's ears go from pink to flaming red.

'She very cold,' Maria remarks, with a raised eyebrow. 'Her ... nipples? They...'

Rogu3 coughs. I press my lips together hard.

'Let's just get what we came here for,' he says furiously.

He opens the wardrobe, heaving out a pile of clothing to reveal an expensive-looking safe. Even Dire Straits didn't boast a model as up-to-date as this one. I knew that Rogu3 made a lot of money out of his hacking ventures, but enough to need this security? Maria and I watch as he bends down and presses the pad of his thumb to open it. It's not quite as secure as the MI7 warehouse but it's not far off; no wonder MI7 offered him a damn job. He reaches inside, pulls out some manila envelopes and stuffs them into an empty bag. Then he carefully closes the safe and stands up.

'Done?' I ask. He nods. 'Do you want to see your parents?' It's a serious question. Now that he's with me and my world has exploded into the mess it's in, there's no telling when he'll get a chance to see them again. We could wake them up. Quietly.

'My mum will only freak and try to get me to stay. And my dad...' His voice trails off. Yeah, his dad will probably try to punch my nose for landing his son in such shit yet again. 'I'll leave them a note.'

He opens a drawer and scrabbles for a pen and a scrap of paper. As he starts to scribble a few words, Maria gasps. I turn to her. Her face is almost pure white and her eyes are fixed on one of Rogu3's photos.

'Maria?' I ask.

She doesn't answer. I follow her frozen gaze to an old photo in a small wooden frame. I scoop it up, my blood chilling as I examine it. 'This?' I ask.

Maria doesn't move. Her eyes dart to Rogu3 who, sensing that something is amiss, slowly turns. He looks from her to the photo and back again. I can hear my heart thudding against my ribcage. Rogu3's a lot younger in this photo. I know for a fact that it was taken long before I met him because his arm is hanging loosely round a young girl's shoulders and they're grinning at each other. I've never met the girl before but I know who she is. The entire country knows who she is. She's also the reason Rogu3 and I met in the first place.

'Alice,' Maria whispers. 'That is Alice.' She stares at Rogu3, the teen infatuation fading from her eyes to be replaced by an unmistakable look of fear.

MARIA DOESN'T SAY a word on the journey back. She curls up in the back seat and, when Rogu3 attempts to sit next to her, she shrinks away and points at the front. He throws me a quick, confused look, as if he's looking for guidance. I shake my head in warning. We need to get back to the relative safety of the warehouse first.

Alice Goldman was exactly seven years and five months old when she was abducted from the street in broad daylight. She was cycling home from a friend's house after an afternoon of playing hide and seek, a journey that should have taken less than ten minutes. Alice was a sensible girl and it was supposed to be a safe neighbourhood. Tell that to her grieving parents – or to the many others who were affected by her disappearance. Her pink bike, with streamers tied on the handlebars, was left discarded and dented by the side of the road. You don't need much of an imagination to shudder with horror at what must have happened to her.

A missing child, especially one with cute, curly blonde hair and huge blue eyes, galvanises even the most apathetic into joining search parties. People searched in their thousands, tracking through nearby woodland, stopping cars, putting up posters. None of it did any good. Her parents were questioned time and time again. Police patrolled the streets, knocked on doors and glared at anyone who looked even remotely suspicious. There was appeal after appeal. Her innocent face was plastered across every newspaper in the country and repeatedly emblazoned on the rolling news channels. But we all know how these stories usually end and Alice had, to all intents and purposes, vanished into thin air. After two weeks of fruitless searching, her bloodstained clothes were found dumped in a bin. And there was a lot of blood. There may not have been a body but it was clear that little Alice would not be returning home.

She'd been a neighbour of Rogu3's. He'd even babysat for her sometimes. And, when I'd been working for a shady insurance company that was searching for ways to avoid paying out on the policy for her, I'd bumped into him. There was no doubt that her disappearance hit him hard but he helped me find a way to force the insurance company to pay up. They tried to suggest that she'd been recruited by one of the Families and, taciturn to the last, the vampires didn't respond when questioned. Rogu3 hacked into their systems and proved they had nothing to do with her disappearance. Bruckheimer and Berryhill had to give the Goldmans what they were owed. I doubt it really changed anything for the family; only the safe return of their daughter could have achieved that.

Rogu3 and I stayed in touch afterwards, initially because his hacking skills were particularly useful to me and then because we became friends. If Alice hadn't gone missing, we'd never have met. I reflect on how much better that would have been for everyone.

Part of me expects Maria to bolt as soon as we get back but I'm not about to let that happen. I keep a close eye on her but she doesn't do anything other than hold herself away from us and shuffle inside.

'I don't understand,' Rogu3 says, as she disappears into one of the small bedrooms and shuts the door. His expression is desperate. 'What's this all about?'

'She knows Alice.'

His brow furrows. 'Everyone knows Alice. Unless you were hiding under a fucking rock when she went missing, you know who she was.' He stops. 'Oh. You don't think…' He takes a deep breath. 'Oh God.' He looks like he's been punched.

'Let's not jump to conclusions. It's four years since Alice was abducted.'

'Five years.'

Time flies. 'Okay, five years. I don't know how long Maria was at that club but it can't have been that long.'

'Why not?'

Because if that's the case, it's just too bloody awful to contemplate. Apart from her outburst this evening, Maria has refused to speak about what happened to her. Maybe if things hadn't spiralled out of control with Tov V'ra and Medici and Hale, I might have pressed her. I don't know if I should have. I don't know if that would have made things better or worse.

I take a deep breath. 'Look, Maria puts on a strong front but she needs our help more than she lets on. We have to be there for her. Don't push her on this. She'll tell us what this is about when she's ready to.'

'But she might know something about Alice!'

I curl up my fists and try not to let him see how desperate I am to rush into Maria's room and demand that she tells us everything. It could be her undoing; Alice was a child but so is Maria. 'You said it yourself. Alice has been gone for five years.' I try to be gentle. It's not bloody easy. 'Alice is dead. If Maria knows anything about who took her then I promise I will go after them and make them rue the day they touched her. But Maria is still living, Alistair. She's suffering more than either of us can imagine. Give her a day or two. Then let's see.'

He wants to argue. I can see his inner turmoil all over his face. It might be only a few short weeks but Rogu3 cares desperately for Maria. He cared for Alice too. 'Alright,' he says finally. 'Alright.' For a brief moment he looks so very, very young. He squeezes his eyes shut. 'When is it going to end, Bo? It's just one shitty thing after another. You think things are getting better and then they fuck up again. Is this really what life is about?'

I grab him and give him a gentle shake. I can't think of what to say. It's on the tip of my tongue to tell him yes, this is what life is about. Instead I go for the inane. 'Don't swear.'

He laughs harshly, opens his eyes and looks at me through a veil of tears. 'Fuck. Fuck you. Fuck life. Fuck all this. Word of the week, Bo. *Fuck.*'

I reach down for his hands and hold them tightly. 'Don't. You're better than this. Look at what Maria's been through. She's not giving up on life. She knows that around the corner anything could be waiting. It might be good and it might be bad but the last thing she's going to do is give up. Life is a struggle. Life's not fair. A three year old could tell you that. But it's not fairness that counts.'

He sniffs. 'Then what does?'

I think of Michael, lying half dead on a bed nearby. I think of how close I've come to losing my sanity and every shred of my own morality. 'Hope,' I say. 'Hope is the most precious thing in the world.'

He heaves in a ragged breath. We stand still for one long moment as I squeeze his fingers and he squeezes back. Then a shadow moves behind him and my grandfather steps forward. 'Devlin has made some disgusting chocolate concoction in the kitchen. Please go and tell him to stay away from all things culinary, would you, Alistair?'

Rogu3 wipes his eyes. 'Sure.' He pulls back his shoulders, looking more like a man than he ever has before, and walks away.

'He's grown up a lot lately,' I comment.

'He's not the only one.' My grandfather gazes at me steadily. 'That was a nice speech.'

'Yeah.' I massage my shoulders. 'And hope is really important.' I pause. 'But revenge runs a close second. Now tell me every damn thing you can about Maria.'

CHAPTER 5
ITCH

I sit next to Michael, smoothing his hair with fluid strokes, while I mull over what I've learnt about Romany gypsies. It's difficult to estimate how many there are in Europe; some say four million, some say nine million. Nomadic by nature, they're scattered across the continent, divided and sub-divided into groups. They're not witches, not in the true sense of the word, but their long heritage means that magic runs through their veins. In some of them it is stronger than in others and, according to my grandfather, Maria's is some of the strongest he's ever seen.

Michael moans softly in his sleep. I run my fingers down his jaw, marvelling at the stubble there. Even the hair on his head seems longer than it did when he was a vampire, as if decades of stunted growth means that now it's taking advantage of this new situation and sprouting at an incredible rate before things change again. I press my palm against his forehead, worrying at the heat of his skin. He subsides again.

Maria can't perform spells. She could buy ingredients from somewhere like Magix and do what O'Shea does from time to time, but she wouldn't be particularly skilled at it. I'd probably do just as good a job. No, my grandfather insists that Maria's speciality comes from within, that the power which sings through her blood is enough to recognise levels of magic in others. He told me a story of a man he once hired at MI7. They used him to infiltrate different triber groups and assess their potential for mayhem. It was only when MI7 got cocky because of the results they were seeing that they pushed him too far and sent him into the bowels of the Kakos daemon world. He was never seen again.

So far it all fits. Maria knew immediately that X was a Kakos daemon and X did everything he could to meet her in person. If, as my grandfather states, her blood is stronger than any Romany he's met before I can only wonder at her potential. She can recognise a Kakos daemon even in full glamour – but can she withstand one? Can X read her mind like he can read mine, or is she somehow immune? I have no idea how to test the theory.

Between the thought that Maria knows what happened to Alice Goldman and the idea that she might be the key to make X pay for what he's done, I can feel desperation clawing beneath my skin. I remind myself of what I told Rogu3: she's a victim. More than any of us, she deserves our support – she doesn't need to be used again. She's had enough of that. I sigh heavily. Maybe the temptation will be too great; maybe I should keep as far away from her as possible.

Beneath my fingers, I feel Michael stir. His eyelids flutter open and fix on me. 'Hey,' he says weakly.

I manage a smile. 'Hey you.'

'I feel like shit.'

'You look like it,' I tell him with a wink, trying to keep my tone light. He doesn't need my anxiety to deal with on top of everything else. 'Why don't you try to eat something?'

Michael grimaces as if he can't possibly think of anything worse. 'I've had enough bloody chicken soup.'

I give him a considering look. 'You're right. You've spent several decades on a liquid diet. Perhaps it's time to expand your taste buds.'

'Bo, I didn't just drink blood. You know that.'

He's right. Although blood provides vampires with the nutrients we need to survive, we can still eat solids. But they don't taste the same; it's not so long since I was human that I can't remember what the difference was. I tap my finger thoughtfully on the side of my mouth. 'Trust me. I have just the thing.'

I pop my head out of the door and call down the corridor. O'Shea's face appears immediately. 'Is there a problem? What's happened?'

'Everything's fine but I think we need to rev Michael's diet up somewhat.'

He wrinkles his nose. 'He rarely keeps the soup down. What else can we try?'

I grin. 'Where's the nearest fast-food restaurant?'

He looks at me sceptically. 'You don't seriously think that's going to help him, do you?'

'At this stage, it's unlikely to hurt.'

He shrugs. 'It's been a while since I had a greasy burger. Connor had me on far too much organic veggie stuff.' I don't move a muscle. 'It's okay, Bo, I can say his name without spontaneously combusting or anything.' He arches an eyebrow. 'But I wonder how MI7's fabulous facility would cope with that scenario. Maybe that can be a little project for later.'

His banter is forced; despite his brave words and lopsided grins, Connor's loss still affects him keenly. Grief isn't some fleeting experience; it colours our lives forever.

As if it's clear that I'm thinking too deeply about it, he gives a business-like nod. 'I'll be back in a jiffy.'

'You'll be careful, won't you?'

'Natch.'

We grin at each other. Unfortunately, the moment is lost when there's a loud clatter and crash from Michael's room. Alarmed, I rush in. He's face down on the floor, his expression contorted.

'What happened?' I dash over and help him up, getting him back onto the bed and into a sitting position while I scan him for fresh injuries.

He turns his head away from me. 'I need the toilet,' he says through gritted teeth.

I curse. 'That's why I'm here!' I hear a rustle in the doorway and look over my shoulder at O'Shea. The daemon raises his hand and nods before bowing out again. 'That's why we're all here. All you need to do is say the word and we can...'

'What? Hold my dick for me? Point it in the right direction? Wipe my arse afterwards?'

Abruptly, I realise what the problem is. 'There's no shame in being ill, Michael,' I say softly.

He snorts. 'I'm not just ill, am I?' His voice is weak and I have to strain to hear him but he's not about to give up. 'I'm human. I was one of the most powerful vampires in the country and now I'm nothing. Nobody.' His fingers curl round the sides of the bed and his knuckles turn white as his tension increases. 'You should have left me to die.'

I straighten my back. 'Piss off. Stop feeling sorry for yourself.' He jerks. 'So you're human. So what? Most of the damn world is human. I didn't want to be a vampire but I am. You don't want to be human but you are. We don't always get what we want.' I pause. 'We get some of it, though. I want you. I *love* you. If that means wiping your hairy arse for the next fifty years then so be it.'

He looks at me levelly. 'I don't love you. I said I did because I wanted to get into your pants. You mean nothing to me, Bo. I've had plenty of women who are more attractive than you – and less psychotic. Whatever was between us has gone.'

I ignore the searing stab of hurt in my chest and stare into his eyes. 'Nice try,' I say. 'But psychotic or not, you don't get rid of me that easily.'

He sucks in a breath through his teeth and slumps down further. 'Bitch.'

'Yeah. But, you know what? I'm your bitch.'

For the briefest of moments something flares in his eyes. I move round until I'm facing him then, as gently as I can, I lean forward and kiss him on the lips. I'm rewarded with another flare.

'You need to let me go,' he whispers.

'No chance.'

He gazes at me. 'No, I'm serious. I'm going to wet myself if I don't get to the damned bathroom.'

Startled, I laugh aloud. 'Come on. I'll help.' I hoist him to his feet.

'No.' He shakes his head. 'Please, Bo. Not this. It's bad enough that you are seeing me this weak. Don't do this.'

'Okay. I'll go and get help.'

'Thank you.'

I place my hand against his rough cheek. He reaches up and covers it with his. 'I hate that you see through me so easily.'

I grin, awash with relief that I hadn't read the situation wrongly. Put me up against a Kakos daemon or a witch or a bastard like Hale and I'll be the toughest son-of-a-gun in the room but I've realised that I don't need to be like that all the time. Pit me against Michael – or anyone else I care for – and the truth is that I'm just mush. 'You see through me too,' I tell him. 'So now we're even.'

~

I LEAVE Michael to my grandfather's brusque and unembarrassed ministrations and go through to check on Rogu3. There's still no sign of Maria and the young teenager is glaring ferociously at the computer screen as if he can blame technology for all that's wrong with the world. Judging from the set of his spine, he's not yet made any progress with his new software, so I leave him where he is and head for the fridge to get some blood. It won't be particularly tasty and it won't do much to stave off my hunger but it'll be better than nothing. I don't need to drink as often I did when I was a newbie but, if I go for too long, strength saps out of me like water from a leaky bucket.

I'm halfway there when my phone rings. I pull it out, a frisson of excitement zipping through me when I see that it's Foxworthy. 'This is Bo.'

'Morning.' The gruff inspector's voice sounds hollow, as if he's in a cave.

'Where are you?' I ask.

'Hiding in a damn cell so no one hears me talking to you,' he answers. 'It appears that there's a new initiative in place.'

Something about the way he says it sets me on edge. 'Go on.'

'Orders from on top. We are to seek out any surviving bloodguzzlers and place them into custody for their own safety.'

'So because giving ourselves up voluntarily didn't work, we're going to be treated as criminals? What happens once we've been taken in?'

He inhales heavily. 'There's a special squad that will take you to an unknown location. All the better to keep you safe, of course.'

I roll my eyes. 'Of course.'

'Bo,' he says, 'I've never seen anything like this before. It's unprecedented. And it's bloody dangerous.'

It's good to know that he's seeing things the same way I am. 'You say that this has come from on top. How far up are we talking?'

'Government level.'

I purse my lips. It doesn't take a genius to work out which damned politician put it into place. 'Wanker,' I mutter.

'It's not my fault,' Foxworthy says, put out.

'Not you.'

'I'm glad to hear it. Now, listen. I can find a way for you to get out of the city. I've been assigned across the river this evening. If I come and pick you up then...'

'Whoa. Who said anything about leaving?'

Rogu3 looks up from the computer, his expression suddenly intent. I gesture to him to get back to what he's doing. He doesn't move.

'Bo,' Foxworthy continues, 'this is getting serious. I understand you are stubborn and you don't want to leave with your tail between your legs but you can come back when things calm down. This is not the time for a vampire to be strolling around the streets!'

'I didn't know you cared.'

'There's been enough damned blood on my streets as it is.'

I don't comment on his use of the personal pronoun because I feel like that about London too. It's the kind of place that gets under your skin, whether you were born here or not, and it stays there like an itch that's annoying but so very, very satisfying to scratch.

'Thank you for the offer,' I tell him. I mean it sincerely; it's nice to know the gruff old policeman cares. 'But I'm fine. Tell me you have other news.'

He sighs. 'I don't suppose I can change your mind.'

'Nope.' I try again. 'Do you have anything else to tell me?'

'Going up against the Kakos daemons is lunacy.'

'Foxworthy...'

'Alright, alright. I've found several addresses for your daemon. The most recent one seems to be 12 Brightside Avenue.'

'That's next to Canary Wharf.' The poshest-of-posh, over-priced scraps of land in the country. It figures.

'It is.' He pauses. 'Am I going to be scraping you off the pavement and into a body bag?'

I feel my fangs lengthen and my heart rate pick up. 'Not if I do this properly. Cheers, Foxworthy.' I end the call.

Rogu3 is still watching me. 'You have an address for X.'

I nod. 'I do.'

'Is this the best thing to do, Bo?'

I consider his words. 'Probably not. But it is the right thing.' I meet his eyes. 'If I don't come back, you know what to do.'

He swallows. 'Yeah.'

'Good.'

O'Shea appears holding a greasy brown paper bag. Despite the overpowering smell of cooked meat and limp cabbage, my stomach growls. I really need to eat.

'I got a kebab,' he trills. 'Yum yum.' From out of nowhere, Kimchi bounds towards him, almost smacking into his legs. The dog whines and starts to slobber, a line of drool landing on O'Shea's shoe. 'These are handmade leather,' the daemon yells, lifting his foot to shake away the spittle. Kimchi's tongue lolls as he tries to decide whether to attack the shoe or leap towards the kebab. O'Shea hisses in disgust then looks from Rogu3 to me and back again. His expression clears abruptly. 'Ah. I see we've made some progress. Let me drop this off with Michael then I'm coming with you.'

'No.'

'Bo, we're partners. Buddies. Where you go, I go.'

'It's too dangerous, Devlin.'

He winces. 'I really hate it when you call me that.' He tilts up his chin. 'You can't stop me, Bo. If you're going to do this, then so am I. I'm more than an errand boy. If you get all your vital organs ripped out of your body then someone's going to need to break the news to Michael.'

I raise an eyebrow. 'You're volunteering to tell him I'm dead?'

'That's what friends are for, darling.'

I look at him. Despite his teasing words, steely determination is etched into his brow. 'Okay.' I sigh. 'Okay.' God save me from my own people.

Kimchi whines, sensing the sombre atmosphere. O'Shea reaches inside the bag, picks out a scrap of brown meat and offers it to him. For once, the dog doesn't go for it. Instead, he lies down and gives both of us a long-suffering look with his large, soulful eyes.

'Dogs don't have special senses, do they?' O'Shea asks nervously. 'Like being able to tell when someone's about to die?'

'Nah. I think that's cats.'

My grandfather's moggy takes that moment to leap down from the desk and wander up to me, rubbing its head against my shins. O'Shea and I stare at each other. Eventually, I shrug. 'Last one to get their heart eaten is a rotten egg.'

<h1 style="text-align:center">CHAPTER 6
LIFE INSURANCE</h1>

The irksome thing about this part of London is that it's all wide streets and glossy facades. You won't a find a dark alley to hide in anywhere near here. However, there are lots of tall buildings. Given that I have no idea how close I have to be to X for him to read my mind, it's important to stay well away in terms of yardage but close enough to spot him. O'Shea and I find his building while keeping our distance, then venture to the corner opposite.

'We need the roof,' I say decisively, looking upwards.

O'Shea cranes his neck. 'It shouldn't be hard to get up there. But it won't be easy to follow Mr X once he's on the move.'

'Don't call him mister,' I say. That bastard doesn't deserve the respect. 'And I don't want to follow him. Right now, I just want to get a handle on him. What he's doing, how he's travelling around and where his vulnerable spots are.'

'He's a Kakos daemon, Bo,' O'Shea says, sounding falsely cheerful. 'He doesn't have any vulnerable spots.'

'No one is invincible, not even him.'

O'Shea gives me a long look. 'Well,' he says finally, 'now I'm wishing I'd bought another kebab. We could be here for some time.'

'Yeah.' I feel a wave of faintness and pinch the bridge of my nose. Damn it.

'You need to eat as well.' O'Shea bites his lip and offers me his wrist.

I frown. 'Ick.'

'You don't like daemon blood? I'll have you know I can be pretty damn tasty.'

'It's human blood I crave. You know that.'

'I'm only a quarter daemon.'

I shrug. 'Doesn't make a difference.'

'Racist,' he mutters.

'Come on. Let's get inside and make our way up. I'll find someone along the way to snack on.'

The doors whoosh open and we're immediately greeted by a blast of cool air. There are a few people milling around inside; the marbled floor shows their blurred reflections as they stare at their phones like zombies. O'Shea lets out a coo of delight.

'We need to be discreet,' I warn. 'The slightest disturbance and X might find out we're here.'

'He can't see us in here, he doesn't have X-ray vision.' O'Shea pauses, his eyes widening. 'Unless that's why he's called X.'

I scoff, although the truth is that I have very little idea of what X is capable of. I damn myself for not doing more when I had the chance to discover his abilities. I seriously doubt X-ray vision is one of them; all the same, I feel a nervous swirl in the pit of my stomach. I really don't want him to know I'm here.

I scan the list of names on the information board, looking for something that will work. I'm thinking that the lawyer on the sixteenth floor could be a good bet until I see who's right above him. My heart suddenly sings in delight. Well, well, well.

'There.' I jab my finger. 'And we can kill two birds with one stone. It's about time something went our way.'

O'Shea leans in. 'Bruckheimer and Berryhill Insurance.' He purses his lips. 'Life insurance? Bo, I hate to say it but I doubt you'll be able to afford the premiums.'

I clap him on the shoulder. 'There's more method to my madness than you realise.' Bruckheimer and Berryhill are my old employers; it's the company I was working for when Alice went missing. 'This is the perfect cover. We don't even need to hide any longer because we have a reason for being here that doesn't involve X.'

Leaving a confused O'Shea to trail behind me, I approach the reception desk. 'Good morning!'

A young man wearing a crisp white shirt, an old school tie and a professional smile glances up. I enjoy watching him go pale. 'Bo Blackman,' he bursts out, before he can stop himself.

I grin and check his name tag. 'One and the same, David. One and the same.'

'My friends and I were discussing you last night,' he beams, almost immediately recovering from his shock. 'What are you planning to do? Are you going to kill all those religious freaks? I said that you wouldn't do that because you're the Red Angel and you're too good, but Barry...'

I don't need to hear what Barry thinks. I interrupt him. 'That's kind of you to say that about me.' I hold out my hand. 'And it's lovely to meet you.'

He's almost overcome. He reaches across and vigorously pumps my hand. 'The pleasure's all mine.'

'I'm here to see Bruckheimer and Berryhill,' I tell him, once I've extricated myself.

He blinks rapidly. 'Of course, of course. Do you have an appointment? You can't see them otherwise. The rules are really strict.' He sounds regretful, as if to emphasise that he'd change things if he could.

I shake my head sadly. 'No appointment. I'm trying to keep my movements secret. It's dangerous out there, you know.' I point at the street.

'Oh my goodness! It must be awful for you. I can't let you in but if there's anything else I can do to help, all you have to do is say the word. I'm a really big fan. It wasn't right what happened to your friends. I know some people are saying that the blood guz— I mean vampires, deserved it but *I* don't think that.'

I'm not sure I've ever met someone who talks this much. 'You know, David, there is something you could do for me.'

His expression transforms into that of an eager puppy. 'Anything,' he breathes. 'Anything for you.'

At least some people are still fans. I lick my lips and eye his jugular. 'I'm really hungry.'

I don't think he was expecting that. He swallows and stares at me. 'You want my...' his voice drops to a whisper '...my blood?'

'I'll only take a teeny bit,' I promise.

He wants to say no, I can see it written all across his face. He's not a wannabe vampette – which is hardly surprising as even the most voracious vampettes are keeping well out of the way at the moment for fear of reprisals – but he's afraid of what I'll do if he says no. He scans round the lobby, looking anxious. Unfortunately for him, my appearance hasn't been enough to drag the others' attention away from their phones. None of them have even noticed I'm here.

'Er, I suppose it's okay. But...'

I interrupt. 'Fantastic!' I give him a wide-mouthed smile and hop round the desk. Before he can say anything else, I let my fangs lengthen and I sink them into his neck. He lets out a tiny yip and there's the unpleasant tang of aftershave on my lips but it's quickly superseded by the salty deliciousness of his blood. I keep an eye on the phone zombies but they still don't look up. Wow. This is how you take over the world, by doing it when no one's watching because they're too busy playing Candy Crush.

I drink quickly and deeply and it's not long before David's body sags. I release him gently onto the floor, where his limp form is hidden from view by the desk, and beckon to O'Shea.

He looks almost fearful. 'Was that necessary, Bo?' he whispers.

I shrug, trying to feel guilty. 'He said he'd do anything for me. He said it was okay. He shouldn't have said it if he didn't mean it.'

'Yeah, but he's passed out.'

'He'll be fine in an hour or two.'

'You used to hate drinking from people, even vampettes. And I've never seen Michael treat someone like that. You had this look in your eye. Like a predator.'

'Michael lived in a different world. And I've changed from the person I was.' I sigh and try to explain. 'I have a heart, O'Shea. It's not the same as it was but it's still there. I'm more ruthless because I need to be. And I *am* a predator. I'm a vampire. I'm also on a mission that could mean life or death for more than just me and X.' O'Shea is patently unconvinced. 'Look, just then my need was greater. You were right before – I had to get some blood. If it makes you happy, I won't do it this way again. But at least David doesn't get into trouble for letting a crazy vampire loose in the building because it'll look like he was attacked. And he has a story to dine out on with Barry and the rest of his friends.'

O'Shea still doesn't look pleased. 'I thought we were trying to keep a low profile.'

'This way is better. If X comes across us, I've got a ready-made excuse.' I say the words confidently, as if I really believe them.

'Eating a receptionist?'

'Nope. Visiting some old friends.' I grin and wipe away the last of David's blood from my mouth. I'm just in time because one of the humans finally gives up on her phone and wanders over.

'Hi,' she says in a perfunctory manner. 'I'm here for Charcoal and Sons.'

'Do you have an appointment, ma'am?' I ask in my most proper accent.

'Yes.' She checks her watch. 'In about five minutes.'

'I'll buzz you right up.'

I search the desk and find the right button. The woman nods and heads for the lift.

'She didn't even notice who you were,' O'Shea marvels.

'All she saw was a worker bee,' I say. 'I wasn't a real person, just a cipher doing a faceless job.' I glance down at David. The colour is already leaking back into his cheeks but I suddenly feel sorry for him. Whether I'm an infamous bloodguzzler or not, it's no wonder he was so happy to talk to me. I noticed him as an individual, a living being. Alright, I amend, an individual, a living being and lunch. I'll put up my hands and admit that I'm not a good person but I could be worse. It's not much of an epitaph but I reckon it means there's hope for me yet.

I tell O'Shea to stay in David's place and watch over him. He bobs his head dutifully and buzzes me up to the insurance company. When I left the warehouse, the last thing I expected from this expedition was some fun. Now I'm actually feeling rather excited.

THE OFFICES for Bruckheimer and Berryhill are a testament to how swimmingly the insurance industry is going. Years ago, when I worked for them, head office was a rather dilapidated affair on an industrial estate on the outskirts of the city. Now they're in the heart of London, with plush carpets, gleaming glass and a whole host of glossy leaflets. I pick one up at random and scan it. Yeah, maybe they are looking better-heeled than they used to but they're still performing the same tricks. This particular leaflet offers life insurance against acts of witchery – but from the very, very small print, they won't pay out if that act results from your own actions. Fair enough – until you realise that this policy is aimed at witches. Screw up a spell, end up dead and your family gets nothing. Alternatively, do something to goad a fellow witch into attacking you and you'll still end up with nothing. I wonder whether they've actually had to make any payments for this product.

A young woman appears. 'May I help you?' she asks politely.

I bare my fangs. Recognition flares in her eyes and she lets out a yelp. Her eyes snap to a wall behind me. Curious, I turn to see several rows of professionally taken photographs of their board members. Underneath are several other photos, including one of yours truly. A half smirk crosses my lips and I take a closer look. Underneath, on a neatly printed card, are the words: 'Bo Blackman, a former operative who helped many of our clients get everything they deserve.' I almost laugh.

'Do you often display images of old investigators?' I ask. 'Or is it just the famous ones?'

'Ms Blackman, let me find Mr Berryhill for you.' She legs it.

I focus on the picture. It's amazing that I could ever have been this young. It's not only that I look barely out of school, it's the naïve optimism shining out of my eyes. I don't need a mirror to know that these days what you see is hard calculation and bitter disappointment. But maybe if you look closely enough, you'll see a flicker of love too.

'Bo!' A warm voice greets me from behind.

I turn and spot Berryhill. His arms are open wide as if he's expecting me to rush in for a hug. Considering I never qualified to meet the man when I worked here, he's got high expectations. I highlight the fact that I used to be nothing more than a faceless minion to him by saying, 'It's Ms Blackman. Who are you?'

The slight flicker in his eyes tells me that I've made a dent in his over-sized ego. 'Mark Berryhill. We met at the end-of-year celebration when you were one of our employees.'

No, we didn't. I curve my lips into a smile. 'Oh.'

He drops his arms, realising that I'm not going to embrace him like we're old friends. 'What can I do for you? Are you seeking re-employment now that the Families have been reduced to dust?'

Score one for the sleaze in the suit. 'The Families might be gone,' I tell him, flicking at an invisible piece of lint on my sleeve, 'but we vampires are hardly dead and buried.' I lick my lips, providing him with a faint glimpse of my teeth. 'I'm actually here to request some old files.'

He blinks, taken aback. 'Oh yes?'

'The Alice Goldman case.'

His expression clears. 'Ah. Such a tragic situation, that one.'

Mm. All the more tragic because Bruckheimer and Berryhill had to pay out a large wad of cash. 'I worked on it for a while,' I say. I'm sure he's well aware of my role; I cost him a pretty penny as a result. 'I'd like to see the file.'

'Why?'

Playing the 'ignorance is bliss' card, I don't drop my gaze. 'It's probably better for you if you don't know.'

He links his fingers. 'Those files are confidential.'

'As I said, my work is included in those papers so I don't think confidentiality is an issue here.'

'Yes, but you are a former employee. And that case is closed.'

My smile widens. 'You have my photo on the wall.' I pause. 'Without my permission. If you're taking advantage of me, Mr Berryhill, I feel I should get something in return.'

His gaze is flat. 'I don't appreciate intimidation or threat tactics, *Ms Blackman.*'

I'm the very picture of innocence. 'Really? I worked for you. I know exactly what tactics you appreciate.'

Berryhill's bonhomie is almost gone. 'And bloodguzzlers are so perfect,' he says sarcastically. 'We help people through tragic circumstances beyond their control. You put them in those circumstances. The difference now is that you're on your own.' He shrugs. 'Sure, you might be able to kill me but I have friends in high places. They'll come after you. You don't have the Families to hide behind any longer.'

'I removed myself from the Families long ago,' I tell him calmly. 'I don't need to hide behind anyone.' I don't take my eyes from his. 'But I fear we're getting off on the wrong foot. I don't want to bother you and I don't want to create a stink because you're using my name to drum up more business. All I want is to see the files on Alice Goldman and then I'll be out of your way.' What I don't state is the obvious: if he continues to block me, I'll do a lot more than just grin at him. I display my fangs once more to make sure he gets the message.

He stares at me for a long moment. There's considerable animosity here. 'Fine,' he snaps. 'I need something from you in return.'

I raise my eyebrows. Interesting. And brave. 'What?'

'A few well-placed attacks. You don't have to kill anyone but it would be good if you could bring them to the brink, so to speak.'

My lip curls. 'Good grief. You're worried about your bottom line, aren't you? How many people have cashed in their policies in the last week? With no vampires to worry about, there's no need for anti-vampire life insurance, is there?' I shake my head in mock dismay. 'Tut tut.'

Berryhill glares but ignores my goading. 'Children would be best.'

The man has no shame. I inspect my fingernails. 'There's an unconscious body downstairs.' I curtsey. 'You're welcome.'

If he's taken aback, he doesn't show it. 'That's not enough.'

'You need headlines.' I eye him with distaste. 'You could just create a new policy, one to guard against attacks by crazed religious groups.' Berryhill doesn't answer. 'Oh,' I say. 'You already have. Silly me.'

He sniffs. 'That's the deal.'

I consider his terms. 'Very well. I will ensure that tomorrow's front page has details of a vamp attack. That will have to do for now.'

'Accepted. Come back tomorrow and I'll get you what you need.'

I step back and look him over. His teeth have been whitened to within an inch of their life and, judging by his lack of facial expression, there's definitely been some Botox action. I allow the silence to draw out. It's not words that give people power – it's control. I've got a damned sight more than Berryhill has. For one thing, I'm not worried about ageing. Not for a long time yet.

As I expected, he can't stop himself filling the silence. 'I can't give you the files now,' he says. 'I've got no guarantee that you'll do what you promise.'

'Unless the Queen drops dead, you'll get your front page. You have my word.' I glance over his shoulder. The door behind him is open and there is a cluster of wide-eyed office bees staring through. 'Otherwise, I'll decimate your pretty little outfit here.'

Berryhill's Adam's apple bobs up and down. There's been enough stuff written about me recently that he believes I'm capable of it. There are some advantages to being psychotic. He mulls over his options and comes to a quick decision. 'Very well,' he snaps. 'Follow me.'

He spins on his heel and heads back through the door. I shake my head at his stupidity. You should never turn your back on a dangerous animal. For now, however, I follow him meekly. The secretaries and insurance agents duck their heads as if to hide from me. It's hard not to laugh.

Berryhill stalks through and points to a nearby office. 'You can wait in there,' he says stiffly.

'Nope,' I say cheerfully. 'Not there.' I look around then spot the room I need. 'That one will do.'

His expression sours even further. 'That's my office.'

I beam. 'Fabulous.'

He mutters something under his breath, obviously tempted to refuse. Eventually, however, he chooses the wiser of two options and nods stiffly. 'As you wish.' His breathing is barely controlled. 'I shall retrieve the files.'

I clap him on the shoulder. 'Thank you.'

CHAPTER 7

THREATS AND PROMISES

I have no idea what Bruckheimer's office looks like but Berryhill has certainly gone all out on his. The desk looks antique, even if the large chair behind it is ergonomically designed, and there's a slim, expensive-looking laptop on top of it. On one wall there's a huge flat screen displaying the day's news. Yet again, the destruction of the five Families is leading the way. Irritated, I turn it off. I open a couple of desk drawers and peer inside, noting the various cards for escort services next to the tidy array of stationery. Then I wander over to the window. I have a perfect view all the way down to X's place. Nobody is coming in or out. I cross my arms and study the darkened windows. Are you in there, X? Do you know I'm coming for you?

I remain where I am for a moment or two, then wheel round and grab Berryhill's chair. I push it out from behind the desk and place it in front of the window just as the man himself returns.

'What are you doing?'

'Rearranging your furniture,' I say, without looking round. 'The energy in this space is all wrong.'

If I was expecting him to complain, I'm disappointed. He huffs slightly and walks up beside me, holding out the files as if he's cradling a bomb. I take them then shoo him away dismissively. Berryhill's jaw works as if he wants to say something. In the end, he gives in and leaves me to it.

'I'll come and find you when I'm done,' I call out after him. Then I smile.

Keeping one eye on X's building, I open up the first of the files. I'm confronted with a gap-toothed, smiling photo of Alice – the one that was broadcast on so many news programmes. Her eyes sparkle with mischief and she grins with so much childish optimism that I feel my heart ache. I quickly flip over to the first report.

The initial pages detail little more than what happened to Alice, although the language is cold. *The insured subject was last pinpointed at location blah blah blah.* That kind of thing. I understand that an insurance or a police report or anything of that ilk has to be dispassionate but there's something very disheartening about reading it. This was a child – not a 'subject'. I suppose I should congratulate myself on proving that I'm not completely heartless after all. When confronted with the stark facts of Alice's abduction, though, there's little congratulating to be done. I suppose things could be worse; I could still be working for these bastards.

Due to the high-profile nature of the case, Bruckheimer and Berryhill used several different investigators to ensure no stone was left unturned. I conjure up a vague sense of professional detachment as I examine their separate reports. It's clear which investigators were trying to do their job as the insurance company saw it – namely finding any way possible to duck out of paying out on the policy. All they needed were a few suggestions that bloodguzzlers were responsible. However, as I read I realise I wasn't the only one who did everything I could to force the company into paying up. I was just more successful because I had Rogu3 to hack into the Families' systems and prove that vampires weren't involved.

There's little new information in the files although it's helpful to see what bases have already been covered. The family friend who Alice was visiting was questioned at length. Even at seven years old, there's a sense of tired exasperation in her words, as if she'd been interviewed so many times that she was repeating what had happened with little emotion. No, Alice had never expressed any interest in vampires, witches, or daemons. Yes, she was her normal self on the day she vanished. No, they hadn't seen anyone strange lurking around the neighbourhood.

Bruckheimer and Berryhill didn't just dispatch investigators to speak to those directly involved with Alice. They also sent at least two agents to speak to everyone in the neighbourhood, coaxing out details to suggest that there had been a vampire sighting in the area. The questions they asked were deliberately vague in order to incite equally vague answers. They didn't want any flat denials. The mere suggestion that a bloodguzzler was hanging around the quiet suburb would cast enough doubt to get the insurance company out of paying. Unfortunately, several locals played along.

I take more time as I read their answers: one suggests that there was a dark-haired man with blood running from his mouth who transformed into a bat and flew away. Yeah, right. Another discusses a strange car that was seen in the area. Sadly for Bruckheimer and Berryhill, the police discounted that one fairly quickly as the car was caught on CCTV at the local petrol station and belonged to an estate agent scoping the area. I jot down notes from each of the statements. There's no telling what could prove useful in the future. Even the crazy old man who is adamant that bug-eyed aliens took Alice off the street in front of his eyes gets a mention on my notepad.

Unfortunately, eyewitnesses are notoriously unreliable – UFO sightings or otherwise. Ask ten people who witnessed the same event to describe what they saw and you'll get ten different answers. The company concluded that the locals could 'provide clues' as to reasons for Alice's disappearance that could help them avoid payment but, even with the varied stories, they couldn't make any of them stick. Vampires might have been the easy target to blame, but there was no evidence to prove it.

I smile humourlessly. No doubt Berryhill and his buddy would have tried to bury the information from Rogu3's hacking efforts if I hadn't inadvertently let it slip to the local press. The simple truth was that the Families weren't involved and everyone knew it. Even Medici wasn't that much of an idiot.

I sigh and close the file, staring out of the window with my chin in my hands. Hundreds of people looked into Alice's disappearance. Every scrap of evidence was pored over; if there was anything to find, it would have already turned up. The only person who can shed any new light on all this is Maria. Maybe she knows where Alice's remains are buried so we can provide closure for the Goldmans. But if Alice ended up in the same place as Maria, I doubt there's any information that will make her family feel better. I suppress the shudder that ripples through my body. If there's one thing I've learnt, it's that I can't change the past. All I can do is affect the future.

There's still no sign of life from X's building. Despite Foxworthy's efforts, this address might not be current. I calculate how long I can wait before I break in and snoop around. The place looks unthreatening but it's probably almost impregnable. I'm confident there will be a chink somewhere, though – there always is.

As far as I can tell, there's only one entrance. I'll be surprised if there's a back door, although it probably merits checking out. My eyes flick from window to window, searching for vulnerabilities. I'd hesitate to scamper up the side of the building itself – there's no telling what alarms that might trigger – but I could probably make the leap from the office block to the left. Maybe it'd be worth getting Rogu3 to leave off Hale for a couple of hours to see if he can seek out any building plans.

I massage my neck. Tempting as it is to storm through the front door and let the chips fall where they may, I'm only going to beat X if I'm smarter than him. Most people would say I've not got a snowball's chance in hell, but I'm very, very motivated. I'll find a way to get to him even if it kills me.

I continue to watch the street, losing myself in an elaborate fantasy of X at my feet begging for mercy before I blow off his head. I'm just getting to the good part when there's a cough behind me. 'What do you want, Berryhill?' I ask, irritated. I turn and look at him. He's loosened his tie but his eyes are harder than before. He's had enough time to stew and he's starting to regret our little 'deal'. Tough.

'There's a phone call for you.' He points to a phone on his desk. 'I've had it diverted to this line.'

My eyes narrow in suspicion. No one knew I was coming here because, until I saw their listing downstairs, I didn't know Bruckheimer and Berryhill were located in this building. 'Who is it?'

'How the fuck should I know?' he snaps.

I point at him. 'Don't move.' I receive a glare in response but he does as he's told. I pick up the receiver. 'Hello?'

'This is Joe at reception,' O'Shea's voice trills out. 'You should come down.'

My blood freezes. 'Why? What's wrong?'

'There's a package for you to collect. You need to sign for it.'

It takes me a moment to understand. 'You can't talk freely.'

'That's correct,' he answers breezily.

I lick my lips, ignoring the suddenly calculating look in Berryhill's eyes. 'Are you in immediate danger?'

'No,' O'Shea squeaks. Then he hangs up.

I swallow. This is most definitely not good. Berryhill snorts at my expression. 'Oh dear. Trouble in paradise?'

I don't have time for more verbal sparring. I toss down the phone and stride towards him. I'm less than a foot away when he realises the danger he's in. 'Hey!' he protests. 'You promised…'

I grab his arm and swing him towards me. After David, I'm not really hungry but this is about more than satiating my physical hunger. I hook one arm round Berryhill's chest and drag him back to the lift; at the same time I sink my teeth into his neck. He tries to struggle but it's futile. His blood fills my mouth, while his employees stare in shock. A few stand up as if they're going to try to rescue him from my evil clutches but, as soon as I glance in their direction, they think better of it. With Berryhill moaning underneath me, I press the button for the lift and march over to my photo.

I release my teeth from his neck and use my index finger to dip into the fresh wound, then I smear Berryhill's blood onto my picture, colouring my lips bright red. The effect is rather impressive. I push him back against the wall so his head is propped next to the picture, pull out my phone and snap a photo.

'Sorry,' I shrug. 'I know there's not much finesse but I need to get downstairs. This should do the trick, though. I did promise.' With one tap, I send the photo off to the first journalist I find in my contacts.

I hear a murmured whisper as one of Berryhill's braver employees calls 999. I nod grimly. That'll help.

Just as the lift opens, I let Berryhill sink down into a heap. He's not dead. Although perhaps he had it coming.

~

O'Shea is waiting beside the lift door as I emerge. When he catches sight of me, he hisses in alarm, 'You're covered in blood!'

I wipe my mouth with the back of my hand. 'Occupational hazard.'

'Goddamnit, Bo. I know I insisted on coming along but the one thing you said was that we were going to be low profile. I don't actually want to die today.'

He jerks his head across the lobby and my eyes follow the movement. The zombies from earlier have been replaced by some new ones but I still don't see any imminent danger. I open my mouth to say so just as O'Shea elbows me sharply in the ribs. 'Look harder.'

I frown and squint. Generic businessman in a generic cheap suit. Another one next to him, tapping his foot. A slick woman with hair so perfect it looks sprayed on is gesturing at reception with fluid movements. There's something about the way she flicks her wrist that's incredibly familiar. I suck in a breath. Oh bugger.

'You see it, right?'

'I see it,' I reply grimly. There's only one other person I know who moves in that kind of precise, almost lyrical manner. And he's a Kakos daemon. 'Let's get out of here.'

There's a groan from behind reception. David, still looking pale, staggers up. The woman quirks her manicured eyebrow in his direction. She doesn't look worried – she looks amused.

'Now,' I whisper urgently. 'There has to be a back door.' I grab O'Shea's arm and start walking quickly. I feel a strange pressure behind my eyes and I pinch the bridge of my nose. This is not the time to start getting a bloody migraine.

David smiles weakly at me as we rush past him. 'Sorry,' I mouth. He gives me a half shrug.

I pick up speed but I'm waiting for the woman to yell out or to feel sudden pain as she springs towards us and rips my heart from my chest. We continue on unimpeded, however, and O'Shea flings open the nearest door. I shove him through before quickly following.

The second the door slams behind us we sprint down the narrow corridor towards the emergency exit at the other end. Nausea swells up through my stomach. Why did I think I could do this? Why did I think I could take on X?

'How did you know?' I gasp to O'Shea. 'She's in full glamour.'

'I'm an Agathos daemon. Partly, anyway. And I've been known to use a bit of glamour myself,' he pants. 'But I wouldn't have been able to tell if she hadn't let her glamour slip. It was only for a half second. That was enough.'

I feel panic rise in my throat. I push down frantically on the bar to the emergency door and we burst out into bright sunlight.

'Which way?' O'Shea yells.

'Right. No, wait.' I point. 'That way. Left.'

We run. My mind turns over the expression in her eyes. She didn't once look directly at me but she knew I was there. It was written all over her face. And she'd been able to read both our minds. 'This is a trap,' I say suddenly. 'We're running into a damn trap. She wanted us to come this way. She let her glamour slip deliberately so that we'd do this.'

'Why?'

There can only be one reason. 'X.' I fling my head round. 'He's here somewhere. He's waiting for us.' I slow down. 'I wasn't here for you!' I yell. 'I was here for Alice!' Even to my own ears, the words sound flat as they echo off the walls around us.

Nobody answers and I damn myself for a naive fool. Why did I think I could fool a Kakos daemon? He knows my lies better than I do. Not only that, but X has got friends and he'll have enlisted them to make sure I don't step out of line. I've brought O'Shea here and into danger; if we die, it's all my fault. I just hope that my grandfather will be able to help Michael once I'm gone. My arrogance has been my undoing.

'There's no one here, Bo,' O'Shea insists.

For the first time in my life, I know what it feels like to be a tiny field mouse stalked by a farm cat with hunger pangs. 'He's here. He's watching us.'

'We're alone.'

I don't believe it. O'Shea touches my arm. 'Bo, you can't let him intimidate you like this. We can't even see him and you're terrified.'

'You know what he's capable of.'

'So let's fight then. Two against one.' He smiles wanly. 'That'll even up the odds up a bit.'

It won't and he knows it. I wait, my fists curled, but X still doesn't show. Neither are we being followed. I breathe in slowly through my nose, trying to bring my heart rate down again. Eventually, when it seems like O'Shea is right, I sag. 'You're right. He's not here.'

O'Shea licks his finger and holds it up in the air. 'Say that again. Say that I'm right again and you're wrong.'

I smooth my hands down against my thighs to get rid of the clammy sweat gathering there. O'Shea watches then pulls me into a hug. 'He doesn't care any more, Bo. He got what he wanted. He's just toying with you.'

I twist away. 'It's not that I'm afraid of dying.'

O'Shea remains calm. 'I know that.'

'I'm not even afraid of the pain.'

He regards me levelly. 'You're afraid that X will continue living and that you won't be able to make him pay for what he's done. It's not just X though. All the damned Kakos daemons were involved in bringing down the Families.'

I meet his eyes. 'But X is the one who made it personal. I don't care about the others.' O'Shea frowns but doesn't argue.

I run my hands through my hair. 'This was a mistake,' I whisper. 'Coming here was a mistake. Staying in the city was a mistake.' I feel as if someone has dunked a bucket of icy water over me and now I finally understand what's real. I've been kidding myself that I could take on X; it's time to wake up and smell the damned blood. I drag in a breath. 'We've not even seen X and I'm a mess.' I tilt up my chin. 'We should leave London. Tonight.'

'What happened to that Bo Blackman determination? This is your city. Are you going to let him force you out?' O'Shea seems puzzled, as if he doesn't understand the severity of the situation.

'It's important to know when to quit.' I glance back. My head is throbbing. 'Nothing happened. No one spoke to us, no one threatened us, but I can feel it. It's like I can taste it in the air. There's nothing I'd like more than vengeance but I need to grow up.' I think of what I said to Rogu3. 'There are more important things. If we leave, there's still hope for the future. Maybe, when we're all back to full strength and we have the numbers, we can do something. But at this moment we're powerless. *I'm* powerless. I was a fool to think otherwise.'

O'Shea nods, loyal to a fault. 'Okay, then. Let's go.'

Since the moment Michael opened his eyes, I've been waiting to confront X. The thought of bringing him to his knees was all that kept me going. That, and wishing for Michael to get better. Now, clichéd as it sounds, it feels like a gigantic weight has been lifted. There are other things apart from X for me to focus on. I can stop worrying about what will happen to London and start worrying about what will happen to me and mine.

I think about Bruckheimer and Berryhill and the witches and Vince Hale. Nah. They can all go hang themselves. I'm going to take the advice that everyone's been giving me for days. I'm going to run away.

O'Shea and I jog to where the van is parked. I can still feel adrenaline firing through me. The female Kakos daemon doesn't appear but there's a prickling along the back of my neck that suggests she's watching. She probably has her arm round X and they're both laughing their heads off. I scowl with considerable ferocity.

'What is it?' O'Shea asks in alarm.

'Too much damn thinking,' I grunt.

'That's always been your problem,' he says as he unlocks the driver's door. 'The old man is the same.'

I open the van door. As I do, something flickers at the edge of my peripheral vision. I glance up and freeze. Not doubled over laughing then. X is leaving his shiny building with the swagger of someone who knows he's at the top of the food chain. I hiss and his head snaps towards me. He stops moving abruptly.

'Get in the van, Devlin,' I say quietly.

'Believe me, that's what I'm...' his voice falters. 'Oh.'

X lifts one hand and crooks his little finger, beckoning me to join him. The urge to leap into the van with O'Shea gunning the engine is almost overwhelming. For what seems like an eternity but is probably less than a few seconds, my feet are rooted to the spot.

O'Shea urges me inside. 'Bo!'

I tilt my chin. X is getting what he wants: I'm going to leave my damn city for him. I fold my arms and glare. He smiles lazily in return and drops his glamour. At once his dark tattoos are visible, writhing across his skin in perpetual motion. He beckons me forward once more.

'Bo, we can still get away,' O'Shea says.

I shake my head. 'No. He could run us down if he wanted.' As I watch, X's smile broadens. 'He's not going to do anything here.'

'You don't know that!'

'Yeah,' I say softly, 'I do. It wouldn't be ... gentlemanly.'

In response, X sweeps a perfectly executed bow. Ignoring the tension in my spine, I mutter, 'Keep the engine running.' Then, as if I don't have a care in the world, I stroll across to meet the creature who destroyed my life.

'Bo,' X drawls, once I'm close enough. 'How utterly wonderful to see you again. Although I have to say, you're looking a little worse for wear.' He frowns. 'You should get more sleep.'

'Say what you have to say, X,' I tell him. 'You know we're leaving.' An image of his lady friend flashes into my mind. So I'm intimidated. That's what they both wanted.

X takes the smallest step backward. His tattoos, which are starting to make me feel nauseous with all their twisting and turning, vanish into his skin as his face melds back into a human façade. 'You *should* leave,' he agrees, his mellifluous voice flowing over me like a caress. A caress from a genocidal dictator, that is. 'The city of London is no longer the place for one of your kind.'

Despite my fear, my anger sparks to the surface. 'One of my

kind?' I spit. 'Whose fault is it that I have to my leave my bloody home? You prick. You vicious, soul-sucking cock. You...'

He holds up a palm. 'I get the message,' he says calmly. He raises an eyebrow. That must be the signature move of every damn Kakos daemon. 'You're very angry, Bo.'

He has got to be kidding me.

'You should be happy,' he continues. 'I saved the love of your life. I wouldn't have done that for just anyone, you know.' He reaches out and draws the tip of his index finger down my cheek. I can't stop myself from recoiling. 'You're special.'

My breath comes in short, sharp gasps. I conjure up my daydream from earlier – the one where I'm holding a bazooka to his head while he begs me for forgiveness that we both know will never come. 'Read my mind, X,' I snarl. 'If there is ever a chance, even the slightest chance, that I can destroy you, then I will do it.'

'Vendettas aren't helpful but you vampires do seem to like them.' He examines me with vague detachment, as if he's a scientist peering through a microscope. 'That's why you're so easy to manipulate.' He laughs although there's no humour in his eyes. 'Don't feel bad about it. It wasn't your fault. And,' he adds, 'it wasn't mine. We all have to dance to our own pipers.' He shrugs as if it's nothing to get worked up about.

I can't help myself. I know it's stupid and I know it's suicidal but I no longer care. I fling myself towards him with every intention of scratching his eyes out. But he knows my moves before I do and he blocks me easily, knocking me to the ground with one swift thrust. Then he bends over and peers at me. 'How's that MI7 stronghold working out for you?' he enquires.

Damn it. I hadn't even been thinking about it. Can he reach into my mind and pull out any bloody information he pleases?

'No,' he smiles, putting out a hand to help me up. 'I just

know. In fact, I could give you the address of every place you've stayed in since you left my apartment.'

I ignore his proffered hand and get stiffly to my feet. 'Fuck you. Fuck you and all your friends.'

X tuts. 'Such language. I expect better from you, Bo. Although I can understand why you're feeling stressed. Little Michael is rather poorly, isn't he? He was a bloodguzzler for a long time. It's always touch and go whether someone will pull through the process or not.' I lift my hand to strike him but he catches my wrist. 'We've already done this dance,' he comments. His eyes drift over my head. 'Take Michael and leave London. And don't come back.' He drops his mouth to my ear. 'And I wouldn't try to turn him again if I were you. He definitely won't make it.'

He smiles soullessly and turns on his heel to re-enter the building. The door slams shut behind him with a thud of excruciating finality.

I stare at the spot where he was standing, still breathing heavily. If I had any doubt about my change of plan, X has quashed it. The implied threat when he said Michael's name was obvious.

'Just go, Bo,' I whisper. 'Just sodding go.'

I turn round. O'Shea has got out of the van again and is standing by its side looking worried. I try to give him a reassuring smile. Then I realise we're not the only ones out here on the street. The female Kakos daemon is also on the pavement, framed by the dark shadows of Bruckheimer and Berryhill's building. She doesn't wave or gesture or blink. She is, however, watching me with a steady, unwavering intensity and I'm struck by a numbing terror.

CHAPTER 8
MIND TRICKS

The moment we get back to the MI7 warehouse, I yell, 'Get your shit together! We are leaving!'

Nobody answers. A trickle of cold air runs down my spine. X knows we're here. Has he already done something? Leaving O'Shea, I sprint to Michael's room. He's lying curled in a half-foetal position while Maria sits on a chair in the corner, her head lolling onto her shoulders and her eyes closed. I rush towards him, only realising as I reach down to shake him that his chest is rising and falling.

Maria stirs. 'What is problem?'

'You need to watch him! You can't just come in here and doze! Anything could happen to him! He could choke or have a fit or die!' A distant part of me is aware that I'm shrieking.

She regards me impassively. 'He okay.'

'Don't say he's okay!' I growl. 'He's not okay! Look at him.'

Michael's eyes flutter open. 'I'm okay,' he wheezes.

I ball up my fists. 'We're leaving,' I manage in a more controlled voice. 'We're getting out of the city.'

He tries and fails to prop himself up. With a muttered curse, he sinks back. 'What's the problem? Has something happened?'

I don't answer him. I look at Maria. 'Get your things together. We're getting out of here.'

'Is something I want say...' she begins hesitantly.

I push back my hair. 'I'm sorry I shouted at you,' I tell her, trying to calm myself. It doesn't work. 'I'm just a bit stressed. Let's talk once we're out of here and on the road.' I whirl round and head for the main room.

Kimchi bounds towards me. I side step and scan round. Rogu3 is frowning at the computer screen and gnawing on his fingernails. 'Rogu3!' I bellow. 'Didn't you hear me calling? I need you to pack everything up.'

He swivels round in his chair. 'What's up?'

'Just get your things together.'

His frown deepens. Before I can urge him to get a sodding move on, my grandfather appears, a tea towel in his hand. 'We have to leave,' I say.

'I heard you the first time,' he replies. 'Are we expecting an imminent attack?'

'Yes. No.' I curse. 'Maybe.'

'Bo, you need to slow down. Start from the beginning.'

'There's no time. We have to leave.' Desperation is starting to claw at me.

Rogu3 stands up and pushes back his chair. Relieved that someone is finally doing what I ask, I turn towards him. 'No,' he says. 'I'm not going.'

My mouth drops open. 'Excuse me?'

He points to the computer screen. 'I'm getting somewhere with Hale's system. In another couple of hours, I think I'll be able to access his hard drive.'

'Forget Hale.'

His eyebrows fly up. 'You've changed your tune.'

'This level of panic is most unbecoming, my dear,' my grandfather says. 'And uncharacteristic.' He steps towards my and cups my face, peering into my eyes. 'Your pupils are dilated.'

'Because I'm bloody scared. We have to get out of here.'

He leans back. 'Hm. Your expedition to find X was a success of sorts, then.'

I throw my hands up in the air. 'Can we please stop talking and get out of here? It's not safe!'

'You're turning into a blithering idiot, Bo. Stop and think.'

I can't believe he's doing this. 'He'll kill Michael! We have to leave. We can get to Dover and then catch a ferry to France. I don't trust the airport right now. We...'

My grandfather slaps me hard. Stunned, I rock back. 'What the hell...?'

'He has got inside your mind.'

I can still only gape. 'I don't know what you're talking about,' I manage.

'Tell me exactly what happened.'

My mind is a muddle of confusion. 'X found us. He threatened me. He threatened Michael.' I start to plead. 'We have to leave.' I drop onto my knees. 'I'm scared. I'm really bloody scared. He's going to kill all of us and eat our hearts.'

'You're babbling.' My grandfather turns to O'Shea. 'Devlin. Explain.'

The daemon licks his lips nervously. 'Well, we went into a building near X's place. Bo decided to go up to talk to some insurance firm.' I receive a sharp look from my grandfather but he doesn't interrupt. 'Then I saw her. The Kakos daemon. I thought she was human to start off with but she flashed me a reveal of her true face and that's when I knew.'

'Knew what?'

His brow furrows. 'That I had to get Bo and we had to leave.'

I nod vigorously in agreement.

'Was there anyone else around?' my grandfather probes.

'Lots of people.'

'And no one else saw her show her true form?'

'They were looking at their phones.'

'Were they indeed?' he murmurs.

'You don't believe us?' I screech. 'You weren't there! You don't know!'

'Fetch Maria,' my grandfather says quietly to Rogu3 then he turns back to me. 'You left here all gung ho. You had a plan. You weren't going to be reckless but you were single-minded in searching for a way to halt the Kakos daemons in their tracks.'

'I was being stupid. I didn't know what I was doing.'

'And now you do?'

'Yes!'

The cat saunters into the room and winds its way round his legs. My grandfather bends down and scoops it up into his arms. 'You know they can read your mind, Bo.'

I still don't understand what he's getting at. 'So? That's not news.'

He sighs. 'How big a stretch is it that they can't just read your mind but that they can manipulate it too?'

I squint. 'What do you mean?'

'You saw this woman? This female daemon Devlin mentioned?'

I nod slowly. 'Yeah.'

'The word is yes.'

I roll my eyes. 'Yes.'

'And how did you feel afterwards? What were you thinking?'

I stare at him. 'That we were foolish to have gone there. That we should leave London and we could come back at a later date to confront the daemons if need be.'

'I see.'

'It was perfectly rational!'

'And yet now,' he comments, 'you are acting far from rationally. You shouted at Maria. You screeched and ran around as if the sky were falling.'

'X threatened us,' I protest.

'What did he say?'

'He implied that…'

'No, Bo. What did he *actually* say? What words did he use?'

'Pedantic much?' When my grandfather doesn't respond, I hiss, 'He asked about this place.' I try to think. '"How is the MI7 stronghold working out for you?"' I gesture as if it's a fait accompli. 'So you see he's coming here and he's going to attack.'

'I don't see how that means he's going to attack.' He regards me intently. 'And I told you, this place is a fortress. Do you really think I'd let my only grandchild be placed in mortal danger?'

'You let me become a vampire,' I point out. 'I could have died then. Besides, I've been in mortal danger plenty of times.'

'If I could have stopped you from being recruited, I would have. And there's a difference between giving you the independence to make mistakes and leading you somewhere mistakes are going to happen. This place is safe.'

'X said that I should take Michael and leave London.'

'Or what?'

I shrug. 'He didn't say. I know what he meant though.' I fidget. 'I'm getting tired of all these questions. We really need to go.'

He ignores me. 'When did you begin panicking?'

'Who cares?'

'Bo,' he says sternly. 'Answer the question.'

'It was when we saw her the second time,' O'Shea says quietly. 'The Kakos daemon. She came out onto the street and stared at you and that was when you started going nuts.'

I glare at him. 'I am not going nuts.' I pause. 'You don't think…?'

Maria edges into the room. 'We leave?' she asks.

'Yes,' I say.

'No,' my grandfather replies. 'Come here, my dear.'

She looks nervous and I immediately feel guilty. I didn't mean to shout at her when I came in but it's my responsibility to keep everyone safe. She does as my grandfather tells her, however.

'Bo's mind has been affected by a Kakos daemon. I need you to help her.'

'I not know how.'

He takes her hand and gently squeezes it. 'Yes, you do.'

Maria flinches. 'Is very serious matter.'

He nods. 'I know. But she needs to be released from its grip.'

I stamp my foot. 'I've had enough of this. If you don't want to pack that's up to you but we are all leaving this instant.'

My grandfather draws something out from his pocket and points it at me. I stare at it uncomprehendingly. 'That's a Magix taser. An anti-vamp one.'

He beams at me, his eyes crinkling. 'Yes. I knew it would come in handy one day.' Then he raises it up and shoots me dead centre in the chest.

I'M STRAPPED TIGHTLY to a chair in the middle of the room. Maria, Rogu3, my grandfather and O'Shea are standing in a semi-circle in front of me. Kimchi is at the side, swinging his head from them to me and back again as if he can't make up his mind what to do. In the end, he whines and hunkers down, dropping his head onto his paws and gazing at me mournfully.

I struggle against the bonds. I can already feel them giving away. 'You bastards! You don't want Michael to be safe. That's what all this about, isn't it? You want to turn him over to the daemons so that...'

'Do be quiet, Bo,' my grandfather says.

I glare at him. 'This won't hold me for long. When I get free, you'll be sorry.'

He glances at me dispassionately. 'Are you threatening me? I'm an old frail man who's barely out of hospital.'

'I don't care.'

He sighs, as if he's under a great imposition. 'Maria,' he says. 'If you will.'

She bites her lip and tiptoes forward. 'Don't you dare,' I warn her. 'I took you in. I gave a roof and a safe place to stay. I bloody rescued you!'

'Ignore her, my dear.'

Maria blanches but she draws closer. I pull at my wrists. These aren't anti-vampire handcuffs; a few more tugs and I'll be free. I stare malevolently at them all as Maria reaches out two delicate, bird-like hands and presses her fingertips against my temples.

'Let me go,' I hiss. 'Let me go or I won't be responsible for my actions.'

She holds steady. And that's when I feel it. Her clear eyes gaze into mine and my body judders. The pressure that has been building in my head from the moment I saw the Kakos daemon in the lobby suddenly starts to fade.

There's a wash of blue. It floats through my senses like a lapping wave, pushing back the panic. I stop struggling and stare wide-eyed at Maria. Her eyes are unfocused and sweat is beading her brow.

Pain flashes through me and I cry out. I'm vaguely aware of Maria biting her lip again – but this time so hard that she draws blood. I smell the tang of it in the air, pervading my senses. Not only that but I can see... Oh God.

Voices waft over me. My head is foggy and I blink rapidly to try and clear the mist. Dizziness swims through me and I'm sure I'm going to throw up.

'I don't understand.'

'Should I get a medical kit?'

I tense, reminding myself that I'm still alive. I'm here. My mind is clear. 'No,' I say, although my voice sounds as if it's coming from far away. 'I'm alright.' I smile faintly. 'I'm okay.'

A face swims in front of me. My grandfather. 'Do you still want to leave London?' he enquires.

'No.' I clench my teeth so hard that my jaw hurts. 'I want to destroy X. Not only has he manipulated me from the get-go, he's invaded my mind. He made me scared.' I grip the arm-rests of the chair. 'He messed with who I am and he's not going to get away with it.'

'Actually,' my grandfather says, 'I rather think it was the female daemon who did this.'

Rogu3 begins to untie the bonds to free me. One sharp tug and I'd break them myself but I let him do it. 'Why do you think that?'

'It started with Devlin,' he explains. 'She planted the seed in his mind that he needed to get you out. Then, when you appeared, she made you want to leave. She began with rational-ity. It made sense to you that you should quit the city, right?'

I nod. 'I guess. I was scared then but not as terrified as later. She must have thought that she'd not done enough and that we were going to stay.' I frown. 'But she read my mind. She knew that wasn't the case. I only felt real terror after...' I pause and swallow. 'After I spoke to X.'

'That's what it sounds like,' my grandfather agrees.

I cast my mind back. The little step back X took when I thought of the woman and the fact that he'd been leaving the building when I first saw him. He hadn't expected to see me there in the street but, rather than continue on his merry way after talking to me, he went straight back inside. 'He's afraid of her as well,' I say. 'But why?'

Rogu3 moves away and looks at me. 'Has X ever tried to manipulate your emotions like this before?'

I rub my wrists and stand up. 'I don't suppose I'd know. Except,' I consider, 'I had a headache when she did it. I've never felt like that before. It was as if something was pounding inside my brain.' I grimace. 'It was. *She* was.'

'Well,' O'Shea says heavily, 'we know two new things at least. The Kakos daemons are desperate for you to leave London.'

'What's the second thing?'

He gives me a grim look. 'They're a damn sight more powerful than we realised.'

I rub my forehead. When are things going to start going my way? I sigh deeply and walk over to Maria. I put my hand under her chin, tilting her head till she's looking at me. 'Thank you,' I tell her. 'I know how difficult that was for you.'

'Is okay.'

'No,' I say softly, 'it's not.' I glance back at the others. 'I'm not sure what can be done about the daemons right now. We need to know more about their agenda and their capabilities.' I shrug helplessly. 'But if they have mind control at their disposal, I think we're pretty much screwed. Right now, there are other things I need to focus on.'

Rogu3 jumps up. 'Vince Hale.'

'He's one of them. But there's something even more pressing.' I swallow. 'What Maria did wasn't just a one-way street. I saw inside her head at the same time as she saw into mine.'

My grandfather doesn't look surprised but O'Shea sucks in a breath. 'And?'

Maria moans slightly and pulls back. The pain in her eyes is overwhelming. I can see her trying to disappear into herself, then she turns and runs out of the room.

I gaze after her. Empathy wells up inside me with such force that I can barely breathe. 'The things that have been done to her.' I suck in air. 'She's stronger than all of us. That's not all though.' I tear my eyes away to look at Rogu3. 'Alice Goldman is still alive.'

CHAPTER 9

FEAR

Maria's earliest memory is from when she was about four years old. She remembers the sun shining brilliantly and the arc of rainbows reflected in oily puddles. When she trailed her finger across the water, she could make the rainbows swirl, creating a kaleidoscope of colour from blues to greens to musky oranges. The puddle turned red when her father smashed his fist into her mother's face above her. She remembers the expressions of those others who were around her. It wasn't shock or horror or fear, they simply closed their faces, their mouths tight and their eyes hard. It was easier to pretend you didn't see. It was smarter not to get involved. It was a lesson Maria learned quickly.

She wasn't much older when she used to sit cross-legged under the rickety kitchen table. She was still short enough that her head remained inches from its flat wooden top but, if she reached up, her fingers could skim the underside of it. She scratched letters, gleaned from snatched moments of education when her mother had time. It was lucky she was a fast learner; those moments were all too few and far between. And she had to be careful. Once she was so absorbed in her task that she didn't notice her father come in. He sat down heavily, his fat thighs dripping over the edge of the seat. When she didn't move out of the way fast enough, he drew one foot back and kicked, connecting with her chest and breaking three ribs. The pain was sharp and instantaneous but she didn't cry out. She knew that would make only things worse. She saved her tears for when her mother bound her up with torn cloth from the cupboard under the sink. It smelled stale and faintly of bleach but the bandages helped turn the agony into a long, dull ache. There were no doctors. They did not speak of such things.

Things could have improved. One wintry day, stern-faced men wearing crisp uniforms appeared. They threw her father to the ground, snapped his wrists together with shiny bracelets and dragged him off. He screamed and yelled the entire way. She cried when she saw him swallowed up by the white van, though whether the tears were because she was relieved at their escape from his fists or because she somehow knew she'd never see him again, she couldn't tell.

Without the income from whatever jobs her father took on, her mother fell on other means to keep them fed. Sometimes, when the weather was warmer and the foliage was greener, she'd pluck grass and flowers and boil them into a thick green sludge. It didn't taste particularly good and Maria was often sick as a result but it stopped the gnawing hunger in her tummy for a short while. When the only plants that remained were too inedible even for them, her mother would take her onto the streets, thrusting her in front of well-dressed passers-by to part them from their money. Sometimes it worked, sometimes it didn't. After particularly bad days, when all they had in their pockets were a few pennies, her mother would cry and slap her and tell her she had to try harder. It wasn't because her mother was a bad person – Maria loved her. She got angry because Maria kept failing.

The taller Maria got, the harder it became to garner sympathy. Younger beggars, who didn't have her drawn, pinched look, did better. Truthfully, someone always did better. It didn't matter how often Maria resolved to be a better daughter, she never did well enough. When her mother stayed at home, entertaining local men or unable to move from her bed, Maria went out on her own and earned more. She learned tricks. Witches, practitioners of both black and white magic, gave her money for blood. They recognised her heritage and could put it to good use. There were scabs all over her arms and legs from the tiny nicks and she had to be careful not to give away too much blood because the vampires would also come looking – and they paid better than the witches. The one time she did sell more than she intended, she collapsed on a street corner before she could get home. When she came to, someone had rifled through her pockets and taken every hard-earned penny of her blood money.

Humans didn't ask for blood but some of them were mean. They'd spit at her and tell her she was scum. Usually the well-dressed, rich-looking ones were the worst, as if they were afraid that if they didn't cling to everything they had and prove how far removed they were from someone like Maria, they too would find themselves in similar precarious situations. The poorer humans, with tatty clothes and pinched expressions, were more generous but they could only give what they could afford.

Strangely, the daemons were the kindest. Agathos daemons muttered at her, tossing her money and a quick smile. Others, whom Maria recognised as Kakos daemons but wouldn't put a name to until years later, did more than the rest put together. It wasn't that they were more generous with their funds – they weren't – but they saw her for who she was. Unlike the rest, they met her eyes, acknowledged her individuality and stopped for conversation. The chats were usually meaningless, comments on the weather or such-like, but they reminded Maria that she wasn't invisible to the rest of the world after all.

If all this sounds like a litany of misery, I'm probably doing her a disservice. Maria wasn't the only young beggar on the streets and, despite the competitive hierarchy among them, she still made friends. Tragic circumstances can often foster camaraderie and, while success often meant the difference between life and death, it was also measured in coins rather than notes. Maria found it difficult to resent someone who earned enough to buy a whole loaf of bread when she could only afford a slice. Besides, cliques formed quickly on the streets and sharing assets was not uncommon. It wasn't long before she found herself in a network of street children. Whispers ran from one end of the city to the other: take care with the man with the crumpled hat, he has grabby hands and doesn't care where he pinches; be nice to the woman in the purple dress and she'll be generous. And if you see the hooded men, be sure to run and don't look back.

Not everyone on the street simply begged. Many stole, with quick fingers that could sneak into the bag of an unwary pedestrian and take phones, wallets, or loose change. Maria tried it once but her approach was clumsy and, even under the professional guidance of a friend, she found a hand wrapped tightly round her wrist and the threat of violence in her face. Only a short sharp kick to the shins of her would-be target allowed her to escape. Some young beggars also sold more than blood, leading 'clients' down dirty back alleys. Maria only had to see the aftermath, grubby faces streaked with tears, purple bruises and dead eyes, to decide she would rather starve first.

Not everyone took no for an answer but she knew enough from watching her father about where to hit or scratch. She was slippery; she could not be caught. But not all evil lurks in shadowy streets; sometimes it comes in bright daylight, clothed in respectability.

When March rolled around, Maria knew things were different. For three whole days her mother smiled. The cupboards, which were usually bare, were full of brightly coloured tins. Each morning, instead of suffering from an empty stomach, Maria was handed chocolate, a luxury she previously couldn't have begun to contemplate. When she questioned where all this bounty had sprung from, she received a pat on her head and a low inconsequential murmur. She stopped asking. She wondered afterwards if it would have made a difference if she hadn't stayed quiet.

On the fourth morning, she was licking delicately at a creamy brown chocolate square when there was a sharp knock at the door. Her mother, wearing her best dress of cornflower blue which made her eyes glimmer brightly in contrast, jerked away from the sink and grabbed Maria's shoulders.

'Don't screw this up!' she hissed, wetting her thumb with saliva and rubbing furiously at the stains around her daughter's mouth. She wiped her hands and, with a ramrod straight back that Maria hadn't seen in years, opened the door to greet the stranger.

Waiting on the porch was a middle-aged man in a suit. He had a warm voice and, when he stepped inside, Maria could see that he was someone who laughed a lot. His eyes crinkled at the sides with tiny crow's feet that gave him a kindly, benign appearance. He smelled of expensive aftershave which filled their small house until Maria could smell nothing else. When he caught sight of her, he beamed widely and strode over.

'This must be little Maria!' He gestured to her to stand up and, when she didn't, her mother hauled her up by the arms and thrust her towards him. 'I'm your Uncle Verne,' he boomed.

Maria blinked. She'd been told that her extended family had

died or moved away. She'd never heard of an Uncle Verne before.

He circled round her, his eyes travelling up and down her frame, lanky even at this age.

'She's tall,' her mother said nervously. 'But she'll fill out. I certainly did.'

Uncle Verne clapped his hands together once. 'She's perfect.' He met Maria's eyes. 'Do you like sweets?'

Maria didn't know where to look. Feeling her mother's anxious gaze upon her, she bit her lip and nodded. When Uncle Verne grinned broadly, she knew she'd given the right answer and she felt a wash of relief. He reached into his pocket, pulled out a small white paper bag and held it out to her. 'These are special,' he promised. 'You won't have tried anything like them before.'

Hesitantly, she took one and placed it on her tongue. It was very sugary and began dissolving almost instantly. It fizzed and tickled. She rolled it around her mouth, curious at the sensation.

Uncle Verne and her mother continued to talk.

'She'll be looked after?' her mother asked.

'Of course! We do everything we can for our charges.'

'And can I call her?'

'It's probably best if you don't. We find that children settle in more easily when they're not constantly reminded of their families. It's also best if you don't tell anyone about this. People will only get jealous or they won't understand.' He passed Maria's mother an envelope. 'Here is what we agreed on.'

Maria turned as their words filtered through. She was already feeling dizzy and her tongue felt thick and clumsy. 'What's happening?'

'Be a good girl, Maria. Uncle Verne will look after you now.' Her mother gazed at her for a long moment, slipped the envelope into her bra, patted it self-consciously and walked out of the door. A second or two later, the world fell sideways.

When Maria woke up, she felt disorientated. Her head hurt and her tongue was furry. At first she thought she was in her own bedroom but it didn't take long to realise she was actually in the back of a lorry, boxes stacked up in front of her and a bottle of water by her side.

It wouldn't take a genius – even if that genius was barely a teenager – to understand what had happened. Maria allowed herself one choked sob and then, because she was nothing if not pragmatic, started to assess her situation. She desperately wanted the water but she was wary of what it might contain. Her head remained fuzzy from whatever had been in 'Uncle Verne's' sweet. In the end, however, thirst won. If the water was spiked, she reasoned, it wouldn't kill her. They wouldn't go to this much trouble if all they wanted was a corpse. Besides, she was a nobody. No one cared enough about her to want her dead – and that apparently included her own mother.

The water was untainted. She gulped it down and began to plan her next move. It took considerable effort to move the boxes that blocked her in; they were extraordinarily heavy and, despite her height, she didn't have many muscles. She managed it eventually, creating enough space so that she could squeeze through. By the time she reached the far end of the lorry, she could feel the vehicle coming to a stop.

Maria was intelligent enough to know that she'd probably have only one chance at escape. She examined herself for bruises or aches but, as far as she could tell, she hadn't been touched. That was something. As harsh voices began to drift over to her from outside, she pressed herself against the far wall, concealed by shadows. Metal clanked on the exterior of the lorry and the door rolled up, revealing the night outside together with three shapeless figures who were barking to each other in a guttural language she didn't understand. Maria shrank against the wall, sure that her heart was thudding so loudly they'd be able to hear her, even if they didn't see her. Apparently they weren't expecting her to have awakened so quickly. They clambered inside and began moving the boxes, their movements calm and unworried. The smell of their acrid sweat tickled Maria's nostrils but she preferred that smell to Uncle Verne's. At least sweat was honest.

As soon as the three ventured far enough inside so that she could leave without being spotted, Maria bolted. She leapt out of the back of the lorry and sprinted for the open ground ahead. There was a chain-link fence which, although it was looped with barbed wire at its top, she was sure she could climb. Unfortunately, however, there were more people outside. Someone shouted, alerting the three men inside who were still struggling with boxes. A dog started to bark, a ferocious sound that spoke of anger and violence.

Maria ran. But while she might have had the gangly limbs to outstrip a fully grown man, she couldn't outrun a dog. She wasn't even close to the fence when it was upon her, leaping onto her back and making her fall forwards. Then its jaws latched onto her arm.

Ten days later, patched up and more terrified than she'd ever been in her life, Maria found herself in a strange building. She was thrown into a room with others just like herself. There were children of all shapes and sizes. Each one had the same look that she knew was in her own eyes, that of the dispossessed, the unwanted, the forgotten. No one complained or cried or spoke but, all the same, the room was filled with fear.

There were cots lining one side of the room but not every

child slept in them; several chose to curl up underneath them, as if they thought they could hide. Unwilling to give in, Maria waited until she thought everyone was asleep before she tiptoed and examined the door. There had to be a way out. She'd even brave another dog if it meant escape from this dark place.

'There's no point,' a quiet voice told her from the corner.

Maria whipped round, unsure who had spoken and unable to understand the words. When nothing else was forthcoming, she shrugged and returned to the door. She tugged at the handle and the bolt on the other side rattled.

The owner of the voice stepped forward, emerging from the shadows. She placed a small hand on Maria's arm and looked at her with concern. She spoke again, and again Maria could not understand what she said. Eventually, the girl seemed to understand this and gently led Maria away, shaking her head in warning. When the door thumped open and an ugly face appeared, glaring round to find who had dared to touch the only exit, Maria was already in the corner with the girl's arm round her for support. Perhaps on this occasion the guard was busy with other matters because he snarled once and left them alone again.

'I'm Alice,' the girl whispered. 'Be quiet or they'll kill you.'

This Maria understood.

TIME LOST all meaning in the strange prison. Meals appeared, bland food but enough to satisfy everyone's appetite. Sometimes booted figures with red hoods walked in and looked around. The hooded men, the ones she had been warned about far away on the distant streets of her homeland.

The first time the men came, Maria didn't understand.

When she felt eyes sweep past her dismissively, however, there was a sense of reprieve which made all the more sense when those same eyes halted on one shivering body. The unlucky child was dragged out. It was the only time Maria ever heard anyone in that terrible place scream. When she tried to ask Alice what happened to those who were chosen, the younger girl shook her head sadly. Maria had the awful sensation that even her imagination couldn't conjure up what happened once you were taken – and her imagination was vivid.

They passed the hours and days and weeks in different ways. They were given nothing to play with; their guards were not interested in keeping the children occupied. Maria realised the guards' sole purpose was to keep their charges alive. Nothing else mattered. Some of the captives withdrew completely into themselves, arms wrapped around bony knees, rocking backwards and forwards in perpetual motion. Others seemed to invent distant places to escape to, their eyes unfocused as they dreamt of anywhere but that room.

Alice and Maria were different. With hushed whispers and increasingly complex gestures and charades, Alice taught Maria to speak and understand this strange new tongue. Maria's mouth wasn't prepared for the unaccustomed syllables and sounds and her attempts were often clumsy but Alice was patient. And between them, they had nothing but time.

New children arrived and other children left. Once, one of the newcomers who was braver than the others flung himself at the door, beating it with his fists. The same ugly guard appeared. He stared at the boy and then shrugged; a moment he later he smashed his fist into the boy's face and left once again. The boy never woke and, three days later, someone came in and removed his body. Maria wondered if perhaps he had chosen the best way out. Waiting like this for what could only be inevitable weighed heavily upon her. Some days it was only

Alice's presence beside her that kept her sane. But on the day they came and chose her, she knew she'd give anything to be waiting once more.

The men entered as they always did, three of them, their hoods covering half of their faces so that little more than their eyes were visible. They walked slowly through the room, ignoring the soft whimpers from the tiny figures in front of them. Somehow, before they even looked at her, Maria knew that it was her turn. The first one stopped and stared at her then nodded. The others agreed by inclining their heads. She got to her feet shakily. She wasn't going to scream. She wasn't going to be like the others.

Alice had other plans. She shrieked loudly and flung herself forward, placing her smaller body in front of Maria's. 'Take me!' she yelled. 'You want me!'

The other children, their terror temporarily forgotten, stared wide-eyed. The ugly guard appeared from behind the men, his fist raised. Maria tried to push her friend out of the way before he could reach them but the nearest hooded man did the job for her, his hand snapping out and stopping the guard. Maria instantly understood why: Alice was different to the others. She was special. She wasn't to be harmed.

The hooded men advanced, knocking Alice out of the way. She was small and weak and a mere shove sufficed. She clattered to the ground and Maria darted forward. If she resisted in any way, Alice would get hurt. Instead she lifted up her chin and stared at the red men, silently telling them that she would come. They dragged her away but Maria was true to her word and didn't scream once. Alice did, though. Even when the heavy door shut behind them, Maria could still hear Alice screaming.

Maria was gagged and bound to a gurney before being wheeled down a long corridor. The lights flickered above her head and the metal beneath her was icy cold. The walls changed from a dirty green to an antiseptic white, so bright it hurt her eyes. She let her body go limp as a white-coated man peered over then gestured to a mirror behind her. Someone was behind there watching, Maria realised. Someone was there who wanted to watch this obscene play through to its finale.

There was a pinprick of pain on the tip of her index finger. She looked down and saw the white-coated man smear a drop of her blood onto a tiny glass plate then turn to a microscope to examine it. Another man, this one wearing a black coat, stepped forward and began to chant. He was barely five words in when the first man bellowed at him to stop. Faltering, he stared.

'Gypsy.' The white-coated man spat the word. 'She's a fucking gypsy. Cut her loose and get another one. And tell Verne if he brings us another like this then he's finished.'

CHAPTER 10

RUMOURS AND SPIES

I'm glossing over most of what I learned from Maria's strange mind. It's her story, not mine, and I came by it involuntarily. The room filled with stolen children and the sinister hooded men are pertinent, however.

'That's barbaric,' O'Shea breathes. 'What were they planning to do with her if she wasn't Romany?'

'I don't know,' I say grimly, 'and neither does Maria. But I think we're agreed that this takes precedence. Hale and X and whatever else is going in the world are definitely our concern but these children might still be out there. Maria doesn't know where this prison is but we can find out.' My voice hardens. 'We *have* to find out. Alice might still be there.'

'So what you're saying, Bo,' my grandfather interjects, 'is that some things are more important than vengeance?'

My mouth tightens. 'That's exactly what I'm saying.'

He smiles. 'Good.'

Rogu3 is struggling to hold back tears. 'Why didn't she tell us about this before?'

'I think to begin with she probably wasn't sure whether she

could trust us. Then later, when she realised she could, other events took over our lives.' Another thing to blame X for.

'What happened?' He swallows. 'What I mean is, how did Maria end up in the place where you found her?'

'She was sold,' I say, giving him the unvarnished truth. 'I suppose the hooded men needed to recoup some of their investment.' Even saying it makes my mouth taste as if it's filled with ash. I look at them all. 'Drop everything else. We need to find out more about these wankers.'

Rogu3 gathers himself together. 'I'll begin a search on the dark net.' His bottom lip trembles and his hands are curled into tight balls. He slams his fist onto a nearby table, splintering the wood. 'Sorry.'

My grandfather waves a hand. 'De nada.' He takes a step forward and stares down at the wood. Then, without warning, he also smashes his fist into it. I draw in a sharp breath but don't say anything. I don't need to. 'I will check on Maria,' he says calmly. Then he turns and walks out of the room.

'Devlin?' I ask.

He won't meet my eyes. I think the horrifying truth is almost too much for him. 'I'll get onto the streets and see what I can learn.'

'Good. As soon as you have anything, no matter how inconsequential, let me know. I'm going to check on Michael.' I need to remind myself that there's still some good left in the world.

'WHAT'S GOING ON?' Michael asks in a weak whisper as soon as I enter the room. 'I could hear a commotion.'

I'm tempted to keep the truth from him. He doesn't need more misery in his life. I can't treat him like a child though. I briefly outline what happened with X and the other Kakos daemon, then what I've learned about Maria and Alice. He closes his eyes.

'There were rumours about these men,' he says. 'Whispers from the street. We heard them from time to time but there was never anything substantial. I sent people to try and find out but...' He sighs.

'But people don't trust vampires, especially those people who are already vulnerable.'

He curses to himself. 'Exactly.' He turns over and looks at me. 'We should never have kept quiet about Alice. I wanted to tell the press we didn't have anything to do with her disappearance.' He meets my eyes. 'You do believe me, don't you?'

'I do. But it wasn't just you, it was centuries of stupid tradition forcing your mouths shut. Things are going to be different from now on.' There's vehement promise in my tone.

Michael gives a short laugh. 'You're a good person, Bo.'

People keep saying that. I wonder what they'd say if they knew just how strong the darkness is inside me now. 'No, I'm not.'

'How many other people would put aside their own interests to save a bunch of strangers?'

'I think, given these circumstances, everyone would.'

'It would be nice to believe that, wouldn't it?' He smiles faintly. With a surge of sudden hope I think that he's starting to look a bit better. He can certainly speak for longer and in real sentences. 'But you're one of the few who are actually in a position to do it.' He reaches out and takes my hand. 'Turn me. I can guide you through the process. Turn me back and I can help.'

I think of X's warning. 'I can't. It's not going to work. Turning you will kill you.'

'I'm willing to take that risk.'

I put my other hand over his. 'I'm not.' I bite my lip and make a decision. 'It's not safe for you here. I can't look into the hooded men and worry about the Kakos daemons and keep you safe all at the same time. I know some people up north. I can send you...'

'No!' His voice rises to a shout and he starts to choke. Alarmed, I reach for a glass of water but he waves it away angrily. For a moment I see the old Michael. He coughs. 'I'm getting better.' He points at the discarded kebab wrappings. 'You were right about the food. I don't know what was in that but it tasted bloody good.'

I try to smile. 'It's probably better that you don't know.'

'Probably,' he agrees. 'But more of that and less of O'Shea's chicken soup and I'll be back on my feet before you know it.'

There's a strange sound. I frown and glance down at him. 'Was that your stomach?'

He shrugs. 'I suppose it was.' A slow grin eases across his face, lessening the shadows I can still see there. There's even a flicker of wonder. How long has it been since his belly rumbled for something other than blood? I feel a wistful jolt of jealousy. 'Get me more of the same,' Michael tells me, 'and I might even be strong enough to take a piss on my own.'

'Them's fighting words,' I say, kissing him on the forehead.

He curves his hand round my neck and draws my mouth down to his lips. 'You're the warrior around here,' he whispers. 'I have to give you something to be proud of.'

Before he can start feeling sorry for himself, I growl, 'You're my hero, Michael. I love you. Even if you're a grouchy prick who's going to get fat on fast food.'

He laughs softly and kisses me. 'I love you too, Bo Blackman.'

We grin stupidly at each other. For that one brief moment, all my other worries are pushed away. As long as I still have him, I can still believe. Just.

AFTER MICHAEL DRIFTS back off to sleep I'm too antsy to get any rest. Maria's door is firmly closed and I'm certain that I'm the last person she wants to see. Rogu3 is hunched over the computer screen muttering something about a possible lead. When I lean over his shoulder he snaps in irritation, so I leave him in peace. O'Shea is out pounding the streets for info. Perhaps I can do that as well and get some more additive-filled food for Michael at the same time. It's better than sitting around here with my mind full of images from Maria's past.

I grab a delighted Kimchi and go outside. There are two shopping areas near here, one filled with farmer's markets and organic produce and artisanal shit and the other with a food bank and discounted products for the less affluent. If I'm going to find anyone who's heard of the hooded men, it's not going to be amongst gleaming aisles of imported lychees or bloody civet-poo coffee beans. We head in the opposite direction.

It's early enough in the morning for the streets to be quiet. There's the occasional jogger from whom I keep a wide berth. Despite that, Kimchi insists on barking at them with such force that I'm sure they think he's an enormous beast – until they look round and realise he's only vast horizontally. Other than that, we're left on our own. It suits me. Although I'm coming round to the idea that the warehouse is pretty much the safest place in London, it does feel rather claustrophobic, especially after my Kakos-daemon induced meltdown. I let the fresh air fill my lungs. I've really missed this sort of freedom.

We pass a small newsagent's that is opening up for the day. I'm pleased to note that the front page on the stack of newspapers waiting outside displays the photo I snapped of Berryhill. It wouldn't normally make the headlines but, as I surmised, people are hungry for any news of vampires now that most of us are dust. It means I've kept my promise – not that I imagine Berryhill is happy about it.

I keep walking. It's amazing, I reflect with a curious detachment, how much of a difference there is between this area and the other side of the warehouse. The further I go, the more unkempt the streets become. There's more litter, less greenery, less sense that anyone cares. It's more than a money thing, it's about pride and respect and believing there's a point in getting up again tomorrow. I'm not sure if there's any way to fix all that.

I massage my shoulders, kick a rusting old shopping trolley out of the way, round the corner and see the small collection of shops right in front of me. At this hour they're all boarded up, their heavy metal shutters keeping out would-be thieves. I check the signs displayed outside; they'll be open within the hour. That gives me enough time to find the right sort of people to ask about the hooded men.

To the right I spot a small park with ragged bushes and some forlorn looking trees. There's a rickety slide and a set of swings which I eye dubiously. I doubt many parents would let their children come here, judging by the air of abandonment and the discarded syringe I've just crushed under my heel. There's a bench in the corner with a lump draped on it. As far as my mission is concerned, this is as good a place as any to begin.

I tie Kimchi to the gate, hop over the fence and approach. I can't see any facial features but there's a mop of stringy grey hair visible over the top of the sleeping bag. Wrong age group but there's no one else around. The nice thing to do would be to wait patiently until this person woke up. I reach out and shake what I presume is a shoulder.

There's a grunt and a moan then, with a sudden movement, the shape sits bolt upright and thrusts a blunt-looking knife at me. 'What?' he snarls.

I hold up my palms. 'Morning,' I say cheerfully. 'I'm Bo.'

He has piercing blue eyes but he's all human. I'd estimate his age at around fifty but he looks a lot older. Living on the streets will do that to you. Still, he doesn't have the vacant, slack-jawed expression of a drug addict, so maybe I can get some sense out of him. He looks me up and down and sighs resignedly before pulling down his grubby shirt to reveal his neck. 'Thought you guzzlers were all dead.'

I stare at the dirt embedded in his skin; I can't imagine anyone more unappealing to drink from. 'I'm not here for blood,' I say softly. 'I'd like information.'

His eyes dart from side to side. He's still clutching the knife; his yellowing fingernails, which are gnawed down to the quick, are curled tightly round the hilt. We both know I can take it from him in an instant. ''Bout what?'

'Missing children.'

'Don't know nothing,' he grunts. 'Piss off.'

I put out a hand and gently squeeze his shoulder. 'I'm looking for the hooded men.'

'You're the bloodguzzler. You should know. Thought you lot knew everything.'

I shake my head. 'Unfortunately not.' I lean forward. 'This is important. They steal children.'

'Kids? Why they do that?' he asks suspiciously.

'I don't know. Have you seen anything? Heard anything? Rumours? Whispers?'

'If I had,' he says, 'why would I tell you?'

'Because they're hurting the innocents.'

He snorts. 'Ain't none of us innocent, darling. Not even kids.' His lip curls. 'Bunch of them here yesterday, throwing things at me, yelling.'

'I'm sorry.'

'Yeah, you're sorry. Everyone's sorry. You're not going to do anything 'bout it though, are you? No one cares.'

It occurs to me how unattractive self-pity can be. I should remember that the next time I start feeling sorry for myself. 'Thank you for your time.'

He mutters to himself and lies down again. 'Whatever. S'not hooded men you should be looking out for, it's the damn aliens.'

I halt my steps and turn. 'What did you say?'

'Go on,' he says sourly. 'Laugh at me.'

'I'm not laughing. What about aliens?'

He raises his head. 'Friend of mine told me about them over in the East End. Googly eyes and green skin.' He wags his knife at me. 'Better watch out or they'll take you. They'll cut you open just to see what's inside.' He cackles loudly. 'They won't find a heart in you, that's for sure.' He pulls the grubby sleeping bag over his head, indicating that this conversation is over.

I wonder if I should press him for more details. 'Where can I find your friend?' I ask finally.

'I'm trying to sleep here!'

'Just tell me where he is and I'll leave you in peace.'

'Unmarked grave in Ashton Cemetery,' he says. There's an air of tragic finality about his words muffled. 'Them January winds'll kill you.'

Sodding hell. I feel like I might be onto something, though. I nod to myself in satisfaction. I wonder whether the aliens belonging to Alice's crazy neighbour had googly eyes and green skin too.

CHAPTER 11
JUNK FOOD

I wait impatiently for the first of the shops to open then dart inside and start throwing things into a basket. My choices would make a nutritionist faint with horror but I reckon Michael can worry about getting his five a day later. O'Shea's kebab gave him more energy than I could have hoped for, so the more salty, sugary, fatty shit I can find, the better. No doctor would prescribe a junk food diet but they've never treated an ex-vampire before. I grab pickled onion crisps, fizzy cola bottles, tinned luncheon meat and noodles coated in a thick sweet and sour sauce that would make a self-respecting Chinese person huddle in a corner and give up on life. At the last minute, when guilt niggles at me, I toss in a bag of apples.

There's only one till, located right at the back of the shop. I'm so focused on the shelves that I don't notice until I'm there that the person manning it has the distinct, throbbing tattoo of a black witch. I stare at her and she stares at me. Uh oh.

I draw myself up and bare my fangs. I might be short but I can look threatening when I need to. The witch isn't intimidated. She just continues to stare.

The door jangles as someone else enters. A female voice calls out a cheery hello. Neither the witch nor I move.

'What are you going to do?' I ask eventually.

The witch doesn't answer.

'You can try to hurt me,' I continue. Her tattoo pulsates faster, flashing at me as if in anger. 'But I'm betting you're not that strong. If you were, you wouldn't be working in this shop.' I pause and drop my voice to a silky whisper. 'I can take you.'

She swallows nervously. I think she's going to speak but the other customer strolls up without even noticing who or what I am. She is a human woman with greying hair and a stiff waddle that suggests years of painful sciatica. 'Have you seen today's headlines? You were right, Thomasina. That Bo Blackman isn't done. I bet we're going to see more bloodshed before long.' There's an unpleasant note of anticipation in her voice. She tosses a newspaper next to the till and jabs at it. 'He runs an insurance company. Maybe he was part of that Toe Rag outfit.'

The witch rips her eyes away from me. 'Tov V'ra,' she says, her voice barely audible. She clears her throat. 'They were called Tov V'ra.'

The woman airily dismisses the correction. 'The police said they'd caught most of them but I bet they're lying. Bo Blackman will sort them out. She'll make sure they pay for what they did.' She nods. 'We need more people like her around here. If Bo Blackman was here, she wouldn't let that prick round the corner keep dealing.' She lowers her voice to a conspiratorial whisper. 'I heard he was hanging around the primary school yesterday. Trying to get them young.'

The witch darts a quick, nervous glance in my direction. I step back, pick up a box of cereal and pretend to read the back. Apparently, if I collect five tokens I can get an orange plastic daemon all of my very own.

'He's not a drug dealer,' the witch says.

'Oh yeah? Then why was he at the school?'

'His son goes there.'

The woman is taken aback. 'Oh. Are you sure?'

'Yes.'

She considers this before declaring, 'I still don't trust him. We should go round to his place later. Tell him that his sort isn't welcome here.'

So much for a community spirit. I raise my eyebrows slightly. The witch is growing more and more uncomfortable. 'What can I get for you anyway?'

'Tin of baccy. And a bottle of vodka.' She rubs the base of her spine. 'Helps ease the pain.'

I try not to snort. She has no problem castigating her neighbour for allegedly taking or selling drugs, yet here she is at eight o'clock in the morning buying hard liquor. What a difference the law makes. Booze will rip families and people apart just as much any illegal substance.

The woman pays for her purchases and walks out without paying me any attention. Once the door shuts, I eye the witch. 'Interesting clientele you have.'

'She's harmless.'

'And the man she was talking about?'

'Same.'

'If you say so.' I smile. 'Now, it's the two of us alone all over again.'

The witch holds out her hand. I jerk, expecting a flare of magic, but her palm remains bare. 'I'll ring up your items,' she says. Her fingers twitch with a nervous tremor. She's a lot more scared of me than I am of her.

I cock my head and observe her then shrug and step forward. I keep my fangs at the ready. Just in case. The witch keeps her head down as she scans my shopping. I have one eye on her and one eye on the door behind her. Maybe there are more witches skulking back there, waiting for the right moment to jump out and attack. I tilt my head back. There's a CCTV camera in the corner. Its little red light blinks at me.

The witch bags everything up. 'Twenty-two pounds and seventy-eight pence.'

I blink. 'For a bunch of junk food?'

'I don't set the prices. You should eat more healthily. All this stuff is full of additives.'

I start to smile, my gaze dropping to her neck. 'Oh,' I purr, 'I eat pretty healthily when I need to.'

The witch pales and steps back. This is kind of fun. I dig into my back pocket, pull out the money and she drops it into the till.

I'm tempted to kill her but we're close to the warehouse and if she lets it be known that I was here some bright spark is bound to put two and two together. It's inevitable that we'll be discovered there sooner or later but, despite my grandfather's assurances that it's as safe a place as we're likely to find, I'd prefer it if our presence is made known later. I have enough hassles as it is. I run my tongue over my lips. The smart thing to do would definitely be to kill her. I can easily destroy the CCTV; there's no way this shop runs anything other than a cheap in-house video recording system. Those images aren't going anywhere.

'I wouldn't tell anyone about this if I were you,' I say eventually.

She nods. I take my shopping and leave.

I'm barely five steps from the door when my phone rings. I dig it out and check the display. O'Shea.

'Hey,' I say. I walk up to the fence and unhook Kimchi's lead. The dog performs a bizarre dance of ecstasy. I've only been out of sight for ten minutes; you'd think I'd abandoned him for a week. He slobbers down my legs.

'It's me,' O'Shea says unnecessarily. 'You won't believe what I've got to tell you. I mean it. I've heard some strange things in my time, I've seen some strange things too, but this is about as weird as it gets.'

I walk briskly. The homeless guy has vanished but other people are starting to emerge onto the street. I glance back at the shop and swear I can see a flutter of movement at the window. Bugger. Is the witch watching where I go so she can find me later? I veer right just in case.

'The hooded men?' I ask.

'Not exactly.'

I pause for a beat. 'Green men?' I say finally.

'Eh? Green men?'

I feel a bit stupid. 'Yeah. Like ... aliens.'

'I think all that sun has made you go a bit soft in the head, Bo. Aliens? I know these kids are being abducted but I doubt it's so they can be taken up in UFOs and experimented on. This isn't Roswell.'

I scratch my ear. 'Well, what then? What have you found out?'

'I asked around about the hooded men. Either no one knows anything or they're keeping quiet. So I asked about missing children. Long before I met you, there was a group of teenagers living rough near one of the poorer Agathos daemon neighbourhoods. Most of them were runaways. I knew a few of them. They were good for errands, running messages, handing over contraband, that kind of thing.'

I stare at him. 'Bloody hell, O'Shea. You used kids to help you break the law?'

'Hey!' he protests. 'They needed the money. It was quid pro quo. Nothing I asked them to do was dangerous – I'm not totally heartless. And pot kettle, Bo Blackman. What about Rogu3? How long have you been using him for illegal activities?'

'That's different.' Sort of. Well, it's not actually. I wince.

'Whatever. Do you want to hear this or not?'

I sigh. Sometimes, where O'Shea's past life is concerned, it's better not to know. And with mine it's better to forget. 'Go on,' I tell him.

'Well,' he drawls, 'I bumped into a mate of mine who said that one of those kids disappeared about three and a half years ago. A Glaswegian boy with red dreadlocks. If you ask me, no white person should ever have dreadlocks. I once offered to get the kid shampoo, I even said I'd pay for it. He looked at me like I was mad and...'

'O'Shea,' I interrupt. 'Is his hair relevant to this story?'

I can almost hear him pouting on the other end of the line. 'Yes. He was very proud of his hair. He told me he'd never wash it and never cut it and he wanted to go to his grave looking like that.'

I turn a corner, the shop now out of sight, and immediately start looping back towards the warehouse. Kimchi picks up the pace too, apparently happy that we're heading home.

'Okay,' I say. 'I'm still not sure why you're telling me this.'

'My mate said that one of these kids disappeared.'

Kimchi, spotting a squirrel, tugs sharply at the lead. I haul him back and hiss. He responds by barking in delight. Idiot dog. 'I imagine that they disappear all the time. Maybe he went back to Glasgow.'

'No chance. There was nothing for him back there. He had a girlfriend here and things were on the up and up. Even the council was involved and had arranged sheltered housing for the whole group. Benjy disappeared two days before he was due to move in.'

I nod slowly. 'Okay. But I don't see any smoking gun.'

'That's the thing. My mate says that last year he saw Benjy over in the West End. He said he called to him and Benjy ignored him. It was like he'd never seen my friend before. No recognition. Nothing.'

I shrug. 'So?'

'So out of interest I went looking for him today. Went to the same place my mate was and hung around. I was there less than three hours when I found him.'

'Benjy?'

'Yep. He was coming out of some swanky apartment – and he was wearing a suit. His hair had been cut and he looked like your average corporate idiot. I said hello and he looked right through me. Then,' O'Shea adds quickly before I can interrupt again, 'I ask the doorman who he is. He says he's related to some bigwig who works in finance. There used to be a man called Colin Fairworthy in the apartment and now his nephew, James, lives there. I'm telling you though, it was Benjy. It was the kid I knew.'

'So he found himself a sugar daddy. Big deal. I'd probably want to forget my past life too if it was me on the streets.'

'You don't get it, Bo,' O'Shea says earnestly. 'He looked like Benjy. He walked like Benjy. But he wasn't Benjy. Not any more.'

I mull this over. 'A glamour?'

'No way. It was too good. And the doorman said he's been living there as James Fairworthy for three years. No one can sustain a glamour for that long.'

I clench my jaw. 'I'm betting a Kakos daemon could.'

'It's not a Kakos daemon. Trust me on this, Bo. Something stole him away and wiped his memory and is now using him for their own nefarious purposes. Maybe even this Colin Fairwor-thy. And if they can do it to one kid, they can do it to hundreds.'

O'Shea sounds very sure but all this is nothing more than circumstantial evidence. And even if it's true, I don't see where Alice would fit in. A homeless kid might be able to melt away into a different life without anyone noticing but Alice was all over the news. She still appeared on television every anniversary of her disappearance. Someone would recognise her. But it's not as if we have much else to work on.

'Okay,' I say finally. 'Do you think you can track down the other kids? The ones who were living rough with Benjy before he vanished?'

'I've already got several names and addresses.'

'Good. Ask *them* about the hooded men.'

'I'm on it. I got a photo of the new and improved Benjy, too. They'll confirm that it's him, I promise you. It's the Manchurian Candidate, Bo. That's what's happening to these kids. I already spoke to your grandfather and he reckons it's possible. He should know. We're staying in MI7's own hideout. Maybe it's time we skedaddled after all.'

I murmur non-committally. If there's one thing I've learnt, it's that jumping to conclusions never does anyone any favours. You start making the evidence fit your assumptions rather than the other way around. And wiping someone's mind? It just seems so implausible. There's no apparent motive either, despite the many conspiracy theories that immediately spring to mind. But then, as O'Shea has already pointed out, the idea of aliens is implausible as well. 'Ask them about green men too,' I say. 'With, er, big eyes.'

'Bo, the government has to be behind all this. We already know how shady Vince Hale is. But aliens from outer space?' He pauses and draws in a breath. 'Although now you come to mention it... You don't really think...?'

'Just ask, O'Shea. That's all.'

'What are you going to do?'

I glance at Kimchi. 'Drop off a few things at the warehouse then go back to Rogu3's neighbourhood. There's someone there I need to talk to.'

IN THE END, I take Kimchi with me. I might be a vampire but people trust dogs. This is the sort of country where if a soap opera highlighted a storyline of terrible domestic abuse a few people would complain, but if they included a story of animal abuse the complaints would run into thousands. With Kimchi in tow, I project an image of being trustworthy. Of course, the image projected onto a million screens a couple of nights ago was of Bo Blackman, thug extraordinaire, not Bo Blackman, caring animal lover. But not everyone recognises me for who I am and I reckon I was justified with what happened with the hybrid witches. If nothing else, it keeps Kimchi happy to be out and about and my grandfather is delighted to have him as far away as possible.

There's still no sign of Maria emerging from her room, but she'd probably be pretty happy to have Kimchi out of the building too. Unfortunately I now understand why. Any time I think about it incandescent rage rises inside me until it's almost overwhelming, but I can't pretend all this shit hasn't happened to her.

Rather than piss around trying to hide my approach, I park outside the crazy guy's house and get out. It looks normal enough; in fact, if you put Rogu3's house next to this it would be nigh on impossible to tell the two apart without going inside. The joys of suburban England.

I go to the front door and knock. Kimchi, trying to be helpful, barks as well. I just hope crazy guy is amenable to blood-guzzlers.

A moment later the door opens and a young woman appears. I'm taken aback; I was certain that the Bruckheimer and Berryhill report said this 'eyewitness' lived alone and had no family. The woman smiles but her expression falters when she sees who is actually on her doorstep.

I force the issue. 'Hi. I'm Bo Blackman.'

She blinks rapidly. 'Yeah. Yeah, I know.' Her hand travels to her throat. I can't blame her but the action makes me wince. 'I'm here because I'm investigating the disappearance of Alice Goldman.'

The woman forgets her fear and stares at me. 'Really? Shouldn't you be investigating what happened to all the vampires?'

'I know what happened to them,' I say, more shortly than I intended. 'But I can't do anything about it.' Yet. I can't do anything about it *yet*. 'Anyway,' I continue briskly, 'I'm looking for Adio Brown.'

Her brow furrows in both puzzlement and relief. 'Oh, he doesn't live here any more.' Sodding hell. I try not to curse aloud. 'He used to own this house,' the woman explains hastily, seeing my expression. She shrugs. 'I only know that because we still get post for him, even after all these years.'

All these years? 'How long have you lived here?'

'We moved in about four months after Alice disappeared. I remember it because,' she looks embarrassed, 'er, because we got it really cheaply as a result of what happened to her. No one else wanted to live round here.'

I scratch my chin. Interesting that Mr Brown left so quickly. 'Did you ever meet him?' I press her. 'Adio Brown?' What I really want is a stranger's opinion of his sanity.

The woman shakes her head. 'No, I'm sorry. To be honest, I thought the house had been re-possessed. We bought it direct from the bank, not from him.'

I consider this. Mortgage defaults were at their height back then so it's certainly credible. Brown had already retired a few years before, though; how many retired people without families to support still had mortgages? Something doesn't ring true. I thank her anyway.

'Nice dog,' she tells me.

Kimchi, instantly aware that he's the topic of conversation, wags his tail furiously. 'Oh, he's wonderful,' I agree, lying through my teeth. 'And so well-behaved.'

We get back into the van. Kimchi hops into the passenger seat and swings his head towards me, his tongue lolling and a long thread of spittle dripping onto the cracked leather. I rub his ears. 'Well done,' I say. 'Even if it didn't get us anywhere, you played your part well. I'm impressed that you managed to hold off drooling until we got back here.'

I glance back to the house; the woman is still standing on her porch. She probably wants to make sure that I leave her quiet little street. She's smiling, no doubt because she can see me holding a conversation with a dog. Daft. 'You know what bothers me, Kimchi?' I ask, as I start the engine. 'That people will think I'm a good person because I have a dog, even though it's been proved that I have a strong thread of psycho. Yet an old man who lived here for decades says once that he saw some aliens and everyone dismisses him as nuts.' I wag my finger. 'Appearances can be very, very deceptive. Remember that.'

We drive off. I'm about to head back to the warehouse – the desperate need to spend more time with Michael is gnawing away at me – but I decide to make one more call while I'm here. I don't want to, in fact I'd rather sink my fangs into Kimchi's hide and drink from him than do this. But I'm here now so I guess I might as well.

~

Alice Goldman's house is less than thirty metres from Rogu3's. I'd like to say that it looks exactly the same as it did years before but there's a haunting air of neglect about it. I've been to houses like this before and it's never fun.

I pull up and wonder whether the Goldmans can smile with genuine emotion now, or whether there's nothing more than well-constructed facades on their faces and an aching, Alice-shaped void in their hearts. I think I know the answer without asking.

I steel myself for the inevitable. This time, I leave Kimchi in the van. Even if his presence would smooth things over, such tricks don't seem fair. I walk up the path alone.

Before I can raise my fist and knock, the door opens and Mrs Goldman's familiar face appears. We never had chance to meet before; I was under orders not to approach the family. Bruck-heimer and Berryhill probably thought that meeting the grieving parents would make me develop a conscience and work against the insurance company to get the family what they deserved. I didn't need to talk to the Goldmans face to face to have a conscience; I was human back then.

'I saw you park outside,' Mrs Goldman says, all in a rush. Her face is flushed and her eyes are anxious. I'm troubled that she might think I'm with the police. It's a ridiculous notion but there's something about the way she's looking at me that sets me on edge.

'Uh, great,' I say. 'I'm Bo Blackman.'

'I know. Of course I know. Everyone knows.'

She knows I'm not a copper then. That's something. I hold my tongue, refraining from plunging straight into my own agenda. Mrs Goldman wants something and she deserves the opportunity to ask for it before I bulldoze my way through and make her spend the rest of the day sobbing.

She takes a deep breath. 'You've been very kind to Alistair.'

For a moment, I don't have the faintest idea what she's

talking about. Then my brain kicks into gear. Rogu3. Of course. 'He's a good kid.'

Mrs Goldman bites her lip and nods. 'He was very helpful with Alice. You know. Before.'

I maintain a professional air. 'Yes, I do know.'

Her words are expelled in a massive rush. 'I wanted to come and talk to you. When you visited his parents. I've been looking out because I thought you might come round again. I thought if we could just speak then you'd understand and you'd help.' She wrings her hands and I see that they're red and raw. She sees me looking and grimaces. 'Sorry. Plumbing.'

I blink. I already know that Mrs Goldman has an inner strength that I couldn't begin to muster – not after the loss of a child – but the last thing I expected was to hear that she's knee-deep in pipes and wrenches. 'Is everything okay?'

'Yes, yes.' She wipes her brow and meets my eyes. Even confronted with the tell-tale red in my pupils, Mrs Goldman doesn't flinch. 'I know it's been a long time and you have other things going on right now, but you did it for Alistair and his family and now I want you to do it for me.'

Suddenly I understand. Although it seems a lifetime ago, it's not that long since Rogu3's life was in danger. I went after those who harmed him and made sure that they wouldn't hurt anyone else ever again. Mrs Goldman wants the same for Alice's killers. But I think that Alice might be alive. I debate whether to tell her and decide against it. There's no point in giving her false hope; it wouldn't be fair.

'That's exactly why I'm here,' I tell her calmly, using her lead.

Her eyes widen. 'It is? Did Alistair's mum talk to you? I told her to pass on a message that I wanted to speak to you. I wasn't sure if she would.' She lowers her voice. 'A lot of my neighbours avoid me. It's as if having a dead child is contagious.' She lets out a tiny snort.

I already like her more than I thought I would. I gloss over Rogu3's mum and the 'message'. 'I like Alistair,' I say simply. 'And he liked Alice. It's the least I can do.'

'I thought you'd be busy. There's so much going on at the moment with all those dead bloodguzz— vampires. I'm so sorry that happened to you.'

There's something incongruous about Alice's mum apologising to me. 'You know,' I say in a soft voice and, for once, with total honesty, 'people keep saying that. They keep saying they're sorry and they keep saying that I must be busy sorting it all out.'

'But sorry doesn't help,' Mrs Goldman fills in. 'And there's nothing left to sort out.'

I nod; she understands it better than I do. Then again, she's had years to think about it. For the briefest and most unexpected moment, my eyes well up with tears. Mrs Goldman reaches out, takes my hand and squeezes it hard. Her comforting me seems ridiculous. I bow my head and bite the inside of my cheek hard until the moment passes. I can't fall apart in front of her; that would be the most unfair cut of all.

'It's been a long time,' I say once I recover control. 'There's not going to be much of a trail to follow. The police looked for whoever did this to your daughter and found nothing.'

'Yes,' she answers. 'They did.' There's no trace of censure in her eyes or in her words. 'They did the best they could. But I can't rest until I've tried every single avenue. I owe that much to Alice's memory.'

I swallow. Without warning, a loud squawl rents the air. I'm so startled that I jump. Mrs Goldman smiles faintly. 'Wait just a minute,' she asks. 'Please?'

She turns and is swallowed up by her house. When she

reappears, there's a pink swaddled baby in her arms. I'm no expert but I'd say she's no older than four months. The sweet smell of talcum powder tickles my nose and, involuntarily, I take a step back. I'm not afraid of a baby, I'm just ... slightly overwhelmed.

'Would you like to hold her?' Mrs Goldman asks.

That's brave. 'I'm a vampire,' I say stupidly.

She smiles. 'I trust you.'

I want to say no. I desperately want to say no. Instead, I reach out my arms.

The baby is heavier than I expected. She yawns at me, her huge blue eyes fixed on mine with no fear or malice. She's just curious. There's a strange lump in my throat. 'What ... what's her name?'

'Hope,' Mrs Goldman replies. 'Because we all need some of that, don't we?'

'She's perfect.'

Her reply is barely audible. 'So was Alice.'

Scared of what could happen if I don't let Baby Hope go, I pass her back. She gurgles and reaches up to grab a curl of her mother's hair. I look away. 'I've been down the revenge path before,' I say finally. 'It's not as satisfying as you might think.'

'This isn't about revenge,' Mrs Goldman tells me calmly and for some reason I believe her. 'This is about justice. I know there aren't any guarantees. I know that every lead has already been followed. But you're different.' Her eyes plead with me. 'I can pay.'

'I don't want your money.' The fact that I'm already looking into Alice's disappearance has nothing to do with this either. Regardless of where Alice is now – dead or alive – I'm not sure I can open myself up to the darkness necessary to bring Mrs Goldman's desired justice to her daughter's abductors. I've been down that road before and it almost destroyed me. Of course the darkness is still there but the worst of it is being held at bay. It's only a thin thread away, though.

'Did you see anything the day Alice went missing? Or in the days before?' I can't believe I'm going to ask this, but it's the reason I'm here. 'Maybe someone wearing a Halloween mask? Like an, um, alien?'

'There was nothing,' Mrs Goldman sighs. 'Believe me, I've been over and over that day a million times. There was nothing out of the ordinary.' She looks sad until Hope gurgles again and her attention is drawn back to the present. 'Whoever did this to Alice deserves to die.'

Yeah, they do. I don't reply.

Aware of my reluctance, Mrs Goldman keeps talking. 'I still see her. Even now, after all this time, I catch sight of her in the street. I run up, screaming her name and then when she turns...' I hold my breath '...it's not her at all. There was even one time...' Her voice falters. 'It doesn't matter.'

'No. Go on. One time what?'

A faint flush stains her cheeks. 'I saw her. I was sure it was her. Her hair was different, it had been dyed dark brown and cropped short. The clothes she was wearing weren't what Alice would have liked at all. But still, I was convinced. I walked up to her and grabbed her. I hugged her and she stood there like a robot. Like I was some mad woman on the street.' She laughs harshly. 'I suppose I was. Of course, then she started screaming and all these passers-by wrenched her from me.' Her tone turns bitter. 'Where were they when my Alice was taken?'

'Mrs Goldman,' I begin.

She shakes her head. 'Sorry. Don't mind me. My psychologist says moments like that are bound to happen. That they're natural.' She sighs. 'I really was so sure.'

I try to sound casual. 'Where was this?'

'Westminster. I only remember because I'd gone to meet my MP. He kept promising to do more.'

For a horrifying moment, I think she means Vince Hale then I remember that he's the MP for some town up north.

'Can you remember when?'

'Two years ago or thereabouts.' Her expression tightens. 'Why?'

'I was just curious.' I glance back at the van. 'Look, my dog is in there. I probably shouldn't leave him for too long.'

'Of course.' She hefts Hope in her arms. 'This little one needs changing.' She lifts her chin. 'You are going to look though, aren't you? I can tell. You have this stubborn set to your mouth that reminds me of Alice when she wanted something.'

The ache in my heart deepens. 'I will look. I can't promise any more than that.'

Walking back to the van, the guilt eats away at me. Why didn't I tell Mrs Goldman what I already know about Alice? I'm sure I'm doing the right thing but I can't help thinking that she deserves to know. If it was me, I'd want to know. I sigh heavily.

Kimchi's bark draws me out my reverie. I open the van door and, with an amazing feat of dexterity, he squeezes past me and leaps out. I curse. Without a care in the world for traffic, people or my pointless shouts, he bolts across the road towards the nearest lamppost, then immediately begins sniffing at it with doggy desperation.

I grab his collar. 'You can't do that! I understand it might smell interesting but there might be cars. You might get run over.'

Kimchi is entirely uninterested. 'Look,' I tell him, remembering Rogu3's litany from the night before. 'There's the Goodsons' car and the shouty neighbour's car and the Lairds' car. Any of those could start up, drive over and not see you. And then you'll be squished dog. Look at that black van! Its suspension is so low that it...'

I freeze. There wasn't a black van here the other night. In fact, I've never seen a black van in this neighbourhood before. My skin prickles. Kimchi looks past me and starts to whine.

I whip round as something purple and noxious is sprayed in my face. I cough and cover my mouth but it's too late. I've already inhaled it and I can feel my head starting to swim. Kimchi barks, a ferocious series of yelps, but the sound is already growing distant. All I can think is that I should have killed that damned black witch in the shop when I had the chance.

CHAPTER 12

UNDERGROUND

I don't think I'm unconscious for long. Whatever chemical was in that sodding gas was enough to knock me out but not to keep me under. When I wake up, my face is pressed against a cold metal floor and there's the sound of an engine in the background. I can feel motion. My hands are cuffed – and this time with the energy-sapping crap from Magix – and when I try to twist round and sit up, my head knocks painfully against something a few inches above me. As I blink and look around, it's clear that I'm being held in what can only be a coffin.

Whoever has captured me doesn't want me dead, at least not yet. If they had then I'd have already breathed my last. The thought of torture flits through my mind; maybe they're looking for Michael and they'll bleed me until I give him up. But hardly anyone knows he's still alive.

I tell myself it doesn't matter what they do to me, I will never break. I know the truth though. Ideas like that are best kept for Hollywood; the truth is that, sooner or later, everyone breaks.

I think of the Kakos daemons. Perhaps this is all their doing but it doesn't feel like their style. During every encounter I've had with X – and the one with the female daemon – they had no qualms about letting me know who they were. They made a point of it.

I try to breathe normally. I have to be logical. Know thy enemy, Bo, I tell myself. Right now it's the only chance I've got.

Eventually, I narrow it down to either the Tov V'ra members who've managed to avoid arrest, the government, or some as yet unknown entity. My bet is on the government. Who else would own a black van that was sitting heavily enough in the road to suggest that it was carrying a lot of expensive equipment? Metallica, perhaps? Last time I checked, they didn't hang around pretty London suburbs. In any case, I already know from Foxworthy about the new initiative to round up all remaining bloodguzzlers. This kidnapping must be connected with Vince Hale. Prick. About the only silver lining I can think of is that either MI7 are beyond clueless, or my grandfather was correct when he said they worked independently to the elected Westminster officials.

Impatience surges through me. Whoever these bastards are, they'd better not take me far away. I've got Alice to deal with and I can't lose precious time being carted to the other side of the country and working out how to escape. If Alice is alive, *she* can't afford that time.

I squirm, pushing against the cuffs with every iota of strength I can muster. I know from past experience that it's next to useless but I have to do something. Only when I'm absolutely certain that I can't free myself do I move on and start banging against the side of the coffin. Every thud is an effort – those bloody cuffs really work – but I'm not about to quit.

After about my twentieth attempt, someone finally bangs back. 'Shut the hell up!'

I pause. Male. Perfect Eton-educated accent. Yep. This is

down to Vince Hale and his cronies. I start banging against the coffin again.

There's a clatter as a lock is drawn and the lid is raised. I blink against the sudden bright light. A smooth face with a carefully tended moustache and cold eyes peers down at me. 'I told you to shut the hell up.'

'I'm claustrophobic.'

'You're a bloodguzzler,' he snarls. 'I thought you all slept in coffins.' He smashes his hand down towards my face. I jerk to the side but there's not enough room to escape the blow fully. His fist connects with my cheekbone and jarring pain shoots down towards my jaw. Now I'm getting pissed off.

The coffin lid is slammed down. I count to three then start throwing myself against the side with even more gusto. The angrier I can make him, the more chance that he'll mess up. This time I only have to do it four times before the lid is flung open again. He grabs the collar of my T-shirt and hauls me up until his face is inches from mine. I don't look at him; I already know what he looks like. This time I want to see where I am.

'If you don't stop that,' he threatens, as I take in two goons – one male and one female – and an array of blinking lights and computer screens, 'then you'll be dead.'

'He won't like that,' the woman remarks. 'He wants to talk to her first.'

I glance past her to the van doors. I can't see a handle, which means they're electronically controlled. Arse.

'I don't give a toss what he'll like. He's not here.' The posh boy glares at me. 'Look at me when I'm talking to you!'

I pull my attention back to him. I'm not getting free until we reach our destination so there's no point in continuing to scan the van. 'What have you done to my dog?' I enquire. Clichéd it might seem but if they've so much as harmed a single hair on Kimchi's back, I will destroy them.

His lip curls. 'I don't harm innocent animals,' he spits. 'Only rabid beasts.'

I take that to mean Kimchi was smart enough to run off before they could grab him, otherwise this tosser would delight in showing me his remains or using him as collateral to get me to behave. In return, I give him a brief taste of what a rabid beast like me is really capable of. I elongate my fangs and I snap my head forwards. He yelps and skitters back, falling over a chair. I smile.

'You bitch! You'll pay for that!'

'I didn't even touch you,' I purr. 'Is that all it takes to get you to piss yourself?'

'Freaking hell!' the woman exclaims aloud. 'Have you wet yourself, you plank? Because if you have, you can be the one to clean it up.'

He's even angrier now. A thick vein bulges in his forehead and starts throbbing. I lick my lips; I don't actually mean to but the sight of all that pulsing blood so close to the surface of his skin is difficult to ignore. He gets to his feet and backhands me but he's not as strong as he looks. It's easy to throw your fist at someone who's trapped in a box but he's going to have to try a lot harder than that if he wants to knock me off my feet.

'Just put her back in the damn coffin.'

'Don't bother,' says the other man, speaking for the first time. 'We're already here.' The words have barely left his mouth when the van rolls to a halt.

I tense. Just like Maria when the lorry she was transported in stopped, I'm aware that this is my best opportunity for escape. Once I'm inside wherever it is they're taking me, it'll be a lot more complicated.

I'm not going to be able to move quickly – the sodding energy-sapping handcuffs will see to it – but I'm still strong. And faster than them.

There are a couple of barked instructions from outside, followed by a thump on the other side of the door. Without saying another word, the men walk over and stand on either side of me, each grabbing an upper arm. I have the unpleasant thought that this isn't the first time they've done this.

'Don't bother trying to get away,' the first one growls in my ear. 'Not unless you really want to know what pain is like.'

I try not to roll my eyes. He's been reading too many Ian Fleming novels; he's already proved that he's not as badass as he thinks he is. All the same, I force my body to become loose and relaxed. I can play meek and mild if it will surprise them when I finally make a bolt for it.

The woman presses a button on one of the blinking machines and the door opens. I peer outside, trying not to obviously scope the area. We're in some kind of garage. Damn it. That makes things a bit harder – but not impossible.

The woman hops out and takes a clipboard from a boiler-suited goon. 'We got her,' she says, satisfaction layering every damn word.

'Bo Blackman? You guys rock.'

I stare at him, half-expecting a fist pump. To have been captured by this lot is starting to become embarrassing.

He lifts his head and stares. 'She's shorter than I expected,' he comments. 'And kind of cute.'

Good grief.

I'm hauled out without ceremony. The air in the garage is dank and oppressive; I think we must be underground until I see daylight at the far end. Nope. This is just a vast space; I can work with that.

I can see two men on the ground, together with the three who got out of the van with me. There's another electronically controlled door about twenty feet away, which I assume is where we're heading. My eyes flick from side to side as I plan my escape route. I've got this.

The two men holding me drag me forward while the woman flips open a keypad. Even with my lack of techie ability, I can tell that this is a far inferior version to the one on the MI7 warehouse entrance. That makes me happy. I wait until she's finished and there's a quiet whoosh then I leap upwards, yanking myself free, and spin ninety degrees. Goon One gets a kick to the balls and Goon Two receives a blow on his nose from the back of my skull. There's a satisfying crunch. As the other three jump to it, I skip away. I can't sprint – not with the cuffs – but I can be smart.

As soon as I reach the side of the garage and the first row of parked vehicles, I drop to the ground and roll under one of them. They'll expect me to make a run for the exit so I head in that direction. When their yelled curses alert me to their location, however, I twist round and roll left to the next row of cars rather than forwards into the sunshine.

Adrenaline is pumping through my system and making my skin prickle with delight. I'm not sure whether my change in direction has gone unnoticed until I scoot round once more and see the feet moving past me. I head away from the door and push myself up so I'm hanging from the undercarriage of a Range Rover. Then I peer out.

As expected, the woman has stayed behind. Her hand is on a remote control and, as she presses it, there's the sound of clanking machinery. The far door begins to trundle closed. I watch her but I also count; I need to know how long it takes the garage door to close. It's not quick. A full eight seconds pass by until it finally judders shut.

'Did she get out?' someone calls.

'No, she's still in here.'

'Turn on the freaking lights! She's under one of the cars.'

Almost immediately, the place is illuminated by fluorescent strip lights hanging from the ceiling. Shadows flicker and move as my captors start ducking down and checking. I adjust my position slightly. Unless they look directly under this vehicle, they won't spot me. I'm going to smell of engine oil, though. That's irritating. Still, the last time I tried this was on a moving vehicle which was heading into a well-guarded army outpost. This is far easier.

The goons skitter around making too much noise. I train my gaze on the woman. She doesn't look anything more than irritated. She might know my name but she still doesn't have a clue who she's dealing with.

I wait until the others are far enough away then drop silently to the ground and roll my body towards her. I can't afford the movement to catch her peripheral vision so I take things easy and it's a good opportunity to rest a bit. The longer the Magix cuffs are on, the more sluggish I feel. I need to conserve as much energy as I can.

There's a shout from the other side of the garage and her head jerks towards it. It provides me with all the time I need to get past her. Now I'm two cars – and less than ten feet – away.

'It's just a bloody cat!'

There's a harsh curse in response. The woman tuts to herself and taps her foot impatiently. I ease out from under the car, taking care not to let the cuffs scrape the ground. With precise movements, and holding my breath, I get to my feet. I can't let her make a sound. Without the use of my hands, this is going to be difficult.

I sneak up, using her body to block me from view should one of the others turn round and look this way. I'm only inches away from her when I stop. I smile to myself then blow gently onto the nape of her neck. Her hand rises and she looks round as I launch myself towards her, aiming for her head. She falls backwards with one sharp yelp which is almost instantly muffled because my shoulder is wedged in her mouth. I wrest the remote from her and shuffle round slightly until I'm the right position. She writhes underneath me. I'm not going to be able to hold her for much longer but I don't need to. I move my shoulder from her face at the same time as my head swings round and slams into hers, knocking her out instantly.

As I hear pounding feet racing back towards me, I leave her where she is and roll again, this time to my right.

'Shit!'

'What's happened?'

'Lane is out cold.'

I pray that they won't notice the absence of the remote but they have other things on their minds.

'She's separating us, then taking us out one by one. We need to stick together.'

I grin. Yeah, you do that, you'll be easier to avoid if you stay in a group. I didn't imagine the tremble of fear in the goon's voice. Let them think I'm the perfect predator rather than their helpless prey. If it helps me get out of this, it's all to the good.

They abandon their companion and start looking under the nearest cars, heading back towards the wall rather than towards the door. They're not the brightest sparks but then again, they do work for the government. As their group edges back, I roll forward. The unfortunate thing is that all this exertion is really beginning to take its toll. It feels as if the handcuffs are tightening round me and I have to keep shaking my head to avoid blacking out.

I heave a sigh of relief when I'm scant feet away from the closed exit. I take a moment to recoup my strength as best as I can and ignore the shouts of frustration from behind me. Blood is roaring in my ears. Come on, Bo. You can do this.

I daren't wait too long. At some point, one of these idiots will call for back-up and the last thing I need is a swarm of goons searching for me. I breathe deeply, press the button on the remote and haul myself back, making sure I'm still out of sight.

There's a shriek. 'The door! The door! She's escaping!'

Booted feet hammer towards me. I don't move a muscle, I just watch the oblong of daylight get wider and wider. One. Two. Three. Four. At five seconds, the first man passes me. He ducks under and out of the door, the other three hot on his heels. Six. Seven. Eight.

'Which way did she go?'

'I don't know! I didn't see!'

'Straight ahead is clear. You two, take the left. We'll go right. We'll find her. She's not going far with those anti-guzzler cuffs.'

I grimace. Ain't that the truth?

I remain where I am, poised to move as the four of them vanish from sight. I wait six beats then roll out and stagger up. I glance in the window of the car I hid under. The keys are in the lock. Excellent.

I twist round, awkwardly opening the door with my fingers before clambering in. I ignore the sweat dripping from my brow and duck down to turn the key with my teeth. The engine revs, thank goodness. I only have seconds.

I lean in the other direction, trying to knock the car into gear. It's not as easy as it sounds and, with one foot on the clutch, I'm forced to move my body into positions it's not been in for years. I manage it though and yank myself upright. It's time to get the hell out of Dodge.

'You broke my nose, bitch.'

I turn just in time to see the woman glaring at me. She's holding something shiny in her hands. I barely manage to register it as a vamp taser before she squeezes the trigger and pain explodes in my chest. Again.

Bugger.

CHAPTER 13

REUNIONS

I'm barely conscious as I'm dragged inside. My vision is blurry and I can't make out much. It doesn't help that I receive several sharp kicks to my ribs and, at one point, someone takes my arm and bends it back until I hear the snap of breaking bone. But if they think they're going to keep me subdued by inducing mind-numbing pain, they've got the wrong Bo Blackman. Physical pain won't stop me; it's emotional pain that's my nemesis.

After what seems like an eternity, we make our way into a narrow corridor. I vaguely hear a lock being turned. There's a sharp cry, I'm flung forward and the door closes behind me. But all is not lost.

'Bo!'

I blink and groan. That voice. A face swims towards me with perfect features and worried eyes. 'Beth?' I whisper.

Cool fingers brush against my cheek. 'It's me,' she answers. 'I'm here.'

There's another voice. Gruffer. 'Her arm is broken.'

A hand clasps mine. 'Hold on, Bo. We've got this.'

There's a sharp yank. Pain flares up stronger than before

then ebbs away until I'm left gasping ragged sobs. I touch my head; it's still there. I wiggle my toes and my fingers. Alright. Things could be worse.

I'm helped into a sitting position and I swallow hard and look around. There are at least twenty other vampires, including Beth. As far as I can tell, only three are former Montserrat; the rest are from the other Families. There's only one Medici minion and he's sporting a rather impressive black eye which looks recent. I point at it. 'Your handiwork, Beth?'

'Mine.' A male vampire wearing a tunic emblazoned with Bancroft colours steps forward. 'He deserved it.'

I nod distractedly and keep my attention on my old friend. 'I thought you were dead. How did you get out?'

'I was lucky,' she says softly. 'I was in the garden.'

'Matt?'

She looks down. 'I don't know. I didn't see where he was.'

I close my eyes briefly. 'You're here,' I say eventually. 'That's enough.'

She kneels down beside me. 'I went looking for you. I looked everywhere I could think of.'

'You went to Rogu3's house.' It's not a question.

She nods. 'It was one of the places I thought you might be. I knew you could help us. I knew you were the only one who could unite us.'

I laugh harshly. 'I can't even stand up, Beth.'

Her expression doesn't change. 'You left the Families. You survived on the outside without them. You know the way forward.'

I sigh. I'm no one's saviour. I can't even stay on the streets long enough to help Alice Goldman. 'I'm afraid I don't know anything. Where were you picked up?'

'Outside New Order. I went there.' She gestures at the

others. 'All of us went there. It was the only other place we knew of where we might be safe.'

An ache blossoms in my chest and it's not from the taser. 'They were there waiting for you?'

'Yes.'

'And Arzo? Peter? The others?'

This time she doesn't look away. 'I'm sorry. They weren't there. I guess they were killed too.'

I ball up my fists. 'Arzo and Peter weren't even fucking vampires.'

'They were Sanguine. That was enough.'

I press the base of my palms against my temples. With Michael's safety to focus on, I'd not allowed myself to think about everyone else. I knew there would be time for that later. Now, confronted with so many deaths, I can't pretend to ignore them all. Hatred for X sparks up inside me once again. He deserves to pay.

I look round what can only be described as a large cell. I can't do much about anything from here. 'Is there any way out?'

'Not that we can tell. The whole place is proofed against bloodguzzlers. All you have to do is touch the door and you'll get a shock strong enough to lay you flat.'

I curse and look at the door, a huge steel thing with a tiny sliding window to look through. 'How long have you all been here?'

A petite woman steps forward. She's pale and shaking and I'm guessing she's not drunk blood for days. Much longer and she'll waste away to nothing. 'I've been here the longest. I was picked up hours after the bombs went off.'

My jaw sets. 'Vince Hale certainly adapts quickly.'

Beth is surprised. 'The politician? He's the one who's doing this?'

'I guess he's not been round to say hello then.'

The window slides across with a thunk and a smarmy, smiling face appears. 'I was waiting for you, Ms Blackman.'

I'M TAKEN to a small interrogation room fitted out with only a table and two chairs. There's not even a two-way mirror or a camera; I guess Hale wants to make sure there are no witnesses. That way he can do away with us all and make up any bloody story he likes.

I sit down and cradle my arm. A blank-faced man chains me up and leaves as Hale takes the chair opposite. 'Would you like something to drink? I can get you some blood.' He smiles disarmingly. 'I know it'll help you heal more quickly.'

Even if I could be sure that it wasn't tainted, I wouldn't give him the satisfaction of seeing me accept something from him. I'd rather starve. 'You can't keep me here,' I tell him. 'It's against the law.'

He throws back his head and laughs. I didn't know I was such a comedian. 'The law's been changed.' He chuckles again. 'It's quite extraordinary what you can get away with when you force people into a panic. Besides, you're here for your own protection. There's no telling how many Tov V'ra members are still out there trying to kill you.'

'You're all heart.'

'My ex-wife would probably disagree. But thank you.' I stare at him. He shrugs. 'For future reference, Ms Blackman, I don't believe in sarcasm.' He pauses. 'Oh wait. You don't have a future.'

I narrow my eyes. 'You're being very brave sitting next to me, considering that last time we met you told me that I was a freak. An affront to God.' I cross my legs. 'That's quite a statement given that I'm not sure that God takes too well to genocide.'

He leans back in his chair and knits his hands behind his head. 'Do you know where the word genocide comes from?' he enquires. '*Cide* derives from the Latin *caedere* meaning to kill. And *geno* comes from the Greek meaning people. You're a bloodguzzler. You're not people.'

It's my turn to laugh. 'And here was me thinking you were well educated. *Geno* means race. Last time I checked, that covered vampires.'

His expression sours. 'You tribers are all the same,' he hisses. 'You don't belong here in our country.'

'Oh, Vinnie, you still don't get it, do you? You think that you pulled the strings and made all this to happen but you were being manipulated by tribers from the very start.'

'Medici wasn't manipulating me. I was the one who—'

'No,' I interrupt. 'You weren't. The Kakos daemons were the ones in charge. They're the puppet masters. Not you.'

'What are you talking about?'

'You heard me,' I say softly. 'Tribers got inside your mind, Vinnie. Tribers played you like a violin and got you do to their bidding. And you're still too stupid to see it. You think you're running this country? It's not you and it's not your cronies. The Kakos daemons are the ones in charge.'

Something flickers in his expression. 'That's not true.'

I cock my head. 'What? You don't believe me?'

'Funnily enough, no.'

Despite his fine words, I can hear the doubt creeping in. 'Look into it,' I tell him. 'You'll find out that I'm telling the truth.'

I have a feeling that Vince Hale doesn't like being played any more than I do. With any luck, he'll do some investigating of his own and X will get pissed off and eat his heart out. It'll be small compensation but it's better than nothing.

'It doesn't matter,' he dismisses. 'Now that you're here, I can put the rest of *my* plan into action. You're the famous face, Ms Blackman. You're the one everyone knows. Once you're out of the picture, the other rats will leave.'

'I'm not leaving.'

He smiles. 'Yes, you are. You and all your buddies are going to be transported to a facility outside the city.' He scratches his chin. 'There's going to be a little accident along the way. An exploding petrol tank will do the trick. Bloodguzzlers don't do well with fire. The smoking remains of five Family mansions prove that.' He eyes me with amusement. 'Do you know, if you walk past each one you can still smell barbecued vampire in the air? I've taken to going there each morning before breakfast. It does wonders for my appetite.'

I can't help myself, I lunge towards him with sharp, vicious anger. The chain is strong, however, and it jerks me back.

Hale laughs. 'You see? You're nothing more than an animal. And not even a well-trained one at that.'

'Last time we met, you said you wouldn't reveal your plans to me. Why are you doing it this time?'

'Because,' he replies, 'I want to see the look on your face when it finally dawns on you that your kind are going to be extinct. Nothing more than ash. When other countries see what's happened here, they'll follow suit.'

'You have to let me go, Hale. I'm on the trail of a lot of missing children. Alice Goldman is one of them. These children—'

'You expect me to fall for that?'

'It's true. You remember Alice, don't you? She went missing five years ago. I think she's still alive. If you let me go, I can find her.'

'You're mine now, Ms Blackman. You're not going anywhere.'

I jerk at the chain in desperation. 'Then at least look into her disappearance. I can give you all the information and you can do something about it. She's not the only one, there could be hundreds of these missing kids. Something's happening to them. Their minds are being wiped or something. You can find them, you—'

'I couldn't give a rat's arse about Alice Goodman.'

'Goldman. Her name is Alice Goldman.'

He shrugs. 'Whatever. What's one more child? There are plenty of them to go round. If she's not a triber, she's not my concern.'

'But—'

'I'm bored with you now. I thought you'd be more entertaining than this, Ms Blackman. Instead you're coming up with silly excuses for why I should spare your life. It's all terribly mundane.' He stands up. 'You did well to escape me once. It won't happen a second time.' He walks to the door. 'Be content that you were one of the last British vampires that ever lived. Maybe someone will write a song about you one day.' He doffs an imaginary hat and departs.

I tug frantically at the chain and yell after him, 'Alice Goldman! You need to do something, Hale! She's just a kid! Listen to me!'

He's not listening, though. No one is. The only thing that answers me back is silence.

I'm not taken back to the cell; instead I'm led straight back to the garage. This time it's clear that Hale's goons aren't taking any chances. Even if I still had the energy to fight them, there are too many of them. I sag against my bonds. I refuse to quit just yet but I can't help feeling an encroaching sense of resignation.

I'm pushed into a vehicle, a prisoner transportation bus with blackened windows which Hale must have appropriated specially for this event. When I get in, I see that the others are there too. Three guards press me down onto a bench which faces away from the side of the bus. I end up seated between two defeated looking Stuart vampires while the guards attach my cuffs to a chain. There's another bench opposite and the vampires sitting on it watch fearfully.

'Don't do this,' I say, keeping my voice calm. 'Do you really want to be responsible for more deaths?' The guards ignore me. I try again. 'Have you heard of Alice Goldman? She went missing years ago. I'm on her trail. I think she's still alive. What you need to do is look around Westminster. I think Alice was abducted and her mind has been wiped. Her hair is short and dark now but...'

The three men walk out without so much as a flicker in their eyes to show that they heard me. My words are swallowed up as the bus doors are slammed shut.

'What's going on, Bo?' Beth asks. 'Where are we going?'

I hiss in frustration. If just one of the guards had listened, there would still be a thread of hope for Alice. I have to believe that. 'They're supposedly taking us somewhere out of the city where we're going to be safe.'

'They're not though, are they?' the Medici guzzler says.

I shake my head. 'No.'

He starts yelling. When that does nothing he throws his head back repeatedly against the window. Each time it smacks off the glass, there's a thud. 'Stop that,' I say tiredly. 'It's not going to make a difference.'

A few others yank at their chains in desperation. Beth is

smarter. She looks at me and raises her eyebrows. 'Do you see a way out?'

'Not yet. But none of us are dead yet. Panic isn't going to help anyone.'

One of the women begins to screech, a high-pitched sound which makes me wince. As if in response, the engine starts up and the bus moves.

'Be quiet,' I snap.

She pauses momentarily and stares at me with crazed eyes. 'Or what? You're going to come over here and hit me?' She laughs wildly. 'We're all dead. We're corpses in the ground. A cautionary note for future generations.' She starts to scream again.

I count to ten.

'What do we do, Bo?' Beth asks.

I glance at her. 'We need to get out of these cuffs and chains.'

'Sure,' the Medici guy drawls sarcastically. 'Then we can blow the roof of this bus and fly away.' A trickle of blood leaks down his forehead where he smashed himself against the window. Fat lot of good that did.

'Does anyone have a hair clip?' I ask. 'A bobby pin I can use to work the lock?'

'You're going to pick a magic lock with your hands tied behind your back?' he snorts.

'It's a better plan than knocking myself out,' I say levelly.

At the far end of the bus, a small voice pipes up, 'I've got some.'

I peer across. A young Bancroft woman. She jerks her head to the left and I catch a glint of metal. I nod. 'Good.' I look at the man next to her. 'You need to get the clip out. You're close enough that if you turn your head, you can use your teeth.'

He glances from me to the Bancroft vamp and back again

then bares his fangs. 'A bloodguzzler's best weapon,' he says with a half grin. There's a flicker of optimism in his eyes. That's what I need.

We all hold our breath as he angles his face so his head is pressed towards Miss Bancroft. It looks as if he's whispering sweet nothings in her ear. She bites her lip in concentration, trying desperately not to move. The bus jerks as it swerves round a corner and she lets out a small moan as his fangs scrape her skull. To give him his due, he doesn't stop trying. A minute later, when he pulls back with dancing eyes and a pin sticking out of his mouth, there are ragged cheers.

I nod again. 'Good. Now you need to pass it along the line. Mouth to mouth like the old kids' party game.' I look hard at them. 'I need you all on board. We have to stay calm if we're going to get out of this.' Several bob their heads in agreement; a few just look scared. I take a deep breath. 'We can do this. We just need to work together.'

The Medici guy draws in a breath as if he's getting ready to argue again. I turn and stare at him and he narrows his eyes but keeps quiet. I've achieved something at least. Even the woman has stopped her shrieking.

'Take it slow,' I urge. 'We can't afford to let the pin drop.'

The first man turns to his right and the woman next to him twists her head. Delicately using her teeth, she takes the pin from him before glancing towards me for approval. I smile at her. She shifts round and passes it to the next vampire. One by one, the little pin moves down the line until it's held between the lips of the Gully vampire opposite me. I pretend not to notice that his hands are shaking.

There's a metre wide gulf between us. I test the chains but I can lean forward only inches; it will never be close enough. The Gully vampire watches me with wide, frightened eyes.

'You must have played spitting contests when you were a kid,' I say softly. 'See who could spit the furthest?'

He looks at me as if I'm crazy. I shrug. 'Perhaps that was just me. It doesn't matter.' I draw back my shoulders and paste on my most confident expression. 'You're going to have to spit the pin in my direction. If you can get it to land on my knees we're on easy street. And if you miss, don't worry about it. I'm sure there are other pins we can use.'

The Bancroft woman clears her throat. 'Actually, I think that's the only one left. The others fell out when I was grabbed.'

I glance at her; her hair does look rather mussed. I make myself relax further. 'No problem because our little Gully friend here has got good aim.'

The panic in his eyes grows. He tries to speak but with the pin in his mouth the words are completely obscured.

'It's probably better if you stay quiet,' I advise. 'And don't over-think it. If the pin falls onto the floor then we can still get it. It'll just be quicker if you can get it to land on me. Okay?'

He nods. The Stuart vampires on either side of me straighten up. They're ready in case the pin veers off course. It's not that difficult, he just needs to make sure the pin has enough propulsion. A child could manage it; I sure as hell hope that he can too.

'I'll stretch out my legs.' I give him a reassuring smile. 'Then you'll have even more chance of getting it to hit me. On a count of three.' I can feel everyone's eyes on me. 'One. Two.' I hold his gaze. 'Three.'

Gully doesn't move. He's blinking rapidly and looking more panicked than ever.

'Good idea,' I tell him briskly. 'It's important to have a practice run. Let's do it for real this time.'

'Mm.'

I smile once more and glance at Beth. 'Do you know his name?'

'Uh ... Chester. It's Chester.'

That's pretty old-fashioned; he must be one of the older vampires. He should have more self-confidence. I try not to let my thoughts betray me. 'Alrighty, Chester. Let's try again. Count of three. Got it?'

'Mm.'

'One. Two.' I take a deep breath. 'Th...' There's a screech as the bus driver slams on the brakes. We must have been going at some speed because the jolt is incredible. A second later there's a godawful sound of crunching metal as something rams into the side. Whatever just hit us, it was bloody large and powerful. The bus begins to tip.

Chester yells. 'I swallowed it! I fucking swallowed it.' He chokes, trying to bring the pin back up even as we lurch and the bus lands on its side. I'm jolted forward violently. Only the chains holding me in place prevent me from falling. Everyone around me looks terrified.

'Well, that's it then,' the Medici guy says. 'See you all on the other side. Wherever that may be.'

I grit my teeth. No, something doesn't compute. We've barely been travelling for twenty minutes so we're still well within the city limits. Hale would have planned for our fiery deaths to take place out on a quiet country road. This isn't right, I know it's not.

Now that gravity is pulling me down, I can feel the place where the chain is attached starting to give. I jiggle around; it's not much but, if I can apply enough pressure, it might give way. There might still be a chance. I ignore the yells and screams from outside and twist harder. Nausea rises through my chest until I can taste the bile on my tongue. I have to do this. It doesn't matter how strong these damn handcuffs are, I have to get free.

There's an odd hiss. I turn my head and frown. A moment later, the hiss turns into an almighty crash as the back of the bus is ripped away, metal peeling off like a tin can to reveal broad daylight and a busy street with gaping pedestrians and stopped cars behind us.

'What the...'

A figure in a balaclava appears, then another and another. Jerkily, they step inside and pick their way across the fallen bodies that are now upside down. The first figure stops right in front of me, raises a long gloved arm and points at me. Blue sparks crackle and my mouth goes dry. It's a witch.

I squeeze my eyes shut, Michael's image floating into my mind. I'm not going to beg. Just make it quick.

Then I'm falling. I'd thought there would be more pain. I fall against something hard and warm and with the faint smell of aftershave. That's when I open my eyes and realise that the witch is holding me and I'm far from dead. Strength is surging back through my veins and firing every impulse. The cuffs have gone.

I push myself away and scramble towards Beth to free her. One of our other rescuers is already there. 'Get out, Ms Blackman. There's a car waiting. We will get the others. I take it you are all old enough to withstand sunlight?'

We nod. I keep my focus on the figure. I can't place the voice and it doesn't matter who it belongs to anyway – I'm not leaving anyone behind. One by one, bolts of magic free each vampire. One or two cry. The Medici guy looks stunned.

I can't do much about the handcuffs but I can help them leave the half-destroyed bus. I grab one after another, easing them outside into the free world. Hands reach out and direct the stumbling vampires into cars with engines that are already running.

This is no time be relieved. 'Who are you? Why are you doing this?' They have to be white witches; black witches would have already taken advantage of my helplessness.

The nearest one grabs me. 'We'll explain later. Right now we have to get away from here. There's no time.'

Sirens are already shrieking towards us. Ambulances and police cars are one thing but as soon as Hale hears of this 'accident' he'll send out his contingent. I could make a run for it and leave the scene; that would make most sense. I see Beth's white face ducking inside the nearest car. Bugger it. I stare at the shadowy figure next to me. 'Fine. Let's go.'

I stumble out unassisted, noting the terrified human faces gaping at the scene of utter destruction visited upon our city once more. The bus is a wreck, fire licking round the engine, smashed glass and twisted metal everywhere. I lurch towards the car Beth disappeared into. She clutches at my hand as I squeeze into the back with several others.

The door shuts and I glance out of the window. There, on the pavement, with her mouth pressed into a tight, thin line, is the female Kakos daemon from Bruckheimer and Berryhill. While I stop breathing, she takes out a phone, mutters something into it then turns away. As the first ambulance finally arrives, we drive away.

CHAPTER 14
GO BE A HERO

I pay close attention to where we're going; I'm not letting them take us to another damned fortress. The other cars follow and, as we get further away, I realise where we're heading. Deep foreboding zips through me. When we eventually pull up outside the MI7 warehouse, my worst fears are confirmed.

I don't even wait for the car to stop, I immediately jump out and back away. 'Who the hell are you people?' I snarl as the first figure, still wearing a bloody balaclava, also leaves.

The reply is mild in tone but doesn't answer my question. 'We thought this was where you would want to come.' She flips back the balaclava and looks at me.

I stiffen, staring at the tattoo on her cheek. 'You're a black witch.'

'That's stating the obvious,' she says, not unpleasantly. 'But yes, I am.'

Others begin to get out of the cars, both vampires and witches. Everyone keeps back, understanding that for now this is between me and this witch. My eyes harden into cold ice. 'Explain to me what is going on.'

'We're not here to harm you. We want to help.' She gestures at the cars. 'As I think we've already demonstrated.'

'Actually, we had things under control.' I don't mention that I'm not sure if I could have performed the contortions required to free anyone, even if Chester had managed to spit the damn pin onto my lap.

The witch snorts. 'Really?'

I cross my arms. 'Really. And you're unlikely rescuers considering that a few nights ago your lot beat a vampire to death.'

I hear several intakes of breath from the watching vampires. The witch doesn't blink. 'I thought you might bring that up. They were not *our* lot, they were hybrids.' Her lip curls. 'An entirely different breed.'

I watch her eyes. 'Is that why you're doing this? You want to get one up on witches who are more powerful than you because they've embraced both sides of magic?'

She shrugs. 'I suppose you could say that's part of it but it's not the real reason.'

I stand my ground. 'Then what is?'

'Stop thinking with your heart, Ms Blackman, and start using your head.' I bristle but the witch continues. 'How stupid do you think we are? Sure, we didn't like the Families. They were far too uppity and close-mouthed, only interested in themselves. But taking the criminal element off the streets and turning them was always going to end in grief. It might have taken longer than we anticipated but we knew it was going to happen.'

'You're still not answering my question.'

She tosses back her hair. 'Once the bloodguzzlers are gone, who do you think will be the next target? You don't really expect that society will just move on and that will be that?'

I think of Hale's derision for all tribers. She has a point but it still doesn't explain why she's helping us. 'There are a lot more of you than there are of us.'

'There are,' she agrees. 'But that doesn't mean we're not vulnerable.' A shadow crosses her face. 'Especially when Kakos daemons are involved.'

My body tenses even more. She laughs, without amusement. 'Yes, we know the part they played in all this. We can feel it when they tamper.'

Anger ripples down my spine. 'And you didn't say anything? You didn't do anything? They're responsible for thousands of deaths. Those deaths are your responsibility now.'

'Do you think the Families would have listened to us if we'd gone to them? You thought you were invulnerable with your traditions and your rules. You'd have ignored us.'

I know Michael wouldn't have. 'That's a shitty excuse.'

She regards me calmly. 'Maybe. But maybe we were tired of the guzzlers thinking they could rule this city. The Families have been above the law for centuries. How can that be allowed? Maybe we thought it was time they were taken down a peg or two.' She pauses. 'I will admit that we did not expect the results to be quite so ... dramatic.'

'So you want us to what? Join forces? I'm a Blackman. You hate me even more than you hate the Families.'

She waves her hand dismissively. 'Old grudges don't concern me. Your grandfather worked against us once but that was a long time ago.'

'I don't believe you.'

'How about I show you can trust me?'

She jerks her head and one of the other witches opens a car door. There's a loud bark and Kimchi bounds out towards me. My heart surges in delight. He barrels forward, almost bowling me over. I hug him tightly then look up at her. 'Thank you.' I consider lying but decide against it. 'It means a lot to me that you rescued him.'

She smiles. 'He's a dog. What else was I going to do?'

'It still doesn't mean I can trust you,' I tell her. I look at the other witches who are watching our exchange. 'Any of you.' I lick my lips and pat Kimchi's head. He subsides, settling beside me but still touching my leg as if he wants to make sure I'm not going to leave him again.

'Then,' she responds, 'we'll have to find another way.'

'Kakos daemons can read minds. They can't be beaten when they know every move you're going to make in advance.'

'You're right. We should all lie down and let them do whatever they want.' She glances round. 'Saddle up, boys. We're leaving. London belongs to the daemons.'

'That's not what I meant.'

'We want you on our side, Ms Blackman. We're already talking to the white witches. The daemons and Vince Hale might have forced our hand but we are adapting. Things are changing.' Her voice is clear and resolute.

'And the hybrids?' I ask. 'What about them?'

She lifts her hand once more. Another figure emerges from which Kimchi was in. This one, however, is dragged out and is wearing a hood rather than a balaclava. Kimchi whines. I stroke his ears to calm him and wait to see what fresh new hell the witch is showing me.

He is brought over and forced onto his knees in front of her. Unease flares in the pit of my stomach; I don't need to witness any more executions. Hybrid or not, there's been enough death – and far too much at my hands.

I recognise him as soon as his hood is whipped off. He was there in Covent Garden and he was involved in the killing of the Medici vampire. His twin black-and-white tattoos pulse in anger and he glares at all of us.

'Watch this,' the black witch tells me, then raises her hand towards him.

I stiffen, unsure whether I should get involved or not. There's a crackle of magic and he starts to scream. It's not like any sound I've heard before; it's imbued with so much pain and fear that even my bones tremble. I start forward but the witch shakes her head and points at his cheek. I follow her finger and gasp. The black tattoo is leeching away, fading from his skin.

'Neat, huh?'

I stare at her. 'You can do that? You can take away their magic?'

She smiles proudly. 'It's something we've been working on. A necessary evil.'

I swallow. It's not only the tattoo that's disappearing; every bit of colour is vanishing from the hybrid. Even his hair is turning white. As I watch, wrinkles begin to form. It's as if he's aging right in front of our eyes. His agony is visible. 'You're vicious,' I breathe.

'We all need to be vicious sometimes, Ms Blackman. Survival demands it.' She smiles again, although this time it's tinged with sadness. 'You know that.'

Every part of me is desperate to run away. I can never trust a black witch, not after everything that's happened. Nobody else says anything. All the vampires are watching me as if they're waiting for my decision.

The Medici guy takes a breath but the Stuart guzzler next to him places a hand on his arm and shakes his head in warning. Even the loudspeaker system from behind us is silent; my grandfather is also leaving this up to me. I push my hair out of my eyes and sigh. I want to talk to Michael, I want him to tell me what to do. This can't be my responsibility.

'I will think this over,' I say aloud. It's hardly a decisive move but it's the best I can offer right now. I see something flicker across Beth's face. 'I might want to talk to you some more in the meantime.' I point at the witch. 'You will come in with me and stay here until I've considered everything further.'

'If you want a hostage,' she says intelligently, 'you should know that my people wouldn't hesitate to think of me as collateral damage.'

Out of the corner of my eye, I see several other witches stiffen. I curve my lips into a smile. 'Oh, somehow I think you're more important than you're letting on.' I raise my head and address the others. 'She comes. The rest of you leave. She'll call you every hour so you know she's alright.'

They don't look happy but, at her nod, they're prepared to agree for now. I bloody well hope I'm doing the right thing. I glance at her. 'What's your name?'

'Hope.'

I start. 'Bullshit.'

She frowns. 'I can assure you I'm not lying.'

I shake my head. 'Okay, if you say so.'

The other witches climb back into the waiting cars and drive off. Beth sidles towards me. 'Well, this is weird,' she whispers.

'You're telling me.'

'Kakos daemons?'

'You have a lot to catch up on,' I say.

'Such as why you're living in a shed,' she replies.

I grin. 'There's more to it than meets the eye.' I nod towards the rest of the vampires. 'Come on. We need to get inside and find some blood for you lot.'

Without being asked, two of them move up and flank Hope. She sighs dramatically but I just smile. 'Things are changing indeed,' I murmur.

∼

My grandfather is waiting for us in the corridor as we enter. I expect him to tell me that I'm being stupid and I need to get rid of all these people at once but he simply gives me a benign smile. 'You've been gone for some time, Bo,' he chides as I pass.

'I ran into a spot of bother. Of the human variety.'

His eyes narrow but he doesn't comment. I lead my troop of bloodguzzlers and one witch into the main hall area, pleased to note as I enter that Rogu3 has dimmed the computer.

'What the hell is this place?' Beth breathes.

'You know my grandfather,' I tell her. 'Take a guess.'

She stares round. 'Oh.'

The Medici vamp pushes his way forward. 'Is it safe?'

It's on the tip of my tongue to tell him he can leave right now if he doesn't like it. Then I realise from the expression on his face that he's asking out of fear. 'As safe as anywhere,' I tell him.

Several of the others exchange glances. One receives a nudge and, swallowing hard, steps forward. 'How long are we going to stay here for?'

I blink. Er...

'What should we do? Most of the other survivors have left the country. Should we join them?'

Beth clears her throat. 'Bo is still here.'

'So we should stay? We should fight?'

Twenty pairs of eyes swing towards me. I lick my lips. 'I don't know.'

'What would you like me to do?' Hope enquires. 'While you decide what to do with the witches?'

I stare at her. 'There's a television somewhere,' I say weakly.

'We should watch television?' a Stuart vamp asks.

Someone else nods. 'That's a good idea. We can scan the news then we'll have a better idea of what's going on. That's what you want, right? Ms Blackman?'

My mouth is dry. I know what *I'd* been planning to do but I'm not prepared to make plans for all these strangers at the same time. Their weight of expectation is palpable. Sodding hell.

The pale woman who was in Hale's clutches the longest sways on her feet. The Gully vampire next to her only just catches her before her legs give way. His worried gaze flicks to mine. I stalk to the fridge. The first three shelves are stocked with blood bags. Taken aback, I blink.

'I had a feeling we might be needing some more,' my grandfather murmurs. 'After what happened to the Medici bloodguzzler the other night, I took the liberty of restocking. It's as fresh as I could make it and there will be a new supply delivered tomorrow. Obviously it's not as good as straight from the vein but it should serve your purposes for now.'

I turn my head and look at him. 'Thank you.'

'You're welcome, my dear.'

'Can you take care of them for now?'

'Of course.' Relief washes over me. Thank goodness. 'Go and see Michael.' My grandfather raises an eyebrow. 'I'm not responsible for telling them what to do with themselves though. This lot are your problem.'

Shit. 'Sure,' I trill. 'I know that.'

I pretend not to notice his worried look and walk out. Hope watches my departure with clever eyes. I ignore her. As much as she might like to think she's my first priority, she doesn't have a clue.

Maria is sitting by Michael's bed and the pair of them are laughing uproariously. I stand in the doorway watching them. It's about as unlikely a pairing as you're likely to get. There's a large pile of rubbish by the bedside – Michael has obviously been partaking in my junk-food fiesta – and he looks like he might actually be getting better.

He lifts his head, as if sensing my gaze. The second his eyes land on me, they crinkle at the edges with laughter lines that were never there when he was a vampire. Having him look at me makes me feel that everything's going to be alright.

'Bo,' Maria exclaims. 'You no look good.'

I glance down at myself. She has a point: I'm covered in oil, dirt and a fair amount of blood, a lot of which is mine. 'Hale made his move,' I say.

Both of them stiffen. Alarmingly, Michael leaps out of bed towards me. 'Are you alright?' he demands. 'Did he hurt you?'

'Lie down! What are you doing? You're ill!'

'I'm fine. I think the strawberry-flavoured Pop Tarts did the trick.'

Maria shakes her head. 'No. It definitely curry Pot Noodle.'

I can't prevent the grin spreading across my face. 'You do look better,' I admit. Relief threatens to overwhelm me; not only does he look like he's going to be alright, Maria is looking more relaxed.

Michael cups my face and stares into my eyes. My knees weaken. 'What did that wanker do to you, Bo? I'll rip his head off if he did anything.'

'You kill him, yes?' Maria says. 'Drink his blood until nothing left.' She nods in satisfaction.

'No,' I demur. 'He's still out there. I'm going to have to do something to sort him for good, though. I don't think he'll stop trying to get rid of all of us.'

Michael's thumb brushes a streak of dirt away from my cheek. 'You're afraid that if you kill him, you'll let the darkness back in.'

'The darkness is still there. It's ... locked away for now.'

Maria stills. 'It never go away. You just manage.'

I give her a shaky smile. For a teenager, she's pretty bloody canny.

There's a loud cheer from the other room. Michael raises his eyebrows. 'Are we having a party?'

'Not exactly.' I point at the bed. He looks irritated but does as he's told. Maria turns as if to go and leave us in peace but I gently touch her arm. 'Stay. You need to hear this too.'

I outline everything that's happened, from what I've learnt about Alice to Vince Hale. When I'm done, Maria bites her lip and frowns. 'I never see these green men.'

'You wouldn't have. My theory is that they dress as aliens to hide who they really are and what they're really doing. With you, there was no need to do that.'

'Because my mother sell me. She no hide.'

I close my eyes, wishing I could make that better for her. It's the ultimate betrayal and there's nothing any of us can do about it. 'Yes,' I say quietly.

'I still don't understand,' Michael says. 'Why aliens?'

'We live in a world with vampires and witches and daemons and ghosts,' I say. 'People will believe almost anything but cast around a rumour that you've seen an alien and you'll be locked away. Everyone will think you're crazy.' I'm convinced that's what happened to Alice's neighbour. The poor guy probably had his house stripped from him by the state to pay for his 'retirement' in an asylum. It won't be difficult to confirm; I'll ask Rogu3 to look him up. 'They dress as aliens so if anyone sees them when they're snatching a kid, the witnesses are automatically disbelieved.'

Michael absorbs this theory, eventually nodding that it makes a warped kind of sense. 'It still doesn't explain why they're taking children in the first place.' He glances at Maria. 'Is it, um...' He can't even say it but I know what he's getting at. I guess his humanity really is coming back in force; he would never have deliberately hurt her before, but there's a different, more considerate, level to him now. And he's worried.

'Sexual abuse,' I say it for him. 'And no, it can't be. Maria's Romany blood wouldn't have stopped them if that were the case.' Plus, she ended up in a damn brothel anyway. My skin twitches in barely concealed rage. Maria pulls her shoulders back as if she's not going to be cowed. Good girl. 'If these children's minds are really being wiped then it's something else.'

Maria mutters something and stands up again. 'I go for walk,' she declares.

I watch her leave. Maybe I shouldn't have asked her to stay but she deserves to be in the loop. After all, we got this far because of her.

Michael's hand covers mine. 'You're doing the right thing,' he tells me, his voice low.

'Are you also reading my mind now?'

'I know you,' he says. His jaw tightens. 'I wish I could do something to help.'

'You can help by getting better.' I brush his hair away from his forehead. 'That's what I need from you. Okay,' I amend, 'that and some advice.'

He waits. I take a deep breath and look up at the ceiling. 'We have these other vampires now. It feels like,' I pause, struggling to find the words, 'like they want me to tell them what to do. Hale was waiting for me before he did anything to the vampires. Hope, the black witch out there, wanted to talk to me.' I ball up my fists. 'I'm no one. In bloodguzzler terms, I'm a baby. I don't need this kind of responsibility and I don't deserve it.' I take a breath. 'I'm not good enough for it. The world is falling apart and everyone seems to think that I have the answers. I don't have anything.'

Michael laughs softly. 'Think about what you've done, Bo. You discovered that Nicky was trying to bring us all down with her crazy plots. You walked away from the Families and helped set up a company where different vampires could work together. You stopped a serial killer. You found a missing billionaire. You beat up a Kakos daemon live on television. You almost stopped Tov V'ra.'

I meet his eyes. 'But the Families were brought down regardless of what I did to stop Nicky. New Order is in ruins. The serial killer captured and almost killed me. Everyone thinks the billionaire is still missing. The Kakos daemon thing on TV was a stunt. They manipulated everything I did. And,' I say sadly, 'Tov V'ra still won.'

'We're not dead yet.'

I point wildly at the door. 'There are twenty vampires out there waiting for me to tell them what to do! I don't have a sodding clue! I'm making all this shit up as I go along, Michael. I've got missing kids to find and a politician to destroy and a host of invincible Kakos daemons to beat and I can't do any of it. Tell me what to do. Tell me how to sort all this out and I'll do whatever you say,' I plead. 'This isn't me. I don't want this.'

He grabs hold of my flailing hands. 'You've got this, Bo Blackman. I know it's scary but I believe in you. You can do it.'

'Michael, I need you to...'

He shakes his head. 'No. You're the vampire. I'm just a lowly human.'

My eyes widen in alarm. 'Don't say that!'

'It's okay. I'm not exactly at peace with that fact but I'm getting there.' He lifts a trembling hand. 'And, as helpful as all that food was, I'm still not strong enough to leave this place. You have to do this, Bo. I have faith in you and so does everyone out there.'

'But...'

'Get a grip,' he says sternly. 'Go be a hero.'

My mouth is dry. I want to argue further but I can see exhaustion creeping back into his face. His expectations of me are too high but he's the love of my life. I have to do what I can.

CHAPTER 15

CIRCLING ROUND THE BOOGEYMAN

Rather than confront the waiting vampires immediately, I go into the nearest unoccupied room and take out my phone. I need to give them something and D'Argneau has had more than enough time. He should have been in touch by now.

He answers on the second ring. 'Thought you'd have called before now,' he says.

'Ditto,' I snap.

He doesn't appear to notice my tone. 'I don't have everything you're looking for. Not yet.'

'But you have some information.'

'Yeah. You're not going to like it.'

Big surprise there. I sigh. 'Hit me.'

'Well, I looked into the legal status of the vampires. It took a long time and I didn't trust anyone else, so I had to do it all myself. Do you have any idea how difficult it is to decipher legal documents that are centuries old?'

'My heart bleeds. What did you discover, D'Argneau?'

'It's not vampires that are above the law, it's the Families. Everything I've found states that categorically. The Families were trusted to keep their bloodguzzlers in line and, without the Families...'

'We revert back to the same rules as the rest of the country.'

'Got it in one. Frankly, I'm surprised no one else has twigged this yet. After all, you left the Families so you should have been subject to those laws too. It's probably because no other lawyers are as good as I am.' He says this without a hint of his typical D'Argneau smugness. 'I traced everything back to a single piece of legislation from 1623. Do you want to hear it?'

'That's alright. I trust you.'

'Really?' He sounds surprised.

'Mm,' I murmur. 'So let me make sure I understand what you're saying. Now that the Families don't exist, vampires are exactly the same as every human, daemon or witch citizen.'

'Yeah. I'm sorry, I know it's not what you wanted to hear.'

'And,' I say, ignoring his pointless apology, 'if a British citizen was rounded up and incarcerated by its own govern-ment without trial, under the pretence that it was for their own safety, that would be illegal?'

'Yes,' he says slowly, finally beginning to understand. 'If they didn't agree to the incarceration, then it's an abuse of both human and triber rights.' He pauses. 'I suppose you'd like me to petition the courts to revoke the government's recent ruling about that?'

'I would indeed.' I doubt that the law will stop Hale in his tracks – after all, it hasn't so far – but it's a step in the right direction. 'I need you to make as loud a noise as possible. Hope-fully the media will pick it up and run with it. If everyone realises that vampires are subject to the same laws as everyone else, it might make them less antagonistic.'

'This is the time to do it,' D'Argneau agrees. 'A lot of the population is sympathetic towards you but that won't last for long. And it's not going to stop people being scared of what you're capable of.'

'Just go ahead and do it. I'll worry about the rest.' I lick my lips. 'What about Kakos daemons? What legal proceedings have you unearthed in relation to them?'

'The last case was about fifteen years ago. A London-based man sued them for killing his wife.'

I feel a rush of optimism. 'Really? I don't remember hearing anything about that.'

'Three days after the first papers were filed, he withdrew the complaint. I thought there must have been some out-of-court settlement because he had a good case. All the evidence was stacked in his favour. I called up his barrister, however, and he told me that there was nothing. Not a penny. The barrister is still disgruntled about it. No win, no fee, you understand. He thought the case was going to make him – it seemed like a slam dunk – but no matter what he did, he couldn't persuade his client to go through with it. All the barrister gets to deal with now are petty speeding fines, that kind of thing.' D'Argneau's voice turns mournful. 'He could have had a glittering career and it was all lost. I'm going to end up like that.'

'They got to him,' I say, thinking aloud. 'The damn Kakos daemons got to the client.'

'Eh? You mean they threatened him?'

I laugh harshly. 'No. They're much smarter than that.' I twirl a curl round my finger so tightly that I cut off the circulation to my fingertip. Bastard freaks. The Kakos daemons have been getting everything they wanted for generations and no one ever realised. That's the cruel beauty of mind control. I shake my head in disgust. 'Tell me about Streets of Fire,' I say through gritted teeth. 'What have you found out about them?'

D'Argneau sounds regretful. 'Nothing. All I know is what is

publicly available. The CEO is a human called Gregory Smith. Everything seems kosher.'

'It's not.'

'There's nothing to find, Bo.'

'Look harder. That sodding company is run by the Kakos daemons.' In fact, with Streets of Fire they don't even need telepathic control. They can control the internet and make people believe what they damn well choose by controlling what information they broadcast. It beggars belief that no one has noticed how powerful they are until now. It's terrifying.

'I've done what I can, Bo. There's nothing else there.'

'Please, Harry.'

He sighs. 'Fine but...'

I hang up. It's not polite and my grandfather would slap me down for doing such a thing but my whole body is shaking. Everyone knows that Kakos daemons are to be feared but they're seen so rarely that they've taken on the guise of the boogeyman. The trouble is that the boogeyman is alive and much, much more powerful than anyone gives him credit for.

'THIS IS THE DEAL,' I say to the small assembly of pale-faced vampires. 'The Families are no more. Stuart, Bancroft, Montserrat, Medici and Gully are dead and buried. Forget which allegiance you used to cling to. It no longer exists.'

You could hear a pin drop in the room. A few of them swallow nervously. My grandfather leans against the wall with his arms folded and an inscrutable expression on his face.

'Our legal status has also been revoked. No one is above the law, not any more. Kill someone, drink from them against their will, steal a damned Mars bar, and expect to end up in prison.

The world has turned upside down and we need to adapt or leave.'

A tentative hand is raised. 'Excuse me?'

I glance over, unsurprised to see that my first dissenter is the Medici guzzler. At least his previous aggressive bluster is muted. 'Yes?'

'We have representatives here from every Family. We can start afresh. There can be a new Lord or Lady for each Family. We can rise up more powerfully than before. We can crush anyone who gets in our way. We can do this.'

There are a few nods at his words. I shrug. I'd been expecting this so it's probably as well to get it out of the way sooner rather than later. 'What's the definition of insanity?' I ask softly.

A half smile curls round Beth's mouth. 'Doing the same thing over and over and expecting different results.'

We share a look of agreement. 'Exactly. Sure we could bring the Families back to life and we might even be successful. The people who did this to us, the Kakos daemons, might leave us in peace.' I wrinkle my nose. 'Somehow I doubt it but it's possible. We could regain our former glory. But then what? Sooner or later the same thing will happen again. The Families failed because they held themselves apart from society. They let tradition dictate how they acted. We need to do things differently if we want to survive. Assimilate into society, be part of this country rather than above it.'

'That's ridiculous!' a Gully woman bursts out. 'The Families gave us security. They gave us a way of life. We can't just throw it all away!'

'If you don't like it, feel free to leave. There are plenty of European Families who will take you in. The Americans are looking to boost their numbers.' I lean forward. 'You don't need to live with a Lord or Lady dictating your every move. You can live by your own standards. Adhere to the law but be an indi-vidual.' I meet my grandfather's eyes. 'Live by your own morality.'

'No.' The Medici vampire shakes his head. 'We can keep Britain great. The Families keep us great.'

'Bullshit.' The voice behind me is quiet but unmistakable. Even if I hadn't known it was Michael, I could have guessed from the look of shock on everyone's face. 'Bo is right. The tradition and rules imposed by the Families were holding the vampires back. Now you're all free. Look to tomorrow, not yesterday.'

Everyone still just gapes.

'Lord Montserrat! You're alive. You're ...' There's a long pause.

'Human,' he says drily. Maria is helping him stay upright but he looks stronger than before. 'Why yes, I am.'

The vampires exchange frightened, confused looks. 'I don't understand,' one says. 'How could this happen?'

'The Kakos daemons,' I say softly. 'They're responsible for all of this.'

'We need to destroy them! We'll kill them! How dare they do this?'

'We'll drain them of every drop of blood they have,' another promises.

I lift up my chin. 'We can't. Even if we knew where they all were, they're more powerful than we are.' I press my lips together. 'For now, anyway.' I'm still going to blow X apart the second I get the chance. 'Look, choose to stay or choose to go. It's up to you. But things will not be the same as they were before. They can't be. We're still vulnerable, we can still be killed. But I'm working on that. I think there's a way out that will make others accept us. It's not going to be easy but I think it's viable.'

'And what about me?' Hope asks, her clear voice ringing over us. 'What about the witches?'

I meet her eyes. I still don't have the foggiest idea what to do with her olive branch. On the one hand, we could really do with their support because right now, the witches are far stronger and more capable than we are. But that doesn't mean that they're not waiting for the chance to take us all out for good. They might have rescued us from Hale but I still can't fathom out their real motives. I search my heart for the right answer.

'What do you really want?' I ask. 'You're not doing all this just because you need a buffer between yourselves and the Kakos daemons.'

Hope exhales in exasperation. 'We're not evil, Bo. Not any more than you are. There are bad apples, sure, but you've experienced that on your own hearth. We're doing this because it's the right thing to do, not because we have an ulterior motive.' She purses her lips. 'Not that an alliance won't help us in the future. Say the word and the black witches will come out in favour of the vampires. It will help your cause. You know it will.'

I look at Michael. He cocks his head slightly. What would you do, I ask him silently. He smiles in response, letting me know that he's keeping out of it. Judging by the way everyone is looking at me, they're going to let him; now that he's no longer a vampire, they've already dismissed him. My heart aches. We have to stop thinking of ourselves as separate from the rest of the world. It's already almost been our undoing.

I stride forward to Hope and hold out my hand. She takes it and shakes. A frisson of electricity travels up my arm and I just manage to avoid wincing. 'It's either face the wolves or jump off the cliff,' I say.

'Which have you chosen?'

I pull back my shoulders and take a deep breath. 'Both.'

Beth steps forward. 'I've never been that bothered by the witches,' she says. 'But I know the Blackmans have had issues with them.'

My grandfather raises an eyebrow. 'Elizabeth,' he chides, 'it is the witches who have had issues with us.' He moves over to Hope. 'I am glad we can finally bury the hatchet.'

Beth clears her throat as the two shake hands. '*As* I was saying, if they can work together then I can work with them too. I'm staying. London is my home.'

The ex-Medici vampire moves up beside her. 'What the hell. I'm not running away with my tail between my legs. I'm not afraid of any Kakos daemon.'

He should be. Regardless, I smile at him. One by one, the others step closer. 'We're with you, Bo. However this goes down, we're with you.'

'I'm not your leader,' I tell them all. 'You need to be masters of your own fate.'

Chester smiles. 'I like the sound of that. I'm still with you, though.'

I tug at my hair. 'Pretty speeches and hand shaking are all well and good but they don't change the fact that we're still in danger.' I take a deep breath. 'If you're up to it, I'd like us to go to Westminster.'

Beth pumps the air. 'Let's confront Hale and sort him out once and for all.'

'No,' I say, 'not yet. First we need to find a girl.'

CHAPTER 16

SEARCH

Although, like Beth, most people think of the Houses of Parliament when they think of Westminster, there's more to it than that. It might not be a particularly large borough, and the majority of the buildings might be historical listed structures, but there is still quite a large residential population. It was here that Alice's mother thought she saw her daughter. There might not have been any alien sightings – I had Rogu3 check through various databases for me – but if Alice still exists this seems the most likely place to start looking for her.

Each vampire has an updated photo of what Alice might look like, complete with short dark hair and five years added on. It's not perfect – photofits rarely are – but it's a good starting point. We fan out across the borough and start asking questions.

It's a dangerous operation, not because of Alice but because of our proximity to Hale's base and all the others out there who are eager to take advantage of our weakened situation. We stay in pairs and I make sure everyone is aware that they need to stay alert at all times. It helps that Hope also musters her troops. Before long, there are more than a hundred of us, all searching for one altered little girl. Unfortunately, even though the streets are starting returning to a semblance of normality, most of the queries follow a pattern:

'Good afternoon.'

Cue stammer and wide eyes. 'You're a vampire.'

'Yes. Can you look at this photo for me? I'm looking for this girl.'

'I thought all the vampires were dead.'

'Please just look at the photo.'

Generally this is followed by a brisk denial that they've seen her and more questions about what's happened to the Families. Without her blonde curls, no one recognises the photo as Alice Goldman. I guess people often don't see what's right in front of their faces. It makes my theory that she might have been hiding in plain sight all the more believable. I make sure that everyone keeps their questions – and their identities – as low key as possible. We don't want to alert the bad guys, whoever they are, to our actions. Every reaction from every passer-by is carefully scrutinised. And so far, no one is having any luck.

O'Shea catches up with me down a leafy street near Westminster Abbey. 'There are no aliens in London,' he informs me stiffly. 'Not of the green-skinned kind anyway.' He appears annoyed at having spent the day searching fruitlessly for creatures that don't exist. It's on the tip of my tongue to tell him that it's better than being held prisoner by a raving loony MP who wants you to burn to death, and better than being rescued from that madman by your mortal enemy, but it doesn't seem worth it.

I shrug. 'Fair enough.'

'Fair enough?' he screeches. 'Do you realise that I've just made every person I've met think that I've lost my marbles? I have a reputation to maintain.'

I pat him on the shoulder. 'It was a lead that had to be followed.'

He grumbles loudly. 'I spoke to all of Benjy's friends. None of them had any clue where he'd gone. They're convinced he wouldn't have just upped and left though. I went back to his posh apartment to try and talk to him again and he's gone. According to his neighbour, an hour after I spoke to him he packed a bag and left.'

I grimace. Another dead end. I'm starting to think we're chasing ghosts.

Hope appears from round the corner from where she's been questioning a bemused couple from Sweden. 'Nope,' she says. 'They've not seen her either.'

O'Shea leaps in front of me, shielding my body from hers. 'Witch,' he hisses.

Hope smiles. 'You must be Devlin.'

O'Shea makes a hex sign and backs up, colliding with me. 'Get thee away from me!'

'You know that doesn't actually work, right?'

'Bo,' he says plaintively, 'what is going on?'

'We have a new ally,' I tell him.

'A black witch?' His voice is rising to a high-pitched shriek. 'Are you nuts? They all want to kill you!'

'Apparently not.'

Hope holds up her palms. 'Listen to your friend,' she says. 'I'm on your side. I'm one of the good guys.'

'Bo, your judgment of people is seriously flawed.'

I grin. 'You got that right.'

O'Shea's brow furrows. 'Hey! I didn't mean me!'

'It's all good,' I soothe.

A grey-haired man hurrying past throws us a look and gives us a wide berth. I dash after him. 'Excuse me, sir!' I say, waving Alice's doctored photo in his face. 'Have you seen this girl?'

He barely looks at it. 'No.' He picks up speed and scurries off.

O'Shea stares at me. 'This is your big plan? Find Alice Goldman by asking people on the street?'

'If you have a better idea...'

'The words needle and haystack come to mind,' he mutters. 'If you're hoping to bump into her, you're crazy. It's a Wednesday and the last time I checked, most kids don't hang around in the open on the streets of London in the middle of a weekday.'

O'Shea's words hit me with the force of a freight train. I keep thinking that Alice was abducted and concealed some-where but, from what her mother told me, that might not be the case. If Alice's mind has been wiped and she's wandering around the streets with an altered appearance, or if she's been brainwashed by Stockholm Syndrome or magic or whatever, she must appear to be undergoing the numbing process of formal education; otherwise the local council would step in. Unless you're going to keep a child locked in a basement – or in a room like Maria's prison dormitory – you have to send them to school. I straighten up. Hiding in plain sight indeed. 'You're right.'

'You bet I am.'

Hope meets my eyes. 'School,' she breathes. A smile spreads across her face. 'We need to hit the schools.'

It doesn't take long to send a message to tell everyone to switch tactics. If Alice is still alive, she's old enough to attend secondary school – and there are only eleven of those in the borough. With witches and vampires heading off in all direc-tions, Hope, a distinctly wary O'Shea and I make a beeline for the local council buildings. Not every child physically goes to school.

Ignoring the cluster of smokers hanging around the front, we march grimly inside. I take off my baseball cap and run my hands through my hair. I get the feeling that my weak disguise won't do much for me here, not if I want to get any real information.

'Which floor for education?' I ask the young woman behind the desk. She doesn't look up from her nail file. Doesn't she realise what a cliché she is?

'S'lunch time,' she mumbles. 'Come back in an hour.'

'No,' I say pleasantly, 'I don't think I will.'

She huffs and looks up. When she sees me, flanked by Hope and O'Shea, her mouth drops open. 'Bo Blackman.'

I smile. 'Hi.'

She swallows and leans forward. 'I heard what you did to that receptionist in Canary Wharf,' she whispers. She pulls away the scarf around her neck. 'Do it to me.'

I stare at her stupidly. 'You want me to drain you of your blood and leave you unconscious for an hour or two?' I feel guilty about what I did to poor David; I don't need to add to my guilt by doing it again.

She doesn't seem to hear me. 'I always wanted to be a vampette.'

I bank down the temptation. No, I feel like we might be getting somewhere with Alice. This isn't the time to stop for a bite – even if everyone else is having lunch. 'Maybe later,' I hedge. 'Where can I find the education department?' They used to occupy their own building but cutbacks have forced them to join the rest of the council workers. I know they're here somewhere.

'Fifth floor,' she says in a cloud of disappointment.

I force a smile. 'Thanks.'

'I never understood why so many people were willing to do that,' Hope comments, as we start up the first flight of stairs. Naturally, the lift is out of order. 'Let vampires drink from them, I mean.'

'I'm equally baffled,' I admit. I shoot a look at O'Shea.

He sighs. 'Connor said it was like sex. Orgasmic was the word he used.' He shrugs. 'Something to do with the chemicals in a bloodguzzler's saliva.'

Huh. No wonder Connor prevaricated whenever I broached the subject. I'd not heard that before. Then I frown. 'Hang on a minute. Is that why you offered to let me drink from you?' I recoil slightly. 'Ick.'

O'Shea arches an eyebrow and pouts. I think he's trying to assume the air of a sex kitten but it doesn't work. 'A woman's never done it for me but if one could, it would be you, Bo.'

My frown deepens. 'Are you saying I'm manly?' I look down at my clothes. Nondescript jeans, leather jacket and black T-shirt. It's not the most feminine look but I've been known to wear dresses. I'd wear them more often if they were practical.

'Well, I find you pretty sexy,' Hope interjects. I can't tell whether she's serious or not and I start feeling flustered.

'She's spoken for,' O'Shea says shortly, glaring at her.

Hope's mouth twitches. 'You mean by the newly resurrected Lord Montserrat.'

'He didn't die,' I say, as we keep climbing.

'No,' she returns. 'He just changed from a vampire into a human. How exactly did that happen?'

'Kakos daemon.'

'So you said. The daemon saved him by turning him back?'

My eyes narrow and I almost spit out the words. 'No. The daemon was getting his revenge on me for not dancing to his tune. It was a trap and I walked straight into it.'

O'Shea reaches out and rubs my arm. Hope, however, looks thoughtful.

We round the last corner and head up the last few steps. A crooked sign at the top reads 'Local Education Authority: Westminster', except the letter 's' is missing from Westminster and someone has taken a Sharpie and changed the 'i' to a 'u'.

'Wet munter,' O'Shea reads. 'That's not very polite. Do you think they knew you were coming, Bo?' I punch him on the arm. He grins. 'Makes me glad to be an Agathos daemon. At least we don't have to go to schools run by this lot.' He peers into a nearby office. 'Those computers look like antiques.'

'Cutbacks,' I say. 'The government is more interested in spending money on running down the last few remaining vampires than on education.'

'I'm guessing not many people come up here.' O'Shea glances into a battered cardboard box filled with bits of paper. 'They'd be horrified if they did. This is supposed to be our tax money hard at work.'

I roll my eyes. 'And when was the last time you paid tax?'

He doesn't get the chance to answer. A ruffled-looking human, with a few crumbs from whatever sandwich he's been eating still attached to his mouth, walks out and adjusts his tie. 'Ms Blackman,' he beams. 'I'm Jonathan Tamworth. What can we do for you?'

I gaze at him suspiciously. Technically, this guy is a civil servant. Surely his first impulse should be to inform his superiors that I'm on the premises, then knock me out so he can drag me back off to Vince sodding Hale.

He notices my look and blusters in a bid to appease me. 'You've been a hero of mine ever since you stopped that school from becoming a bloodbath.' I nod in sudden understanding. He's referring to the incident where I stopped Rogu3 from being gunned down. 'We don't expect snipers to show up at school dances and try to take out our students. I think you'll find that many of us in education are sympathetic to your cause. What's happened to the Families is a terrible business.'

I think he's being genuinely sincere, despite his sycophantic tone. I test the water to see if I'm right. 'I'm here because another of your students is in danger, Mr Tamworth.'

'Oh my goodness.' He knits his fingers together anxiously. 'Who? We can let the police know and...'

'We need to keep her identity secret,' I tell him, making things up as I go along. 'For her own safety.'

'Of course, of course! What can I do to help?'

'I'm very worried that innocent children are going to get hurt.' Although I'm not lying, I still lay it on thick. 'We are sending small teams to watch every school in the area to check that they're safe. If you could phone ahead and alert the schools so that our people aren't ... challenged, that would be extraordinarily helpful.' Let's face it, the last thing we need is a panic on our hands because the last of the country's bloodguzzlers are hanging around schools as if they're waiting to get their revenge on those who deserve it least.

'Yes!' He almost trips over himself, he's so eager to help. 'I can do that.'

'And,' I continue, 'I'd like a list of all the children in Westminster who are being home-schooled.'

He nods vigorously. 'Indeed. Come right this way.'

I exchange glances with Hope and O'Shea. This is going far more swimmingly than I expected so it automatically puts me on edge. It's a shame that I'm forced to look for shadows at every turn, even when people are genuinely helpful.

Tamworth settles himself into a chair which squeals in distress when his arse lands on it. He grimaces. 'Sorry.' He pats his stomach. 'The wife keeps telling me to lose some weight.'

'I think it's the cheap furniture rather than your trim self,

Mr Tamworth.' He's not the only one who can play the sycophancy game.

It works. He beams at me and turns to his computer to tap on a few keys. 'Now,' he says, 'would you like photos to go along with that list?'

I try to keep my mouth closed. Aside from the fact that he's probably breaking about a million laws by giving me the list in the first place, having photos will enhance our investigation considerably. 'That would be wonderful,' I manage.

He lifts his chin and looks at me. 'You know I'll lose my job if anyone finds out I've done this.' He takes a breath. 'I might even be sent to jail.'

I meet his eyes and silently acknowledge the truth of his words. Apparently my sucking up isn't the reason he's helping us. I don't think telling him he's not fat is enough for him to risk getting locked up.

'But,' Tamworth continues, 'I trust you. You're a bloodguzzling fiend who probably should have died several times over by now, but you're doing more for this country than anyone else I can think of.'

'How do you figure that?'

'You're still here,' he answers simply. 'You've not given up on us.'

Without thinking, I reach out, grab his hand and squeeze it. It's a strange moment, grasping the flesh of someone who's a stranger and sharing genuine gratitude and understanding. Most people aren't bastards, I remind myself. Most are just trying to get along with their lives as best as they can.

O'Shea clears his throat. 'As much as I hate to break up this little tête-à-tête...'

I nod and pull back. 'He's right. We need to get a move on.'

Tamworth's expression transforms into business mode and he returns to the screen. 'There are fewer than two hundred children being home-schooled in this borough,' he says. 'Would you like printouts of all their names?'

'Addresses would be very helpful,' I say, pushing my luck.

'I can do that,' he agrees. 'But we'll need to move fast before everyone else comes back from lunch.' His nose twitches. 'Now about the photos. Of course, some are a bit dated…'

Eagerness overtakes me. 'Can I see them?'

Tamworth shrugs and angles the screen so I can see it. 'I'm just going to check on reception,' he says, 'to see if any messages have been left for me.' He stands up and shoves his hands in his pockets. 'Don't touch anything while I'm gone.' He taps the top of the computer and wanders off.

Hope, O'Shea and I glance at each other then we all lunge forward.

It doesn't take long to scroll through the pictures. We can discount all the boys and we know the age of the child we're looking for. I flick through the photos of girls around Alice's age. She's not there. I scowl to myself. Bugger it.

'I guess she's not being home-schooled then,' I say, irritated. 'She must be in one of the schools – if she's being educated at all. We need to hear back from the others.'

Hope taps her mouth thoughtfully. 'I'm new to all this investigation stuff.'

'Perhaps you should keep quiet then,' O'Shea suggests brightly.

She ignores him. 'But if I wanted to avoid anyone looking for a kid, I'd alter their age.'

I nibble at my bottom lip and shrug. 'It's easier to make someone look older rather than younger.' I start to scroll down to the older children. 'No. No. That one?' I squint. 'No.' I keep going until I hit the last photo. 'There's no one that looks remotely like Alice Goldman.'

'Go back up again,' O'Shea says. 'Slowly.'

I do as he asks. Images of gap-toothed, freckled, chubby, pretty, bespectacled children flash up. None of them are her.

'Stop.' He jabs at the screen. 'There.'

It's a professional-looking picture. A winsome girl smiles out at the camera. I touch my hair self-consciously. How does a kid get theirs to be so shiny and bouncy? I shake my head. 'That's not Alice. Her face is too long.'

'Yeah,' he agrees, 'it's not her. But if the bitch ... sorry, Freudian slip ... if the witch here is right about her age being altered, then why wouldn't her photo be altered too? Look at how perfect that kid is. In this photo she has to be ... what? Ten years old? Yet she's got straight white teeth, a model's pose, barely a hair out of place... She's too good to be true. Kids are messy. If girls that age wear make-up then they wear too much. They don't look like that.'

I stare at the photo. She does look rather airbrushed but it seems too much of a stretch. 'If Alice has been brainwashed so she doesn't remember who she is,' I say, 'and if whoever did that to her registered her with the council to avoid questions and they changed her age and her photo, then it could be her. That's a hell of a lot of ifs though.'

'It still begs the question why,' Hope muses.

O'Shea throws up his hands. 'Look, until you hear back from all your little guzzling buddies who are staking out the schools, we might as well follow this up. I'm telling you there's something not right about this photo.'

'Some children are more photogenic than others. They grow up with selfies and Instagram and goodness knows what else.'

'Bo...'

'Alright, alright. We'll look into her.' I read her details. 'Millicent Beatty. She might be younger in the photo but she's actually fourteen years old now. British citizen born in Dubai, only returned here three years ago. She doesn't live far from here.' I lift up my shoulders in resignation. 'Let's go say hello.'

Tamworth appears in the doorway. There's a troubled look on his face. 'Someone's tipped off the police,' he says. 'They're on their way up here. I can stall them but...'

I mutter a curse. I guess D'Argneau hasn't managed to get very far with that injunction. 'It's okay. We're leaving. Is there a back way out of here?'

Tamworth points towards a fire door. 'You can go that way.' He presses his lips together. 'I really hope you found what you needed. If there's anything else you need, don't hesitate to get in touch.' He passes me a card. 'That's my personal number.' He hesitates as if he wants to say something more.

'Go on.'

'Just,' he expels a rush of air. 'Don't go. Don't leave London. I know a lot of people don't like vampires, and I know you have a lot of reasons to leave, but you've done a lot of good here. I'd like you to stay. And I'm not the only one who thinks that way.'

I manage a smile. Then I join O'Shea and Hope and we run down the stairs and dash for the exit.

CHAPTER 17
MILLIE

We keep to the back streets as I get a message out to everyone else to keep a low profile while they stake out the Westminster schools. Even with Tamworth's help in getting the schools on board, the last thing we need is for one of us to end up back in Hale's clutches. I doubt it'll be so easy to escape a second time. He probably won't give us the chance: it'll be a swift execution in a deserted room. He really does want to get rid of all the vampires that much. Hope is right, though – even if he does achieve his current mission, he'll just move onto another target. It's as if he wants the country to be a homogenized, human-only place. He doesn't see that tribers do a lot of good. I rub the back of my neck. We need some better PR.

Fortunately, it doesn't take long to reach Millicent's address and we avoid trouble along the way. I can't stop scanning every street corner and, if I'm honest, it's because I'm more worried about Kakos daemons than about Vince Hale. But our progress is unimpeded and there's no sign that anyone is watching us. All the same, when I see the liveried doorman in front of the swanky block of flats, I'm not in the mood to hang around until we can sneak in. I walk straight up to him. 'I'm here to see Millicent Beatty,' I announce.

He pales, obviously recognising me. He's no Jonathan Tamworth. I'm pretty certain when he starts to reach round the side of the door that he's going for a panic button. I dart forward and knee him in the groin. He groans and collapses.

O'Shea winces. 'Was that necessary?'

I shrug. 'I didn't eat him.' The doorman flicks a pained look at me from the ground. 'There's still time, though. Stay here and find out what he knows.'

O'Shea salutes. 'Yes, boss.'

Hope and I take the lift to the penthouse. Whoever Millicent is, her family certainly has a lot of money at their disposal. Not only do they live in the heart of London with an address that a lot of people would kill for, but it's all gleaming gilt and polished floors. I wave at the CCTV camera and smile, posing first one way then another. When Hope looks at me strangely, I grin. 'It's not like we can hide,' I point out. 'There's too much security for that.'

'You're an odd person,' she comments. 'One minute you're attacking a doorman because he's in your way and the next you're acting like a bad comedian.'

I consider her words. 'I have my vampire half,' I say finally. 'The part that's dark and nasty and wants to destroy things. And I have my human half that wants the world to be a happier place. I'm still finding a balance between the two. I have the capacity to do some very bad things but, if I temper those desires with the better part of me, I can be a better person.'

Hope snorts. 'Everyone has the capacity to do bad things. Nothing's ever black and white, not even witches.'

I think of the hybrid witch whose magic Hope sucked away but, before I can say anything, the lift pings open. 'Let's see if

Millicent is the same girl as her photo,' I murmur and knock sharply on the shiny lacquered door.

When it swings open, and a girl peers out, disappointment engulfs me. She looks a few years older but in every other way she perfectly matches the photo in Tamworth's database. It really was too much to ask that this would be Alice. She takes in both Hope and me then blinks rapidly. A beat later, she slams the door shut in our faces. Uh, okay then.

Neither of us moves. 'She was wearing a twin set and pearls,' Hope says. 'What kind of teenager dresses like that?'

My phone buzzes in my pocket. I pull it out. O'Shea. 'Yep?'

'Our friend downstairs is suddenly very chatty,' he says. 'And apparently Miss Millicent Beatty has been living on her own for years. She's supposed to be with her aunt, a rather stern lady of older years. Andrew here hasn't seen the aunt for quite some time. Millicent has told him that the aunt's not been well and she's convalescing indoors. But...'

'But that sounds remarkably like that other kid you knew,' I finish.

'Benjy has a rich uncle who no one's seen for years. Millicent has a rich aunt. Maybe it's not the adults we need to worry about, Bo. Maybe it's the children.'

I run my tongue over my fangs and wish I had some chocolate to nibble on. Then I knock on the door again.

'Go away!' a muffled voice calls out. 'Or I'll call the police!'

'Why hasn't she called the police already?' I murmur to Hope. I cup my hand to my ear and press it against the door. I can't hear a thing. I pull back. 'I can't enter without an invitation.'

Hope smiles. 'Don't worry,' she says sunnily. 'I've got this.' Her brows draw together and her eyes fix on the door. Ever so slowly, the knob turns then the door swings open once more.

I whistle. 'Neat trick.'

'We all have the capacity to do bad things,' she answers with a droll wink. 'Let's hope that Millicent Beatty really is more than an oddly dressed, home-schooled teenager or I'm going to be in trouble.' She cracks her knuckles and steps inside.

'Get out!' Millicent shrieks. 'Get out!'

I hear a thump. A moment later, Hope appears, dragging the unfortunate girl by her ear. 'Invite my friend in.'

'No way.'

'Let's try that again, shall we? Invite her in or I'll take you outside to her.' She bends down to Millicent's ear. 'That'll be much worse. Trust me.'

Millicent's eyes swing wildly from side to side.

'I'm not going to hurt you,' I say, holding up my palms. 'I don't hurt children.'

'Really? What about...' Her voice falters and her shoulders sag. There's no mistaking the flare of panic in her eyes though.

'Go on,' I urge.

She swallows, seeming even more nervous and scared than she was before. 'The ... the ... other night. There was a ... boy. You attacked him and knocked him out. It was all over the wireless.'

I wince slightly. 'Alright,' I admit. 'I hurt him a bit but he deserved it. *You've* not done anything, Millie.' Wireless is a strange word for a kid to use to describe a radio. I continue to watch her carefully. Oddly, she seems to relax infinitesimally enough to throw me a glare.

'It's Millicent. And you're right, I've not done anything. You're trespassing. You'll pay for this, I promise you that.'

Hope sniffs. 'You've been drinking.'

I flare my nostrils and inhale. 'Gin and tonic? Sophisticated tastes for a teenager.'

'We're not all uncultured louts from backwater suburbs,' Millicent retorts.

'It's not even two o'clock,' I point out. I look her up and down. 'Bring her closer, Hope,' I instruct.

The witch does as I ask. Millicent fights every step of the way but she's too small to do much against Hope's strength. When only a few inches of threshold separate us, I gaze into her eyes. Millicent flinches but I keep looking. I think about the intelligence that shines out of Rogu3 and the haunted fear that's reflected in Maria. Millicent possesses both but there's something else there too. I'm sure of it.

'Where's Alice Goldman?' I ask.

'I don't know who you're talking about.' Her eyebrow twitches almost imperceptibly.

'You're lying.' I look past her into the immaculate apartment. 'Where's your aunt? She's your guardian, right?'

'She's out.'

I paste on an expression of dramatic surprise. 'But I thought she was ill.'

'Convalescing,' Hope agrees.

Millicent's anger only grows. 'What is it to you where she is?'

'You're under age. There must be someone looking after you. Who were you calling just now?'

She draws herself up, an imperious light in her eyes. 'You have no right to do this to me,' she says. 'It's no business of yours who my guardian is. In any case, I am more than capable of looking after myself.'

A kernel of an idea unfurls in my brain. 'Millicent,' I say gently. 'Who's in One Direction?'

She screws up her face. 'What?'

'Tell me the name of one member.'

'You're crazy.' She pulls against Hope's grip. 'You're both absolutely insane.'

Hope keeps her attention on me. 'What are you thinking, Bo?'

Butterflies flap at the corners of my stomach. 'That there's only one person who can tell us exactly what's going on here.'

And he's the last person in the world I want to ask for help.

~

'ARE YOU SURE ABOUT THIS?' O'Shea asks, his orange pupils dilated. I've never seen him so scared. He's not the only one quaking in his boots.

'No,' I answer honestly, staring at the imposing façade of X's building. 'Just keep an eye out for that damned female daemon. If any of us starts acting strangely or out of character then...' My voice trails off.

'Then what? We bop them on the head? I don't think that's much of a solution.'

I look at Millicent, who's being held in his arms. 'There's no choice.'

'There is if she's just a fourteen-year-old girl. Admittedly, a weirdly dressed fourteen-year-old girl whose parents need to be called immediately but,' he purses his lips, 'teenagers are weird by definition.'

'You're the one who thought there was something strange about her,' I point out.

'True. I still think you should have told that witch to stick around, though. We could have used her as bait.'

'Hope doesn't need to prove herself any more than she already has,' I say firmly. 'And she says she had things to do. Keeping her as a hostage is getting stupid.' Strange as it seems, it feels good that the cold war I've been fighting with the black witches all my life seems to be at an end.

A van pulls up next to us and my grandfather, Rogu3 and

Maria get out. 'Hello, my dear,' my grandfather says. He walks up to Millicent and circles her. 'How interesting.' He takes her chin and stares into her eyes. 'Hmm.'

'I looked up that old guy for you,' Rogu3 says. 'Alice's neighbour. He's not in a home or anything like that. He's dead. He was killed in a hit and run.'

'When?'

'Less than a week after he gave a statement to the police about seeing aliens abduct her.'

'How convenient,' I murmur. 'Thanks for that.'

Rogu3 bobs his head in satisfaction. 'I'm making progress with Hale, too. I can't break all his passwords yet because he's spending a lot of time out of the office right now. I'm getting close though. I'm inside his system.'

'You and me both,' I say. Rogu3 looks at me quizzically but I wave in dismissal. 'Maria?'

She edges forward. I point at Millicent. 'Do you know her?' I ask. 'Do you recognise her?'

Maria swallows and looks. She takes her time, examining Millicent carefully. 'I think yes. Not like this. Before she is more...' She looks upwards, searching for the right word.

'Messy?'

Maria nods. I exhale. It seems like my suspicions are correct. I'd really hoped I was wrong.

'What?' Millicent gabbles. Her fear is growing more palpable. 'I don't know this girl! I don't know who any of you people are but you have to let me go!'

I ignore her and focus on my grandfather. 'Thanks for coming. I know it was a long way. You'd better take Maria and Rogu3 back now. Take O'Shea too.'

Rogu3's mouth drops open. 'What? We didn't come all this way just to say hello and then be taken back home again. Fuck's sake, Bo.'

'Don't swear. And you know it's too dangerous.' I look at Bruckheimer and Berryhill's glossy building as if I'm expecting to see Madame Kakos daemon appear at any moment.

Maria licks her lips. 'Not for me.'

'Yes, for you. Thanks for coming. Please leave.'

She glances at my grandfather. He nods, his expression sombre. 'Go on.'

My eyes narrow. 'What?'

'It's for the best, my dear.'

Maria looks at me defiantly. 'Is my idea.'

A chill descends down my spine. 'You'd better not be suggesting what I think you are.'

She pulls up her sleeve and thrusts out her arm. 'Take blood.'

'Maria's Romany heritage means that the Kakos daemons are unable to read her mind, manipulate her thoughts or generally use telepathic means to control her in any way, shape or form.'

I'd been starting to suspect as much. While it's nice to be right, it doesn't stop my uneasiness from growing.

My grandfather continues. 'If you drink from her, you should be able to shield your own mind. Her platelets will last at least a couple of hours in your system.'

I grit my teeth. 'She's a child.'

'She's fully aware of what she's doing, Bo.'

'She's my friend. And my responsibility.' I fold my arms. 'No way.'

'Do it.' Maria's voice is quiet but insistent. 'I want you do it.'

'No,' I say. 'You don't.' I think of O'Shea's revelation about how it made Connor feel when I drank from him and shudder. Hell, no. She deserves better. I spin round and try to walk away but Maria skirts round in front and blocks my path. She holds her arm out once more. 'This for Alice.'

Millicent gags. 'This is disgusting. You are all disgusting.'

'Shut up, Millie.' She flinches and looks away while I shake my head firmly. 'It's not happening.'

Rogu3 snorts. 'Told you she wouldn't do it.'

I meet my grandfather's eyes. 'It's called morality,' I tell him. 'Remember?'

He doesn't answer. Instead, he turns round and retrieves something from the van. When I see what's in his hands, I glare at him.

'You can throw me all the dirty looks you want, my dear, but this is for all our safety. We can't have him planting thoughts in your mind.' He holds up a blood bag. 'Maria decanted this for us on the way here. It's about as fresh as you're likely to get.'

My glare intensifies. 'So she's already lost blood and you were suggesting she lose even more?'

He smiles disarmingly. 'I knew you'd refuse.' He waggles the blood in my face. 'This is the compromise. It's already out of Maria's system. Not using it would be a stupid waste.'

I curse aloud. 'Who needs Kakos daemons to manipulate my mind when you're around?' I take the bag from him then I point at Maria. 'If you ever do this again, I will ground you for the rest of your life.'

A giggle escapes her as if the very idea is absurd. 'Sure.'

'I'm glad someone finds this funny,' I huff.

'Stop complaining, Bo,' my grandfather orders. 'And get a move on. We're very visible out here.' His warning is clear. We have no idea when X's friend/boss/nemesis is going to show up again. I hiss in annoyance, tear the edge of the bag with my teeth then start to drink.

Maria's blood tingles on my tongue. It's not like anything I've tasted before. I can tell she's O negative but it's as if there's something else there too, like Tabasco or a dash of paprika. I only intend to take a few small sips but once I start, and the warm salty liquid slides with such ease down my throat, it's difficult to stop. When I finally pull the bag away from my mouth, I'm breathing heavily.

'Do you feel any different?' Rogu3 asks curiously.

Everyone is watching me; even Millicent appears to have set aside her fear and is staring. I start to shake my head then realise that I do feel different. Lightheaded and almost ... dizzy. I blink a few times but the feeling doesn't subside.

'That's bloody weird,' I mutter.

There's a shout from further down the street and we all freeze in alarm. I whip my head round, only relaxing when I see a bloke in a suit run to catch up with another man. They both look human; I hope they are anyway.

'Get back to base,' I say to everyone. 'Now.' I glance at the almost empty bag in my hands then toss it to Hope. 'Don't let that out of your sight.'

She frowns but nods. As soon as they've all piled back into the van and driven off, I take a deep breath. It's time to face the real monster.

There's no alarm when Millicent and I enter the building. There are no doormen or security cameras or welcome mats; in fact, there's nothing apart from a rather grubby floor and a single lift. I suppose X is so powerful that he doesn't need to protect himself. There's a quiet whoosh and the LED numbers displayed above the lift door start to decrease. Someone is on their way down. I hold my ground. I'm not scared. I'm not scared. I'm not scared.

Millicent squeaks, 'I don't like this. Tell me what you want and I'll do it. I'll tell you whatever you want to know.'

If I thought for one minute that I could trust her, I'd take her arm and run out of here. But I'm doing this for Alice and for Maria and for all those children who've ended up goodness knows where. I don't know whether drinking Maria's blood is going to work or not, but this might be my only chance to attack X and get away with it. Once I've finished questioning him, of course.

The doors open. X glides out, wearing his natural daemon face and a black, funereal suit. He adjusts his cuffs and smiles while Millicent cowers. 'Hello, Bo.'

I watch his tattoos writhe and twist across his skin. 'Does that itch?' I ask with detached curiosity.

He continues to smile. My fists curl without me realising and he starts to laugh. 'I might not be able to read your thoughts,' he says while I hold my breath and hope he's telling the truth, 'but you still give yourself away.' He steps closer. 'How badly do you want me dead?'

'Let's just say I'm imagining your bloody entrails decorating this floor.' I look around. 'It would be an improvement.'

'I saved Michael for you.'

'You manipulated me. You worked with your buddies to commit genocide.'

'The Families deserved it.'

My gaze doesn't flicker. 'No, they didn't.'

Millicent struggles against my hold. 'What the goddamn hell is going here? Let me go! I demand you let me go!'

X raises an eyebrow. 'The lady demands.'

'Bully for her.'

'Always the tough façade, little Bo.' X reaches out and caresses my face. I will myself not to flinch but it takes almost everything I have. 'I've missed you. I had hoped we could stay friends.'

I stare. 'You're insane.'

He sighs. 'I tried to protect you. I shielded you as best I could. You're still alive.'

'Am I supposed to be grateful, you wanker?' I snarl.

He winces. 'There's no need for such language.'

I bare my fangs and lunge forward, dragging Millicent with me. X sidesteps. 'I'm not all bad, Bo,' he says softly, his mellifluous voice trying to seduce me into relaxing.

I concentrate. I'm going to kick you where it hurts, I think, broadcasting my thoughts as best as I can. Then I do just that. My foot connects with his hard body. He turns just in time to avoid getting caught in the groin but he still expels a satisfying oomph.

'That was unnecessary,' he grimaces.

He might be bluffing, there's no way of telling for sure. Still, I think that Maria's blood might be working. 'Where's your boss?' I ask. 'The woman.'

His grimace deepens. 'I am sorry that she attacked you.'

'Is she the one who messed with my mind?'

X inclines his head. 'Yes.'

'Have you ever done that?'

'No.' He doesn't qualify his response but for some reason I believe him. There's something about his tone of voice. Or maybe I'm just an idiot.

'I don't know what the hell is going on here,' Millicent shrieks. 'But you need to...'

'Let you go,' I finish for her. 'So you keep saying.' I thrust her forward into X's face. 'Tell me what she is.'

A smile plays around his lips. 'You're asking me for a favour. What do I get in return?'

I ignore every atom in my body that tells me to smash his stupid, handsome face in. 'You get me not killing you.'

He eyes me with interest. 'You think you could?'

'If you can't read my mind, you don't know what move I'm about to pull,' I growl, my desire for violence throbbing through every word. 'For once the playing field is level.'

X shakes his head sadly. 'I'll still beat you.'

Millicent gapes. 'She's a freaking bloodguzzler! You can't

beat her. She's got preternatural strength. Plus, she's obviously a maniac.'

I swing towards the teenager. 'What do you see when you look at him? What is he?'

She tries again to pull away from me. 'What is wrong with you?'

I watch her flailing movements then I smile. He wasn't lying before then. 'Maria's blood. It really is working. You're glamoured up and that's all Millicent can see. I, on the other hand, can't see your glamour because of Maria's magic. The magic that's now in me.' My smile broadens.

X doesn't disagree. 'It's only temporary, Bo. I wouldn't get too excited. Not unless you're going to drag Maria around and keep drinking from her every couple of hours.'

'Oh, I wouldn't worry about that,' I tell him. I still can't keep the smile off my face. I point to Millicent once more. 'For old times' sake. What is she?'

'You already know.'

'Spell it out for me.'

X regards me silently for a moment. 'Very well, I will. But only because it's the right thing to do. And because no matter what you think of me, I do like you, Bo.'

It's on the tip of my tongue to tell him to sod off but I remind myself that this is more important than my need for revenge.

Millicent, for her part, is starting to realise that things aren't going in her favour. 'What's happening here? I'm going to sue the shit out of both of you! When my lawyers get involved, you'll be sorry you ever laid eyes on me!'

X glances at me. 'Methinks the lady doth protest too much.'

For once I agree. 'Come on, X,' I say. 'Enlighten me. Who is this?'

'Her name is not Millicent Beatty. It's Mildred.'

Mildred? I shoot her a look. 'Poor you.'

She swallows and stares at him. 'No, I'm not! I don't know any Mildred! I'm Millicent!'

X doesn't pay her any attention. 'She's seventy-seven years old. This is not her original body; that lies somewhere else. This body was stolen from its original occupier. I can't tell you who it was because no vestiges of that person remain. She paid a considerable amount of money, both for the body and the procedure.'

I forget to breathe. I'd started to suspect this much but I hadn't been sure. It's not mind-wiping or brainwashing or anything like that; it's bodysnatching. That's why all those children disappeared, because a bunch of wrinkly rich people wanted to live longer. Disgust courses through me.

'How could you do this?' I whisper.

Millicent/Mildred stares at me and I think she's going to continue to protest her innocence. Instead, she sags against my grip. 'Like you could ask that,' she sneers. 'You're a vampire. You live four lifetimes. We humans only get one. I don't have to drink blood to survive. Other people don't get hurt because I live a bit longer. Not like in your case.'

And she thinks I'm a maniac? 'What about the child whose body you took? What about her?'

She looks away. 'She'll get her body back one day.'

I doubt that will ever happen but I fix on her statement. 'So it's reversible? Whatever you did?'

She presses her lips together, making it clear that she's not going to say anything else. I'm tempted to thump her – but it's not *her* body I'd be thumping. Instead, I glance questioningly at X.

'It's not a procedure I'm familiar with but there's no reason why it wouldn't be reversible. All you would need to do is to find her original body. That'll be where this body's soul is being housed.'

'Soul?'

He shrugs elegantly. 'For want of a better word. And before you ask, no, Mildred here doesn't know where it is.'

'Who does?'

'I don't know.'

I take a threatening step towards him. 'X...'

He holds up his hands. 'I don't know because she doesn't know. Her contacts were removed when her swap was completed.' He smiles without humour. 'She was blindfolded every time she visited their premises. Apparently the outfit who do this work on a need-to-know basis.'

'How did she hear about them in the first place?'

'Friend of a friend. That trail is cold.' He regards me calmly. 'Not all of the transitions were successful.'

I feel sick. Transitions? I shake my head. 'It all makes sense. Kids like Maria, who no one would ever miss, were snatched or sold or trafficked or whatever, and then their bodies were used for people like ... *her*. Alice Goldman doesn't fit though. She had a family. Her disappearance was big news.'

'I can't help you with that.'

I snort. 'Fat lot of good you are.'

'I think I've helped you out rather a lot.'

My lip curls. 'Yeah. Whatever.'

'Your gratitude is truly heart-warming.'

My face twists. 'You're still alive, aren't you?' I consider my options. With Mildred in tow, I'm not sure I can do anything about X. I can't keep hold of her and kill him at the same time. Save the innocent or kill the guilty? It's no choice. Shame, though. Still, I can always come back.

I move up until my face is in his. 'I know your weak spot

now,' I say. 'Don't think that your help today has changed anything between us. I'm still going to destroy you.'

X's expression is surprisingly rueful. 'I think you'll have to get in line.' He grabs my arm. 'Don't underestimate the others, Bo. They desperately want to be rid of all the vampires and they don't like losing.'

'You're hiding here, aren't you? Hiding from them. Your *buddies*,' I sneer.

His response is simple. 'Protecting you cost me.'

Am I supposed to feel sorry for him? Before I can snarl another response, his grip tightens. 'Leave London, Bo. Take Michael and your family and your friends and get out of here. You won't win.'

I stand on my tiptoes until our noses are almost touching. 'Bite me.' And then, with Mildred squirming by my side, I pull my arm away and stride out.

CHAPTER 18

DEAL WITH THE DEVIL

Because I don't have the faintest idea what else to do with her, Mildred is safely locked away in one of the bedrooms while the rest of us cluster round the television. No one has found any trace of a girl who looks like Alice Goldman in Westminster. I send a message to Foxworthy explaining what I've discovered. He has resources that I don't but I have no idea whether he'll be able to round up other stolen children. There's no doubt that there are more than Mildred, Alice and Benjy. With Mildred unable to help us find the people who organised her 'transition', I can feel my chances of succeeding in finding any of the children slipping away. The gnawing chasm of futility and helplessness inside me grows and grows.

On television, Harry D'Argneau's familiar face beams out at us from the steps of Parliament.

'I still hate that guy,' Michael mutters by my side. I turn and give him a small smile, curving an arm round his waist. He remains far too pale for my liking but he can stand up unassisted. Score one for additives and greasy food.

D'Argneau licks his lips; it's clear he's loving every minute of

209

the spotlight. 'The current initiative against the remaining British vampires has been declared unlawful. Every vampire in the land deserves the right to be treated as a legal citizen. By that, not only are they bound by the same laws which bind everyone else and keep law and order on the streets, but they are also to be accorded the same freedom which everyone else enjoys. What happened to the five Families is an extraordinary tragedy but it is one from which we must move on. There will be a lot of questions in the days, weeks and months to come and a lot of issues which must be resolved. The vampires, however, are not our enemies. They are us.'

'Nice speech,' I murmur.

My grandfather smiles. 'I may have thrown a few suggestions his way.'

I raise my eyebrows. He probably wrote the whole thing. D'Argneau continues talking. While the others watch, I draw Michael away. 'How do you feel about all this?' I ask softly.

He trails his fingers gently down my face. 'I don't know. It's hard to see your life's work obliterated. Harder still to know that most of the people you knew are now nothing more than dust and ashes. I know the Families had their faults but I was part of it for a long time, Bo.' He sighs. 'Not just part of it, I was in charge of it. You think *you* have doubts about what you're doing? I failed everyone.'

There's a loud whoop as a network pundit comes on television and starts to talk about the benefits of vampirism. Michael and I move sit in the corner, away from all the noise.

'You were Head of one sodding Family. You weren't God. And your way wasn't the wrong way. *This* way isn't the right way.' I struggle to find the right words and wish I was more eloquent, especially about something so important. 'They're just different paths. Not good ones or bad ones just ... different.'

He smiles sadly. 'You're doing a better job than you know, Bo.'

'I'm not doing a job. I'm not in charge and I don't want to be. I'm not you, I don't enjoy leadership. If I could be on my own all the time, then I would be.' I realise how that sounds and trip over my words in a bid to explain myself. 'I don't mean without you or family or things like that.'

'I know what you mean.'

We look at each other. We may have already had a conversation like this but I feel it bears repeating. I wouldn't let Michael dismiss me when he was at death's door but he deserves the option now he's getting better.

'If you want to walk away,' I say, forcing down the stabbing pain that attacks my heart, 'then you can. At any time. I love you and I'm not going anywhere. But I understand if you want to.'

He doesn't even hesitate. 'The truth is, I don't want to be anywhere but with you.' He studies my face. 'If that means being wholly selfish and making you stay with me when I'm wrinkly and doubled over and eating nothing but baby food, then that's the way it's going to be. Because I'm not going to let you go.'

I hold my breath. 'That won't bother you?'

He shrugs. 'Maybe we'll find a way so I can turn back.'

I bite my lip. I know in my heart of hearts that's not going to happen, just like I know that if I got down on my hands and knees and begged X to make me human, he wouldn't.

'You still want to be a vampire?' I ask.

'You still want to be human?'

I let out a short laugh. 'That's a complicated question.'

'Yeah,' he says. 'It is. I guess when it comes down to it, most people don't get the happy endings they want.'

I glance at O'Shea. He catches my eye and gives me a quick

smile and I note the envy in his eyes. He'd give his eye teeth and then some to have Connor back with him, regardless of what that relationship might entail in the future. I should be happy with what I've got. My grandfather can castigate me all he wants for my relationship with Michael; he's not the one who's in it.

Beth lets out a loud shriek. 'Bo! Get your skinny arse over here!'

'What?'

'Look!' She's jumping up and down and pointing at the screen. A spokesperson for one of the French Families is outside the Eiffel Tower, speaking earnestly to a journalist. I frown, not sure why she's so excited. Then I see who's hovering in the background.

'Matt,' I breathe. My old Montserrat buddy. 'He made it out.'

'And,' she crows, 'he can't speak a word of French.' She laughs uproariously. 'He must be having the time of his life!' Even Kimchi barks, as if recognising his old friend.

The camera shifts. Matt's not alone, both Arzo and Peter are by his side. Some of my tension dissipates and I relax into a genuine smile. It's hard to feel entirely happy when so many of us are dead and so much is going to shit, but suddenly it feels as if there's a glimmer of hope. Until the camera shifts again, switching back to London, and Vince Hale's face appears.

'Mr Hale,' the journalist intones, 'you've been one of the most ardent advocates against the vampires. How do you feel about the court's new ruling?'

The politician's expression remains studiously serious. 'What happened to the five Families is an extraordinary tragedy and, believe me, I take no pleasure in it. I have spoken person-ally to Scotland Yard and they do not believe the threat is over. We have indeed captured many of the members of this group calling itself Tov V'ra. However, it is possible that some remain.'

'Yeah,' Rogu3 snorts. 'Like Vince Hale himself.'

I hush him. Hale is up to something and I want to hear what.

'Neither can we deny that the vampires are a threat to our civilized society. I appreciate the court's ruling and I am fully sympathetic to the vampires' cause but these are creatures who prey on innocent victims. They drink blood to stay alive, for goodness' sake. It's all well and good to integrate them into society and let them live amongst us but,' his face now turns sad, 'what about the danger to our children? Let us not forget what happened to young Thomas Glass when a bloodguzzler attacked him in his own yard. I believe that the vampires want to be good. I believe that they mean it when they say they will abide by our laws. But their baser instincts mean that they simply cannot control themselves enough for that to happen.'

'So, Mr Hale, what exactly are you proposing?' asks the journalist, feeding him what is no doubt a pre-prepared question.

'Exactly what I've been planning all along: we transport all vampires to a facility out of the capital. It will be comfortable. We will provide them with all the blood they require. They don't recruit anyone new and no one else is made to suffer because of their existence. They will die out naturally instead of living their lives in fear – and Britain will be safer for it.'

Beth folds her arms and glares. 'He's putting himself across as the calm voice of reason as if he's telling a child to eat their smegging vegetables. It's for your own good,' she mimics. 'Tosser.'

I look at my grandfather and he smiles back with grim resolve. 'The black witches will put out a statement in support of the vampires. They have no desire to be rounded up and placed in some internment camp either.'

I draw in a ragged breath. 'It won't be enough. As long as people believe that Hale is a sensible human who stands for law, order and safety, sooner or later people will rally to his cause. We don't have a strong enough plan for ourselves now that the Families no longer exist. We can't counteract what he's saying.'

'We could come up with a plan.'

'Yeah, but it would be rushed and he'll find holes in it. We have to take our time deciding what we're going to do next and how we're going to live. He wants us to trip over ourselves and make a mistake, then he'll pounce on it, court ruling or no court ruling.'

'So what do we do?'

Everyone looks at me, even Michael. My mouth is dry and my palms are clammy. What I really want to do is to end Hale once for all and leave him bleeding out in some dark alley but that would only play into his hands. It's what he's probably hoping for.

I lick my lips. 'Rogu3, have you got anywhere with his computer? Is there anything we can use to discredit him?'

'I'm sorry, Bo.' He drops his head and looks ashamed. 'So far his files are clean.'

'What about the barrister?' Chester asks. 'Can't he do something else? Tell everyone that Hale's proposal is still illegal?'

'He can shout about the law all he wants,' I answer. 'Once public opinion is against us, there won't be much comeback.'

Michael clears his throat. 'I can do an interview. Present a human face that people will believe because I was one of you.'

'In theory that would be good but Hale will jump on it as a reason why we should all be returned to a human state.'

His response is quiet. 'Isn't that what you want?'

On some level, yes but this isn't about me. I look at the remaining vampires. I'm not imagining the fear in their eyes; they don't want to be human any more than Michael does. I need to put aside my personal feelings and think about what's best for everyone. What's going to give us a future? The only answer I can come up with is getting rid of Vince Hale. I pinch the bridge of my nose and try desperately to think.

'Okay,' I say slowly, 'we've got the Kakos daemons, Vince Hale and a seventy-seven-year-old woman who's stolen a teenager's body. Somehow we need to deal with them all.'

O'Shea grins weakly. 'Well, when you put it like that, it's a piece of piss. Only the most powerful beings on the planet, a Member of Parliament and a body snatcher.' He shrugs. 'What could be easier?'

I scratch my nose. 'What can we control?'

'None of the above,' my grandfather says. 'But if Hale is going after public opinion then that's what we focus on. The faster the black witches come out in support, the better things will be.'

I nod. 'The witches are just one group, though.' I straighten my shoulders. 'There are other people who will benefit from our continued existence and who might be in a position to help us.' I tighten my jaw. 'I'm going into town.'

I'LL BE the first to admit that I'm not good at asking for help. I wasn't lying when I told Michael that I prefer to work alone. Owning up to the fact that I'm not all-powerful and can't do everything solo is one of the hardest things I've done. It's one thing getting help from Foxworthy or D'Argneau, or having Hope and her witches approach me; coming here to initiate a meeting and beg for assistance is entirely different.

Compared to a few days ago, it's obvious that people are slowly starting to return to their normal routine. The streets are busier with both foot traffic and cars. You can't keep a good city down. There are still a lot of bloody people heading towards

Magix, however. There's nothing like a good protection spell to make you believe that you're safe from all the nasty things out there. That desire is what I'm counting on.

I hold my head up high and cross the road, then stroll through the giant glass doors that lead to Magix's shop floor. A young woman, laden with shopping bags and on her way out, immediately notices me and lets out a small shriek. If she's shopping at Magix, I'm pretty certain that she's not a fan.

'Guzzler! Bo ... Bo ... Bo Blackman!'

Heads begin to turn and people drop to the floor as if I'm about to pull out an Uzi and fire indiscriminately. I walk past the woman to the centre of the shop. I spread my arms out wide and yell, 'I want to talk to the manager!'

Two burly security guards march towards me, tasers in front of them. 'Get down on the ground,' the nearest one shouts.

I do as I'm told. I'm not here to appear threatening, I have far grander plans in mind. As much as I hate those damned anti-vampire handcuffs, I press my wrists together and wait patiently for the guards to secure me. It's only when energy starts to sap out of me as the cuffs click into place that they haul me back up to my feet.

'What do you want?' the second guard snarls in my face.

'I want you to see a dentist to sort out that halitosis,' I retort without thinking. He reaches back and slams his fist into the side of my head. I reel. 'Pretty birdies,' I mutter, shaking my head to clear the pain. 'I apologise. I didn't mean to be rude. As I already said, I want to see the woman in charge. Take me to the manager.'

There are a few whimpers from the cowering shoppers. 'You're not going anywhere near her,' the guard spits.

'It's fine,' rings out a clear, imperious voice. We all turn.

Standing less than a few metres away is a well-dressed woman in a tailored suit.

'Ma'am…'

She flicks a hand dismissively at the guards. 'Bring her up.' She turns on her heel, leaving them no choice but to drag me along as we follow.

The top-floor offices of Magix have changed since the last time I was here. A woman's touch, I suppose. There are soft furnishings and bright colours. It looks more like a comfortable living room than the headquarters of one of the wealthiest shopping conglomerates in the world. The woman sees me looking around. 'Do you like it?' she enquires.

I shrug; I don't really give a hoot what the Magix offices look like. Then I remember I'm trying to get on her good side. 'It's wonderful,' I say. 'So bright and airy. The way the pink accents the olive green is inspired.'

A muscle tightens in her jaw and I realise I've injected a tad too much enthusiasm into my voice. 'Sorry. I'm on edge and I don't mean to sound insincere.'

Her eyes widen a fraction. 'Is that an apology from the great, infallible Bo Blackman?' She places a hand over her heart. 'I'm shocked.'

'I'm not infallible,' I say stiffly. 'Especially not with these cuffs on.'

She smiles. 'Yes, my predecessor did get some things right.'

Considering I put her predecessor in jail, where he managed to get himself killed, I decide that this isn't the direction I'd like the conversation to going. 'What's your name?' I ask instead.

'You may call me Isabella.'

I wonder if she's like Madonna and has no surname. This time, however, I manage to be more circumspect. 'It's lovely to meet you.'

Isabella smiles again and sits down, elegantly crossing her

ankles. She gestures to the seat opposite and I plonk my arse down awkwardly. But I am still wearing the stupid handcuffs so it's not entirely my fault.

'Why have you come here?' she enquires.

I lean back and try to look nonchalant, countering her question with one of my own. 'How's your profit margin these days?'

'We're not in any danger of going under,' Isabella replies. 'But thank you for your concern.' She already looks bored.

'I used to work for an insurance company,' I say.

'Bruckheimer and Berryhill.' She's done her homework.

'Yeah. I paid them a visit this week. Mr Berryhill was concerned that they would lose a lot of their clients now that there aren't so many vampires to worry about.'

Her eyes dance. 'So you helped him out by drinking a pint of his blood and snapping a photo. Don't tell me you're here to offer me the same service because, if that's the case, I shall respectfully decline.'

'I'm told the experience is rather orgasmic,' I say before adding hastily, 'but no. That's not exactly why I'm here.'

Her eyebrows rise. 'Not exactly?'

'Look, I know your company has put a lot of money into anti-vampire stuff. These handcuffs, the tasers, all that other shit. If there aren't any vampires, then all that will go to waste. You need tribers like us.'

Her mouth twitches. 'So you're here to ask us to come out in public in support of you.' She pauses. 'And against Mr Hale.'

It's good to know she's been keeping up with current events. 'I am.'

'It is true,' Isabella states carefully, 'that we will lose some custom. But you saw what things are like downstairs. We are not worried. We can recoup our lost profits elsewhere. I understand your position, Ms Blackman, but going against a powerful member of the government would not be in our best interests.'

'Hale won't be around for long,' I growl.

She looks only mildly interested. 'You can't kill him. You know that if you do, his message will become all the stronger.'

I grit my teeth. 'I am aware of that.'

'Well, then.'

I repeat my point. 'More vampires mean more profit for you.'

'We will manage.' She stands up. 'If that's all…'

'What about Kakos daemons?' I burst out.

For the first time I see real interest in her eyes, although her response is controlled. 'What about them?'

'Kakos daemons are far more of a danger to the public than vampires.'

'They are,' she agrees. 'But apart from the odd heart banquet, they tend to keep out of the way.'

'That's not true. They have more power and more control than anyone realises.'

'Which is the key point. If people don't realise the Kakos daemons are a serious threat, they won't spend money on protecting themselves against them.' She gestures towards me. 'Impasse.'

I swallow. 'There are ways to inform the public of the danger. Streets of Fire is owned by a Kakos daemon. I bet there are other high-profile companies too.'

She tilts her head to the side. 'Perhaps this one.'

Buggering hell. Fortunately, she just laughs. 'I jest. Besides, even if the public wanted to find ways to keep themselves safe from daemons, we don't have anything that would work. We're not in the business of lying to our customers, Ms Blackman.'

'Kakos daemons can read minds. They can manipulate thoughts and feelings.'

That's obviously not news to Isabella because her expression doesn't change. 'We can't guard against that.'

'Actually,' I tell her, 'you can.' I stand up, wobbling slightly. 'I have the secret ingredient.'

I'm rewarded with a sudden flare in her eyes. She masks it quickly but I'm satisfied that I've caught her interest. 'Go on,' she says.

'Lobby parliament on our behalf and I'll give it to you.' Hope has the remnants of Maria's blood donation; just a few drops will be enough for Magix to get their boffins onto creating a synthetic version. I get a wealthy corporation helping out the vampires – and a means for all of us to guard against the Kakos daemons. It's win-win. And then some.

'What a fascinating proposition,' she murmurs.

I smile. I've got her and we both know it. Now all I need is to find out what she knows about the art of bodysnatching and I'll really be getting somewhere.

Footsteps sound behind us. I glance over my shoulder and frown as one of the guards appears. He's holding out a phone. 'For you, Miss Isabella.'

'Thank you.' She takes the phone and puts it to her ear. I tap my foot impatiently on the floor. I wish she'd get on with it.

She hangs up and jerks her head at the guard. 'Release Ms Blackman.'

He doesn't look happy but he does as he's told while she turns to a television set, picks up the remote control and changes the channel. 'Oh dear,' she tuts. 'You might be too late.'

I have no idea what she's talking about until I see what she's watching. It's CCTV footage of me posing in Mildred's lift, followed by Mildred herself being dragged out, obviously against her will. Sodding hell. The camera flashes to Vince Hale looking sorrowful. Although the sound is off, there's no doubt what he's saying; he's telling the world that I'm a monster, that vampires are irredeemable.

Screw him. I've had just about enough of this.

CHAPTER 19

TO THE POINT OF NO RETURN

The rage which burns through me is cold and dangerous. It's not simply that Hale is making me – and by extension all vampires – look like crazed criminals, it's that he's using Mildred to do it. Whoever the hooded men really are, they'll now know we've got her. Anyone who's used their services will go underground and any faint hope we had of finding them and those responsible will fade away.

I don't know how many children are involved but even if only one loses their chance of a real life because of Hale's actions, it's one too many. A tiny voice prods me, insisting that he thinks he's doing the right thing and that he doesn't understand what's really happening. I don't care. He's pushed and he's pushed and this is the last straw. I've been holding it together since the bombs went off. Now I'm not.

I march out of Magix like a whirlwind. Plenty of people notice me but no one dares get in my way; whether that's because they've seen the Mildred footage or because I just look damned scary, I'm not sure. I don't bloody care either way.

I step onto the road, into the path of an oncoming car. The

driver slams and flings open the door. 'You crazy bitch! What do you think you...?' His voice falters as he recognises me. 'I didn't see who you were,' he babbles, abruptly backtracking. 'I'm sorry. I...'

I shove him out of the way and get into his car, leaving him gaping after me as the tyres squeal and I speed away. My phone rings but I ignore it. I only have two things on my mind: get to Hale and kill him.

The lights ahead flick to red but I squeak through. A car coming in the opposite direction smacks into my tail end and I'm jolted painfully to the side. I lick my lips. Pain is good; pain is my friend. My phone starts ringing again; vexed by the sound, I'm about to throw it out of the window into the oncoming traffic when I see the caller display. I pause and breathe. Then I answer.

'Hello, Bo,' Michael's familiar voice drawls. 'What are you up to?'

I swerve round a cyclist. 'Oh, you know the usual,' I mutter. 'I'm going to kill a guy. Drink his blood. Make him scream. That kind of thing.'

'Mm. I saw the news. I thought you might be upset.'

'Upset? Upset is what happens the corner shop runs out of blue raspberry lollipops. Or when Kimchi eats my shoes. I'm not upset, Michael. I'm incandescent.'

'You're going to kill Hale.' It's not a question.

'You bet your sweet arse I am.'

He sighs heavily. 'Bo, you won't get past security.'

'He won't stay locked up inside the Houses of Parliament forever,' I growl. 'I'll wait for him to come back out and talk to his adoring public. Then, when they're all watching, I'll...'

'What? Sink your teeth into his neck and kill him live on air? That'll really endear vampires to the watching public.'

'The man is a liability. He's not going to stop coming after us. Either we take him out or he'll do the same to us. It's dog eat dog – and I'm the pit bull.' I nod to myself and speed up even more. I rather like the image of Vince Hale as a yapping Chihuahua.

'Bo, this isn't sensible. You're better than this.'

'Nope. *You're* better than this. I'm not.'

A woman with a pram steps onto the street. I slam on the brakes and glare at her. She pulls back abruptly, her features frozen with fear.

'There are smarter ways to bring him down,' Michael says. 'If you want to do this, then of course I can't stop you.'

'Got that right.'

'But you'll regret it.'

My lip curls and I pull up the handbrake, ignoring the honks from the cars behind me. 'Is that a threat? Or a promise?'

'You're not a crazed guzzler. You're Bo Blackman. People are looking to you to know how to act, Bo. We need you calm and level-headed.' He laughs. 'I admit that it's not often I've seen you in that mode but you're certainly capable of it. Do you remember when you told me you loved me? The look on your face... I wasn't sure whether you were going to attack every Montserrat vampire who was staring at you like you were nuts or get down on your knees and propose.' His voice softens. 'You were so magnificent. You *are* so magnificent.'

I reach forward and turn the ignition key. The engine clicks off. 'Your faith in me is misplaced,' I tell him, not for the first time.

'No, it's not.'

I rub my eyes. 'He's never going to stop, Michael. Hale is going to keep going until every one of us is dead.'

'Rogu3 is inside Hale's computer.'

'He won't find anything incriminating.' My back straightens. 'Hale is too clever to leave a digital trail.'

'But you're cleverer. Think, Bo. How do you stop him without physically attacking him? How do you keep people on the vampires' side?'

'I can't.' The car horns behind me reach a deafening crescendo that make it difficult to hear Michael. 'Hang on.' I start the engine again and pull into the side of the road, letting them pass. Several drivers wrench their heads round, snarls visible on their faces. When they see who's been blocking their path, their expressions go slack. I'm the stuff of nightmares. Apparently.

'There has to be a way,' Michael says.

'There isn't. Hale doesn't care about anything apart from his mission to destroy us. I even told him about Alice Goldman and he made it clear he couldn't give a flying...' I falter.

'Bo?'

'Is Rogu3 there?' I ask suddenly.

Michael sounds satisfied. 'You've thought of a way.'

I flex my fingers. 'Yeah. Maybe I have. Put him on the line.'

THERE'S STILL a group of journalists outside Parliament, some talking to camera and others fiddling with their microphones. There's no sign of Hale. I grab hold of the nearest guy. 'Where is he?' I ask gently. 'Where's Hale?'

The journalist stares at me. 'He went back to his office,' he stammers. He points to the left towards Portcullis House where all the MPs are housed. Well, at least it'll be easier to get in there than into the Houses of Parliament themselves.

I nod once, release the man and stalk away. The journalists try to follow but, when I spin round, glare at them and bare my fangs, they think better of it. That's a first, I think sardonically. I should try it more often.

I loosen my shoulders and try to appear relaxed. A group of wide-eyed tourists gawks at me. When one pulls out their phone to take a photo, for once I take advantage and stop momentarily and pose. I'm not threatening, I project with my smile; I'm just here to plead my case with calm conviction.

As I swing left towards the Portcullis House entrance, something catches my eye. I frown and turn, my relaxed demeanour transforming in an instant. Standing less than twenty feet away is the female Kakos daemon. She's in full human glamour, proving that whatever magic my body gained from drinking Maria's blood has now dissipated. My feet try to spin away, my body telling me to run. I clench my fists and turn towards her.

She tilts her head as if amused and walks towards me. 'Ms Blackman.' Her voice flows over me and I can feel goose bumps rise up on my skin. I pay close attention to my thoughts; the last thing I want is for her to mess with my mind again.

'You worked it out,' she says mildly. 'That's a shame. It would have been so much easier on you if you'd simply done as I'd requested.'

'Is that how you knew I was coming here?' I demand. 'Because you're still in my mind? You're still reading my thoughts, no matter where I am?'

She tinkles out a laugh. 'Oh no, it's just that you're so very predictable. It wouldn't take a genius to realise that, after your most recent starring role, you'd come here to confront the human responsible. I wanted a ringside seat. It's unfortunate that Michael Montserrat calmed you down before you got here.' She wrinkles her nose. 'He can be so pesky. It's only going to get worse now he's human, you know.'

I fold my arms. 'Well, you're the one to blame for that.'

'Hmm. His turning is more complicated than you think.' She shrugs fluidly. 'It doesn't matter, though. He's not going to survive for long. None of you are. We would have let you escape.' Her smile is so evil that I shudder. 'Now we'll just kill you all.'

She takes another step forward as if she's about to make good on her promise right here and now, in front of everyone. Maybe she wants witnesses. Maybe that's her plan. I flinch then I lift up my chin and meet her eyes. I replay the meeting I just had with Magix in my head and the daemon freezes.

'It won't work,' she says, her expression masked. 'They won't be able to reproduce the gypsy's blood.'

In that instant, I know I have her. I drop my hands and smile – and this time it's genuine. 'Are you willing to bet the city on that?' I enquire.

'We'll kill her.' She licks her lips. 'It'll be a pleasure. Young hearts are tender morsels.'

I know she's reading my mind but it doesn't matter. Read away, bitch. I've got you now. 'You know how I'll feel about that but it won't change anything. I already have enough of her blood to give to Magix. I'm not going to take any more from her because I don't need to.' I eye her with amusement. 'How different will things be for you when you can't tell what your victims are thinking? How easy will it be then to rule the city?'

Her calm façade is slipping. 'We have been far more lenient than the vampires ever were.'

'You've been responsible for thousands of deaths. Blood is on your hands,' I hiss. 'Although you and I both know that the truth doesn't matter. It's all a matter of perception. If London perceives just how powerful Kakos daemons really are, you'll be finished. People are afraid of you but they don't know the truth. Not yet. When they do, you'll rue the day you attacked the Families. It'll go down in history as the day you sealed your fate.' I lean forward. 'Manipulate my mind again and it's a fait accompli. A fated fait accompli. Get it?'

I can see from her stance that she's itching to attack me. She can bring me down in a heartbeat but I'll still have enough time to yell out what she really is to the journalists behind me. Even if they don't believe me, my words will sow a kernel of doubt and that will be enough. Hope will make sure that Magix get Maria's blood. If it brings the Kakos daemons down then it works for me.

For the briefest moment, the daemon almost loses control. Shadows of her tattoos appear across her unblemished skin. My smile broadens. 'Another time, Bo Blackman,' she spits. Then she turns and melts away, disappearing into the crowds which are starting to gather.

Despite my confidence, I can't deny my relief. I pause for a moment, checking myself over mentally. I don't seem to have a headache so I think I'm still me.

I take a breath and address the watching humans. 'I'm here to talk to Vince Hale,' I say loudly. 'I want to come to an arrangement with him whereby the remaining vampires are left free. Our country is built on ideals of justice and liberty. I want to ensure it remains that way.' I resist the urge to add a wink. He can't kill me now, at least not today.

As soon as I go inside Portcullis House, alarms begin to shriek as they recognise that a vampire has entered the premises. The sound is high-pitched and piercing. I stop and, as slowly as possible, lower myself to the ground. Security guards rush in from all directions. Michael was probably right: I'd never have got close to Hale in the mood I was in before.

'I'm here to see Vince Hale!' I yell. 'I just want to talk.' I wait to be cuffed but it appears that politicians are more concerned with propriety – or at least the appearance of propriety. There are a few barked orders then I'm hauled to my feet.

A phone rings somewhere. I hear a mutter as it's answered, then one of the guards glances in my direction. 'Let her go. The

Right Honourable Vincent Hale would be delighted to meet her. I'll escort her to him.'

Good grief. Do they really use MPs' full titles when they talk about them? No wonder hardly anything gets accomplished here; they're all too busy showing each other deference and regurgitating meaningless words.

I don't wait to be hauled to my feet. I pull myself up and dust down my clothes. 'I have to look respectable for the Right Honourable Vincent Hale,' I say, arching an eyebrow at the guards. Their expressions range from downright terrified to awestruck.

The guard who answered the phone steps forward. 'This way, ma'am,' he says. He holds out his arm.

Like an eighteenth-century lady in a castle, I take it. Someone finally manages to turn off the alarm and we get into the lift. I'm half-expecting to see a long-coated, white-gloved man whose job is to press the lift buttons but we are alone.

The moment the lift doors close, the guard turns to me. 'I must know your intentions, Ms Blackman.'

I blink. He gives off an impression of coiled strength and concealed power. 'I told you, I'm here to chat to Vince Hale.'

'Is chatting all you plan on doing?'

For a security guard, he asks a lot of questions. I meet his eyes. 'Who are you?'

'Just answer the question.'

I take a shot in the dark. 'MI7?'

The guard doesn't react. 'Ms Blackman...'

The lift doors ping open. I use my arm to wedge them and look at him. 'There is a group based somewhere in London,' I say. 'It's been trafficking children and implanting their bodies with the souls of adults. Vincent Hale has released footage of me capturing one of them. The other "children" will have been alerted to the situation and will be trying to flee the country. I suggest you watch all exit points for unaccompanied minors before there's a real tragedy on your hands.' Without waiting for an answer, I sweep out.

Hale's office is in prime position in the corner of the building. His secretary appears to have done the sensible thing and made herself scarce. I glide through the door without knocking. Hale is waiting for me. 'You have some nerve coming here.' His voice grates on my ears.

'I don't see why,' I remark. 'You've been doing everything you can to get hold of me for weeks. You should be pleased that I've come to you.'

He emerges from behind his desk and perches on the side of it, drumming his fingers on its top. 'If you try to hurt me, it'll be the nail in the coffin of every bloodguzzler in the country.' He smiles coldly. 'So do it. Bite me and end the vampires.'

I raise my eyebrows. 'You'll die for your cause?'

'I'll go down in history. The fourth plinth will be filled with a statue of me.'

I tut. 'Delusions of grandeur are always dangerous.' I scan the room. Despite his words, Hale is convinced he's untouchable. He used that knowledge against the Families but he doesn't realise I can use it against him as well. He's been in power for far too long; if this goes to plan, I'll be able to change that.

Hale's laptop is on his desk, facing away from us. That doesn't work for me so I walk past him, the laptop and the desk, then stand in front of the window and glance down. 'Does it make you feel important to be up here?' I ask. 'Looking down on the city?'

'Is that why you're here?' he asks, sounding bored. He turns his head. 'To admire my view?'

I need him next to me. I blow onto the pane of glass and draw a smiley face in the condensation with the tip of my index finger. Hale still doesn't move. I curse inwardly and turn round.

His desk is expensive looking and old. One side is piled high with paper. 'Is this your in-tray?' I enquire. I reach over and take the top sheet of paper. When I see what it is, I grin. 'Hey! This is your tax return. I've always been curious about what you guys really make.'

He stands up and walks towards me before yanking the paper out of my hands. 'That's private,' he spits. 'Get to the point, Ms Blackman. Why are you really here?'

'Alice Goldman.'

'What?' He looks at me as if I'm mad. 'Her again?'

I nod. 'Yes. I've already tried to tell you about her. She was abducted five years ago and I think she's still alive. We can put our differences aside and work towards finding her.'

'Why would I care about some girl?'

I look surprised. 'She's a young, innocent human who's in trouble. And it's not just her; there may be hundreds of children in the same boat. I'm convinced they've been stolen from their homes and the streets for some terrible purpose. That's why I took that teenager from her apartment, not because I'm evil but because she's one of them. We have the chance to save her and others like her.'

'Oh please.' He rolls his eyes. 'Do you have any idea how many cases like this come across my desk? The important thing is stopping monsters like you. I don't care about this Alice. I care about seeing you and your kind destroyed for good.'

'Stop worrying about me and start worrying about the people you can save,' I snap. 'Alice Goldman needs your help. I've got twenty vampires ready to help. We can work together and find her. She's in the city somewhere and so are these other children. If we can just...'

'I'll see a thousand children dead before I work with the

likes of you,' Hale snarls. 'You're worthless. And so are children. They don't vote. Why should I care about them?'

Despite the situation, I can't stop myself from staring at him in disgust. 'Because they're children. They need our help.'

'Like I give a shit. Get out of my office, Ms Blackman. Tell the press downstairs whatever you like. Next time you see me, you'll be breathing your last. I'm going to kill you and all of your kind.'

I glance at the laptop. 'Why is that little red light on?' I ask innocently.

'What?' He looks over.

Obviously Hale is not very knowledgeable about technology because it takes a moment or two for the penny to drop. The piece of paper falls from his hands as his expression goes slack. I snap my fingers and the red light blinks off. Nifty. I'll have to thank Rogu3 for that later.

'As people keep reminding me,' I say, picking up the paper Hale has dropped and idly folding it into an aeroplane, 'public opinion is very important. This little chat has been streamed live around the country. I wonder what your constituents will think of someone who doesn't care about children being abducted.'

Hale looks from me to the computer and back again. His mouth drops open just as a figure appears in the door. So this is his secretary. The young man swallows nervously. 'Mr Hale, there's a problem.' He holds up his phone, showing a website replaying our conversation.

'Get that off there!' Hale roars.

I leapfrog over his desk and skirt past the hapless paper-pusher. My work here is done. Doors along the corridor are starting to open as more and more people come out to gawk. I note several approving glances; I guess Hale isn't as popular as he likes to think. I smile and get back into the lift. Hale is finished and I didn't need a single drop of his blood to get rid of him. Michael was right.

I press the button for the ground floor and rock back on my heels. That's when I realise I'm still holding the paper aeroplane in my hands. It'll be a cool memento. I turn it over in my hands — and suddenly I know how to find the people who've been stealing children.

CHAPTER 20
PAPER TRAIL

'How much did you pay them, Mildred?' She folds her arms and looks away. 'Come on,' I coax. 'There's no point pretending any longer. We know that's not your body. We know what you've done. Now it's time to make things right.'

There's a knock on the door then my grandfather walks in and hands me a piece of paper. I glance down at it and suck in a breath. 'That's ninety-eight in total.'

He nods. 'That we know of.'

'Ninety-eight lives,' I breathe. 'So many children who've slipped through the cracks because no one cared enough.' I shake my head. 'What about Alice?'

'No sign of her yet, although it seems that she was probably the first one they took. When there was such a fuss about her disappearance, the people responsible switched tactics and went for street children instead.' His voice is grim. 'The ones no one would miss.'

'I guess they held back on using her until some of the brouhaha died down. She's out there somewhere.'

'We'll find her. The education authorities have been extraordinarily helpful. Together with the ones who've been rounded up by MI7, most of the lost ones have been home-schooled.'

It makes sense. 'Home-schooling can easily be faked and it means they don't have to go through the rigmarole of actually going to school. I don't suppose there are many pensioners willing to sit through Maths lessons.'

Mildred rolls her eyes and breaks into the conversation. 'It's not the lessons that are the issue, it's teenagers. Who wants to hang around with those raging hormones on display all the time?'

I sit up. Finally she's giving us something. 'Did they suggest home-schooling, Mildred? The people who arranged your body swap?'

'Yes,' she huffs. 'They did.'

'And who are *they*?'

She turns back towards me disdainfully. 'You won't catch them. What are you going to do? Keep us all imprisoned? Torture us? You won't know who you're punishing. Is it me or is it the body I've taken that is suffering?'

'You don't care about anyone but yourself, do you?' I grab her arm. 'How much did it cost you to steal a life?'

'More than you'll ever see.'

My voice hardens. 'How much, Mildred?'

'Two million. Happy now?'

I exhale. 'Thank you.' I leave her where she is and follow my grandfather out of the room. Anger reverberates through me as the door closes behind us. 'A lucrative business.'

'Assuming you don't get caught,' my grandfather mutters.

I grimace. 'We don't have them yet.' I reach for my phone. 'But we will.'

～

'WE'VE UNCOVERED a considerable number of companies who pay the amount of tax you're talking about,' Foxworthy says. 'I still don't see how this is going to help. We've got ninety-eight minors in custody, courtesy of MI7, but nobody can tell for sure who's genuinely a child and who's a freaking body-snatcher. That is, apart from one we released this morning who was apparently attempting to flee the country because his parents didn't like his girlfriend.'

'I think, generally speaking,' I say drily, 'if you can trace their parents, then you'll know they are who they say they are.'

'These are lost children, Bo. Most of them *want* to be lost. They don't want us to know where they've come from.'

'If they're children at all,' I point out. 'But I see your problem. I really appreciate all the time you've taken on this.'

'The tax stuff is scut work but it makes a pleasant change from dealing with the mess left by the Families.' He says it without thinking and realises as soon as the words have left his mouth. 'Bugger. Sorry, Bo, I didn't mean it like that. I...'

'I understand what you meant. Don't worry about it. I kind of feel the same.' I smile up at Michael as he enters the room. Now he's looking healthier, my habitual feelings of lust stir. It doesn't help that he's wearing next to nothing. I eye his tight boxer shorts which leave little to the imagination and lick my lips. 'How many companies are we talking about?'

'Over three thousand.'

My attention snaps away from Michael and my jaw drops open. 'You're kidding me.'

'I wish I were. It's three thousand two hundred and thirty-three, to be exact,' Foxworthy says.

I pinch the bridge of my nose. That's a hell of a lot more than I expected. I guess the economy isn't doing as badly as I thought.

'I'm emailing you the list,' he says heavily. 'But you have to realise that these are only the companies that are paying their taxes in full. Anyone who's evading their bills isn't on here and, given how nefarious this activity, is, I don't think you're going to find them this way.'

'Oh, they'll be on the list. If Mildred gave us the correct information and my arithmetic is up to scratch, one of those companies is responsible for all this. They're hiding in plain sight. It's been their strategy all along.' A bloody clever one as well – but it's not clever enough. I'm going to find these bastards.

'If you say so.' Foxworthy still sounds doubtful. 'There's something else you should know. It's being kept out of the press for now but they'll pick it up sooner or later.'

'What's that?'

'Vincent Hale was attacked last night. He's in hospital. It was some group calling themselves the Parents' League for Justice. They've already claimed responsibility.'

I smile. 'Well, would you look at that?' I murmur. 'Strike one for the vigilantes.' Hale has also already resigned his position so at least I've achieved something this week. I'm not going to waste any more time on him. He's done.

Michael hands me a glass of warm blood and my skin tingles when our fingers brush. I give myself a little shake. 'You need to keep looking for more children, Foxworthy. Alice Goldman hasn't turned up yet and there will be others who've gone to ground rather than try to escape the country.'

'You know we will,' he growls.

On that promise, I hang up. 'Thank you,' I say quietly to Michael.

He waves a hand. '*De nada*. There's plenty of blood to go around, thanks to your grandfather. I haven't even had to offer myself up yet.'

I shudder at the thought. 'I wasn't referring to the blood.' I meet his eyes. 'You talked me down from a bad place, Michael. Things could have gone very differently if it wasn't for you.'

He sits down beside me. 'You forget sometimes that you're still very young for a vampire, Bo. And you didn't stick around long enough with the Families to get the kind of training in self-control that the others did.'

I raise my eyebrows. 'And whose fault was that?'

He covers my hand with his. 'You're going to get there. I'll keep you on the straight and narrow.'

The strange thing is that I know he will. Physically I'm stronger than he is now; I'm the one the others are looking to for leadership but I know I can't do this without him. I lean my head against his shoulder and take a sip of the blood. 'You're wonderful.'

He grins. 'I am.'

My phone beeps as Foxworthy's email comes through. With some reluctance I get to my feet. 'We've got work to do.'

I LOOK ROUND my motley crew. I'm still trying to remember all their bloody names, yet each and every one of them is watching me with grim eagerness. Horrifying as what's happening to these children is, it's also doing what Foxworthy said: it's giving us something to focus on. Instead of wallowing in our own grief and misery, we've got a mission.

I clear my throat. 'You've each been given a list of companies whose tax bracket resembles what we believe the bodysnatchers are making. Look into each one and be thorough. We need to know who's legit and who isn't. If you can find physical products, they're probably not what we're looking for. Any company that offers nothing more than vague services, is going to need a second and a third look. This is the way it goes, ladies and gentlemen. Detective work is dull but necessary. Just bear in mind that we're going to be saving lives.'

'Uh, Miss Blackman?'

I search round and find the ex-Medici vampire. 'Please don't call me that. It's Bo.' I try and remember his name in return. 'What is it, William?'

'Are we looking for specific examples of illegal activity?'

I grimace. 'Unfortunately, no. Whoever these bastards are, the face they present to the world is one of legitimate, law-abiding wealth. I know it's not going to be easy but we're searching for bland and boring. On the surface, anyway. Any company which fits that bill should be passed to Rogu3.'

The teen hacker raises his hand and waves at everyone.

'This isn't going to be easy,' O'Shea mutters by my side.

I glance at Maria. She's no longer hiding away but she's still hunched in the corner, never straying far from Rogu3. 'It'll be worth it,' I say. 'Let's do this.'

Although following the paper trail is vital, it's painstakingly dull and slow. I discount eight of the companies from my own list almost immediately as I've already heard of them. I'm fairly certain that the manufacturer of sugar-filled fizzy drinks isn't stealing bodies on the side. There are several others which I manage to cross off easily but others are bloody difficult, partly because the work they do is so incomprehensible. What happened to our nation of shopkeepers?

'What on earth is a ballast equities and transmissions firm?'

Billie, one of the Bancroft vampires, is sitting next to me. 'You think you've got it hard. Try this one. They do natural meditative enhancement holidays to South East Asia. They pulled down more money than Croesus last year.' She shakes her head. 'There are lots of IT companies as well. Most of what they do is gobbledegook to me.'

'Pass anything you're not sure about to Rogu3,' I say,

although the pile of paper next to him is growing by the minute. He doesn't appear fazed but there's a look of intense concentration on his face that I've not seen before. I raise my eyebrows at Maria and beckon her over.

'Is problem?' she asks.

'You need to watch Rogu3,' I say to her quietly.

She gazes at me suspiciously. 'Why?'

'He's desperate to find these people.'

She nods. 'For Alice.'

'And for you.' Maria looks away and I bite my lip. 'I'm worried that he'll overdo things though. Make sure he eats and takes breaks. I'm counting on you to look after him.'

Something flickers in Maria's eyes and her shoulders straighten. 'I do this,' she declares and strides off. Maria is a nurturer at heart; she'll take her responsibility seriously and stop dwelling on everything else we're doing. And everything that's been done to her.

Minutes meld into hours. For a long time, nothing can be heard in the room apart from the tapping of computer keys, the shuffling of paper and long, drawn-out sighs. The more time passes, the more desperately futile this search seems, despite my confident words to Foxworthy. I'm aware that the longer it takes us to find them, the more time they'll have to plot their escape.

I discard my fiftieth name and celebrate by standing up and cricking my neck. My body aches from staying too long in the same position. I hear a whine and glance over to see Kimchi gazing at me with sad eyes. Bugger.

'I'm going to take my dog out for a walk,' I declare to no one in particular. He bounces to his feet and lets out an excited howl, then he skitters towards me, tail wagging.

From out of nowhere, there's a hiss followed by a blur of movement. My grandfather's damn cat hurtles across the floor towards Kimchi. Too late, Kimchi realises he's suddenly prey and yelps, abruptly changing direction to get away from the flying teeth and claws. He crashes into Rogu3's chair and sends a pile of papers down to the ground. The cat, however, isn't giving up yet. It also veers off, smacking against Beth's legs in its haste to get to Kimchi. Beth jerks and spills the cup of blood she's holding, causing it to spatter in an arc across the shiny floor. The others stand up.

My grandfather, who had been dozing briefly in the corner, barks out an order. The cat skids to a halt although its tail lashes from side to side to indicate its displeasure.

'It's clearly not Kimchi that's the problem,' I say through gritted teeth. 'You should put that cat outside.' I stalk over and start helping to gather up the strewn paper.

'We're all on edge, my dear. The animals are sensitive to it.'

'Actually,' O'Shea pipes up, 'I feel pretty good. I had five Red Bulls earlier and I think I can do this. If the rest of you want to get some sleep, I can keep going.'

'I'll help,' Michael adds. 'I'm on a sugar high.'

I sigh in exasperation and toss the papers onto a nearby table. A photo on the top one catches my eye and I freeze.

'That sounds like an excellent plan,' O'Shea beams. 'Mikey darling and I will stay up. Alone. We'll work together to find the bodysnatching wankers, our eyes meeting occasionally across the room. When I find the company we're looking for, he'll be so delighted that he'll grab hold of me. He won't be able to stop himself sweeping me into his arms and...'

'You do know I'm in love with Bo, right?'

'She's very short. You'll end up with terrible backache. I'm much more your size.'

'Bo,' Michael says. 'Please rescue me from the crazy daemon.'

I don't answer. I pick the piece of paper back up and stare at it.

'Bo?'

I take a deep breath. 'Rogu3, do you still have that video of the hybrid witch attack?'

He blinks. 'Yeah.'

'Can you bring it up?'

Everyone else watches me. 'Bo,' Michael asks, 'what is it?'

I hand him the piece of paper. He glances down and frowns. Rogu3 taps a few keys and the video flashes up. I watch the silent flickering images and then point. 'Pause it there.' I look at Michael.

'They're the same person,' he breathes. 'The owner of this company and that man speaking to you. The human. They're the same.'

I bite my lip. 'Yeah.'

Beth peers down. 'Renascentia. Weird name.'

'It means rebirth in Latin,' my grandfather says. We exchange pointed looks.

'What do they do, Bo?'

I scan the details, aware that we're all holding our breath. Even Kimchi and the cat seem to be frozen as they wait for the answer. 'Consultancy,' I answer. 'It doesn't say what exactly they consult in.'

'It's vague,' O'Shea says. 'It fits.'

I clutch the paper tightly and stride out, straight into Mildred's room. She's asleep on the bed and none too impressed when I shake her awake. 'What the hell is your problem?' she yells at me.

I grab her arm and haul her up, half dragging her to the main room. She protests but when she sees all the taut faces – most of which belong to vampires – she subsides.

I point to Rogu3's chair. 'Sit down. When I knocked on your

door,' I say, circling round her, 'one of the things I told you was that I don't hurt children.'

She crosses her arms. 'Yeah? So?'

'Can you remember what you said?'

'That I knew that was a lie.' She scowls. 'What exactly is this about?'

'How did you know?'

She blows air out in exasperation. 'There was a bloody video! It was all over the internet!'

'Did you see the video?'

'I heard about it on the wireless. I already told you that. What difference does it make whether I saw it or not?'

I spin the chair round until she's facing the screen. 'Play it again, Rogu3,' I say. He starts it from the beginning.

Mildred glares. 'Why are you doing this? To prove that you're big and bad and scary? I've already got that memorandum, thank you very much.'

'Just watch it,' I snap. When the human steps out from the crowd, I jerk my head at Rogu3 to freeze it once more. 'There.' I point. 'Do you know him?'

There's a slight pause. 'The man? I've never seen him before in my life.'

I watch her face. Is this another dead end? Mere coincidence? 'Are you sure about that?' I prod.

She throws her hands up into the air. 'Yes! Now leave me in peace! The Geneva Convention is supposed to prevent this sort of abuse, you know.'

I roll my eyes. 'You're not a prisoner of war.'

'Certainly seems like it,' she grumbles.

'Mildred,' Michael interjects smoothly, 'do you know anyone else in the video?'

She looks away. 'No.'

Michael and I share a look. 'Mildred,' I say, 'who do you recognise?'

She presses her lips together.

'It'll go easier on you if you tell us.'

My grandfather strolls over. 'My dear Mildred, you and I both know that this is it for you. I can plead leniency in your case if you help us. You still have the chance to do the right thing.'

She still doesn't say anything.

He continues. 'That annoying vampire is my granddaughter. Before she was recruited into the Montserrat Family, she worked a series of dead-end jobs and had some badly chosen lovers.'

'Hey!' I protest.

My grandfather ignores me. His attention is fixed on Mildred. 'After she was recruited, she became a dark creature. She has done bad things and she will probably continue to do bad things. In fact, it appears the only person capable of affecting her conscience is her new lover. He used to be a vampire but is now human and he will grow old and die before her very eyes, causing them both unnecessary heartache and pain.'

Now he's really starting to piss me off. I straighten up and open my mouth but Michael shakes his head imperceptibly. I grit my teeth. My grandfather might be my own flesh and blood but he's straying perilously close to the line – and, for him, that's saying something.

'However,' he says, 'she is still my granddaughter. She is the light and love of my life. Her existence brings me joy and I will do my best to destroy anyone who hurts her.' He leans down. 'Mildred Beatty has no grandchildren but she could have had. That body she's wearing belongs to someone's grandchild, someone who deserves their own shot at life.' He smiles. 'Tell us who you recognise in the video.'

Mildred blinks. Her head drops. The silence draws out while we wait. I curl my hands into tight fists. Come on, Millie.

'The boy,' she whispers finally. 'I recognise the boy. The one you grabbed and knocked out. I saw him just before I transitioned. I wasn't supposed to. I was nervous and going to back out so they took me to meet him. He told me it was perfectly safe. He reassured me that it wouldn't hurt.'

Beth spins round and holds up a laptop. 'Look,' she says grimly. 'That kid is in virtually every photo. His name is Stephen MacIntyre. What's the betting that he's the mastermind of this entire operation and he's availing himself of its benefits along with his clients? That adult guy is probably just his minder.'

I stare at the screen, taking in MacIntyre's smiling face across an array of images, while my blood runs ice cold. I had him. I had him in my arms and unconscious, and I didn't know who or what I was holding. I can't believe it.

'We've found them,' I whisper. I look at the address for Renascentia. It's on the outskirts of the city. We can be there within the hour. 'Saddle up, people.'

'You'll tell the police, right?' Mildred shouts. 'You'll tell them I helped you? They'll be nicer to me. I'll return this body and get a suspended sentence or probation or something, right?'

My grandfather smiles and pats her arm. 'My dear, they're going to throw away the key and you will rot in prison for the rest of your short, miserable life.'

I have to force myself not to cheer.

CHAPTER 21
A SILVER PLATTER

The address we have on file for Renascentia is doubtless a front intended for people like Her Majesty's Revenue and Customs. The real business of stealing bodies will take place elsewhere. If we storm the place straight away, without putting a decent plan into place first, those in charge will have time to make their escape – and will possibly take all the remaining children with them. Let's face it, Renascentia is already going to be on red alert and we still need to find a way to reverse the bodysnatching process. But neither do we have time to pussyfoot around. Maybe the smart thing to do would be to wait for Foxworthy or to contact MI7 and let them deal with things from here. But Renascentia is already going to ground and I want to act now.

We fan out. Their building is in an industrial estate, surrounded by warehouses and nondescript offices. 'It's not exactly where you'd expect a well-heeled consultancy firm to be located,' O'Shea mutters.

I nod grimly. Hope waves at me, gesturing that she's annulled any protection spells or wards that were in place. Much as I hate to admit it, it's rather handy having her around.

I take a deep breath. It's not midday yet so we can expect that everyone who works there is already inside.

Chester ambles across the car park, a cheesy grin on his face. 'All the cars are taken care of,' he beams.

I glance at the Beth. 'The exits?'

'Covered.' Her expression is taut. I've seen the looks she was giving Maria back at base. She might not have exchanged more than three words with the teenager but she wants to destroy these people as much as I do.

I pull out my walkie-talkie. 'Rogu3?'

'I'm ready.'

I take a deep breath. William, the ex-Medici vampire, meets my gaze. I give him the signal and he jerks his head briskly in response. I might have worried about him before but he's proving a real asset. All that working against the well-oiled machinery of four vampire Families has come in useful.

The signal travels down the line. I stand up, flex my arms and crack my knuckles. And then we're off.

Beth and I stroll ahead. I push open the front door and find myself in front of an abandoned reception desk. I tense. Are we already too late? Beth nudges me and points to a closed door. She's right; I can hear the murmur of voices from the other side.

Without wasting any more time, I reach forward and turn the handle. The door opens without a sound and we're confronted by fourteen people, all sitting in a circle and all with worried expressions. Yeah, they'd better be damn well worried.

One man is on his feet. I don't recognise him from any of Renascentia's photos, so he's probably just middle manage-ment. Right now, however, everyone's attention is firmly focused on him.

'People,' he soothes, 'there's no need to worry. Everything is under control.'

'Three-quarters of our clients are in custody! One of them is going to start talking sooner or later and then we're finished!'

'No one is going to talk.' His voice is calm but there's a line of tension down his spine.

'Of course they bloody are!' someone else interrupts.

'No one is going to talk because we're pulling the plug. We're cutting our losses and getting out of here.'

'What does that mean, Phil? You're going to kill them?'

I cock my head. 'Yeah, Phil,' I say aloud. 'What *does* that mean?'

Fourteen heads snap in my direction. A few brave souls get to their feet but most simply look terrified. A middle-aged woman at the far side of the circle makes a run for it, dashing towards the emergency exit, but she's only human. We're vampires. Beth brings her down before her fingers can even scrape against the door.

'Nice try,' Beth hisses, yanking the woman up.

Phil, the manager, lunges to the side, going for a desk rather than an exit. Before he gets there, the cheap strip lights overhead flicker out and the computer screens dotted around the room go dark; Rogu3 has done what I asked and cut the power to the building. There are a few gasps from the others but most remain silent and frozen.

'Is that a panic button, Phil?' I enquire jauntily.

His fingers are still fumbling underneath the desk top. I tut and shake my head. 'It's not going to work.' I wave my hand around. 'We've cut the electricity.'

His chin jerks up and he scans the room. His jaw falls slack as he finally realises the futility of his situation. I wander over and clap him on the shoulder. 'Stand up, old boy. You look like an idiot.'

'How ... how...'

I tap my mouth. 'How did we find you?' I bend down until

my face is in his and he's getting an eyeful of my fangs. 'Because you lot aren't as smart as you think you are. Where are the bodies? Where are the people in charge of this shithole?'

Phil takes a weak stab at making a brave stand. 'You'll never find them.'

I smile. 'I wouldn't count on that.'

'I'm telling the truth!' he babbles. 'They're going to pull the plug. The ancients will die and so will the kids. And it will all be your fault.'

I keep my face mask-like, unwilling to let him see how worried his words make me. 'Ancients? That's what you call them? It's not very inspired.' I lick my lips. 'Don't worry though, Philly boy.' I run my tongue across my fangs. 'Ve have vays of making you talk.'

'I can't say what I don't know!' he yells back. 'None of us know where they're kept.' A self-satisfied smirk crosses his face. 'Renascentia isn't quite so dumb after all, is it?'

I step back and glance at Beth. 'They're shutting down operations.'

'Got that right!' Phil bursts out.

I wince. His voice is becoming painfully high and whiny. 'Shut up, Phil.' I pause and look around. 'And they've sent someone who's low down the food chain to tell everyone, calm their nerves and soothe the savage beasts. Why wouldn't they send a more well-known face?' I look Phil up and down. 'He's a nobody.'

'Screw you!' he spits.

'I told you to be quiet,' I say mildly. 'Beth, try that emergency exit, will you?'

Her brow furrows. 'What are you thinking?'

'Just give it a shot.'

She walks over and presses down on the bar. It doesn't budge. She tries again.

'Try and escape,' a vampire yells from the other side, 'and I'll rip out your throat! We've got you surrounded.'

I lift up the walkie-talkie. 'Rogu3, tell everyone to get away from the building now. You too. Get out of there. We need to run.'

'Eh?'

'Do it now.' I look at the terrified group. 'If you want to live to the end of day, you'll get out of here now too.' I nod to Beth and we both sprint for the door. I'd help the humans out if I could be arsed but they obviously know what sort of company they've been working for. None of them are innocent.

We burst out into the car park and keep running. I gesture wildly to the other confused vampires. 'Get away from the building!'

They do as they're told. I exhale with relief when I spot Rogu3's familiar head bobbing alongside two of the others. There are shouts as some of the more sensible Renascentia employees come out after us.

We're halfway across the carpark and nearly safe when the building blows.

I go flying. I might be strong and I might be able to face down most foes but, as the Kakos daemons have already proved, there's not much I – or any other vampire for that matter – can do against a bloody bomb. Glass flies everywhere and car alarms start to shriek. Acrid smoke fills the air.

Several metres away, Beth rolls onto her back and chokes. 'I smegging hate explosives,' she hisses.

I push myself up. 'Yeah, you and me both.' I look around. The others are getting to their feet, staring in horror at what's behind them. More than one of the vampires seems unable to move. Given the horror of a few weeks ago, I'm hardly surprised. 'Trigger warning,' I mutter.

The walkie-talkie buzzes ineffectually in my hand, its

wiring fried. I toss it to one side. 'If you can move and you're alright,' I shout, 'round the Renascentia staff up. We still have a job to do.' I stalk over to the nearest human. 'How do you like your boss now?' I ask. 'Rather than leave any loose ends, they tried to kill you all.'

Dull, shocked eyes stare at me and I hiss in exasperation. 'Renascentia tried to execute the lot of you!' I shout. 'Someone must know where Stephen MacIntyre is. Someone must know where the original bodies are being kept.'

There's a wheeze. It's Phil. Guess he managed to escape. That's a shame. 'I told you, we don't know a damn thing,' he says.

'You know enough,' I tell him. 'You're fully aware of what they were doing and you still chose to work here. They've been stealing children.'

'Homeless kids! Kids without futures! They lose their bodies for a while but when they get them back they get a nice fat wad of money to compensate for their loss. It's win-win.'

I shake my head. 'If you believe that, you're a fool.'

'We're a charitable institution! We...'

I draw back my fist and smash it into his solar plexus. He collapses without another word and I gaze at him impassively. 'You talk far too much.'

O'Shea, a few abrasions marring his normally perfect skin, walks up and looks down at him. 'Bo, you shouldn't have done that. If anyone knew where to look, it was him. If they're killing their own employees then they're on the way out. We've probably only got minutes to locate the kids before it's too late.'

'The half-breed has a point.'

I freeze at this new voice and slowly turn round. Standing right in front of me, and looking as if she just stepped out of the pages of a sodding fashion magazine, is the female Kakos daemon. 'I don't have time for you right now,' I spit.

She smiles in such a way that my very intestines quake in terror. 'Oh, but Ms Blackman,' she purrs, 'I can help you.'

'I doubt that very much.' I force down my fear and step towards her. 'Either kill me now or get out of my face. I've got more important things than you to deal with.'

'But we want to deal. That's why I'm here. Your earlier threat was most irritating and we'd like to ensure that you don't do anything silly.'

I raise my eyebrows. 'Silly? That's an interesting choice of words considering what your lot have been doing. Are you going to manipulate my mind? Plant thoughts into my head? Kill everyone I know? Would those things be considered *silly*?'

She inspects her fingernails. 'We are prepared to let you live.'

'Really?' I scoff. 'Is that because my death will ensure that Magix gets every drop of Maria's blood and you will be finished? Or because you're such a good and kind person?'

She drops her hands and looks at me with detached interest. 'Your aggression is most unbecoming.'

'Just as well I'm not trying to flirt with you then.' I turn to go. 'Now piss off.'

Her hand shoots and grabs my arm. 'Wait.'

I look back. I don't feel like I have much choice.

'We want you gone,' she says.

'Yeah, yeah. Tell me something I don't know.'

She continues as if I've not spoken. 'But given your negotiations with Magix, we are prepared to compromise. Remain quiet about the Romany blood and we will give you a choice.' She smiles. 'Leave the country with all of your bloodguzzling friends in tow and never come back.'

'Not happening.'

'Do that and I'll give you what you really want.' She drops her voice. 'Your humanity.'

The others are all back on their feet. Everyone is silent and watching me. 'I don't speak for them,' I say eventually, ignoring the wrench in my heart. 'And I'm not going to bargain on their behalf, regardless of what I might get out of it.'

'They'll follow you.'

I think of Michael. 'Not if I'm human.'

'Then keep your bloodguzzling nature, stay away from Magix and we'll give you X.' Her eyes dance. 'His head on a platter.'

Somehow I don't think she means that as a euphemism; she really would deliver his head to me. She nods, reading my thoughts. 'I'll even make the platter silver.'

'Gee. You're so thoughtful.' I cross my arms. 'Why would you do that to one of your own?'

'He broke our laws.'

'What?' I ask sarcastically. 'Genocide?'

She tinkles out a laugh. 'Please.' She shakes her head. 'No, X gave you blood.'

I frown. 'What are you talking about?'

'You used it on the boy.' Her lip curls and her gaze flicks to Rogu3. 'X gave you blood and you returned the boy to a human state. Then X did the same for the Michael Montserrat. We are only permitted to turn one vampire. X, however, did it twice. He deserves to pay for his actions.'

I stare at her. 'Seriously? That's what's annoyed you?'

'It's not about being annoyed, Ms Blackman, it's about our morality. Bloodguzzlers make their own choices. If we went around changing everyone, there would be chaos. Our blood is precious and is not to be thrown around like water.'

I can imagine there probably *would* be chaos. I remember X telling me the first time around that I wouldn't get any more of his magic blood. But right now, I couldn't give a cat's arse about all of this. 'I don't have time for this.'

'It's a good offer.'

'Screw you.'

She drops her glamour and her tattoos flash, snaking across her skin. Some of the watching vampires cry out. 'Think about it,' she says. 'And as a gesture of good faith, that woman in the red skirt knows where you need to go to save those children. I'd hurry if I were you.'

I look round, my eyes falling on one of the Renascentia employees – the one who initially tried to escape. When I turn back, the Kakos daemon has gone.

CHAPTER 22

TRANSITIONS

No matter which way I look at it, there's only one thing that counts now. Much as I hate to admit it, the daemon was right. The middle-aged woman has worked for Renascentia since its inception. One of her jobs is purchasing and she's sent a large amount of interesting medical equipment to the address we're now in front of. Unfortunately for her boss, she was quick enough to give up everything she knew after the attempt to kill her and all her colleagues. I guess assassination attempts and loyalty don't mix. Funny that.

Foxworthy has been alerted and even MI7 are on their way. In fact, every damn law enforcement official in a twenty-mile radius is probably screeching over here. I can already hear the sirens. I'm mindful of Phil's comment about pulling the plug, however. I need to find a way in and I need to find it now.

With my posse of bloodguzzlers at my heels, I stride to the front door.

'Let's go,' William growls. 'We burst in and take them all down.'

He's right. About the only thing we have on our side is the element of surprise. I nod grimly. 'Rock and roll.'

I gesture to the others to keep back then I kick open the door. There's no sudden alarm shriek but that doesn't mean Stephen MacIntyre – whoever he really is – and his buddies inside haven't already been alerted to our presence. I pull back my shoulders and step across the threshold.

A long white corridor stretches out in front. It's Spartan and pristine in equal measure. There are no doors but there's a lift at the far end. Bingo. I march forward, my eyes searching for booby traps or cameras or people. There's nothing.

I stop in front of the lift. There's a single call button on the left-hand side and I examine it for a moment. A hand snakes from behind me to press it but I grab it and pull it back, then shake my head. 'No. We take the lift and we're sitting ducks. There's only one way in and one way out.'

'That's good,' Beth says. 'It means they can't escape.'

I keep my gaze on the lift doors. 'A cornered animal is the most dangerous of all.' I mull it over for a full second and then wrench the doors open to reveal the dark lift shaft. It's a long drop. Of course, I think sourly. If you're going to build a secret lab to do evil things, then it stands to reason that it'll be deep underground.

There's a screech of tyres outside as the first armed police arrive. I frown. 'If you were an evil scientist who abuses magic and you were surrounded by police and vampires and there was no logical way out, what would you do?' I ask.

'Hostages,' O'Shea says from behind me. 'I'd take hostages.'

'And,' William interjects, 'I'd kill a few first to prove that I'm not kidding around.'

'Yeah,' I agree through gritted teeth. 'That's what I'd do too.' I take a deep breath and jump.

I'm halfway down the shaft before I manage to grab hold of the thick steel wires of the lift mechanism. My shoulder feels as if it's being yanked out of its socket but at least I stop my descent. Hand over hand, I lower myself down until I'm standing on top of the lift itself. It's a narrow, claustrophobic space but the ventilation grid in front of me offers some potential. Using my fingernails, I claw the cover off just as Beth lands beside me.

She looks at me dubiously. 'I'm not a sardine.'

I glance down the dark, cramped tunnel. 'I've done this before,' I whisper, assailed by memories from my former life – and a bloodbath that took place in front of my eyes. I was human then; now I'm considerably more powerful. *Now* I'm in a position to act, rather than just watch.

'Not all of us are petite, pocket-sized imps, you know.' Although her voice is low, I can still hear a glimmer of amusement.

I shrug at her. 'If you can't fit, then wait until I call.'

'Screw that.' Her mouth flattens. 'I saw the look in your girl's eyes. These wankers deserve to suffer.'

'You're preaching to the converted.' I take a deep breath and wiggle into the vent.

Stephen McIntyre, whoever he really is, might be a criminal mastermind and an evil genius who's responsible for more heartache than most other bastards I could mention, but he's not one for keeping up with his housework. I'm constantly forced to stop and brush long sticky cobwebs from my face and hair. The smell is worse than a ten-day-old corpse that's been left in the sun for too long. I breathe through my mouth and force my way along. I'm aware there's at least one person right behind me but I'm in too much of a hurry to turn round to see if it's Beth.

I push forward, trying to stay quiet while listening out for any sounds. I have no doubt that, when it comes to pulling the proverbial plug on all the stolen bodies, Phil was telling the truth. I just hope that MacIntyre really will use them as hostages to make his escape first. It's the only way I'll have any leverage.

After several minutes, when the stench is almost unbearable and I still can't hear a bloody thing, I give up on the vent. I can't see anything below but I can't hang around up here forever. I link my fingers together and smash them down on the aluminium. It creates a terrible sound and I pause, but there are no shouts or sounds of running feet. That makes me even more nervous. I slam down onto the floor of the vent once more; this time several rivets fly off. I kick out the panel and drop down.

I'm in a large, darkened room. Apart from some stacked furniture at the far end, it's completely empty. As I slowly turn and take it in, I realise I've been here before, not physically but via Maria's mind. This is the room where she was held, she and Alice and dozens of others. Even if I hadn't recognised it, the lingering air of despair and hopelessness is palpable. It reminds me of a school trip I took when I was a child, back when life was so very different. The silence which hovers over those old World War I battlefields tells of a grim and bloody past even without a history teacher barking in your ear. This room has that same tragic aura. I swallow the lump in my throat. If nothing else, being here hardens my resolve to do whatever is necessary. I'm going to ground Renascentia into dust.

There's a muffled squeak then another shape drops down from the vent. I glance back, freezing when I see who it is.

Maria straightens up slowly and looks around. Even in this gloom, and without my superior night sight, her pale face would be visible. The horrors she experienced here are etched into every pore.

'No way.' I march up to her. 'How did you get here?'

Her jaw works slowly, as if she's struggling to find the right words. 'I crawl through vent,' she whispers eventually. I have to strain to hear her.

I wave my arms around in angry panic. 'No, I mean here. This damn building! Why aren't you back at the warehouse?'

She gives me a blank stare. 'I come in car. With Alistair.'

'You shouldn't be here, Maria.'

'Smegging hell!' mutters a voice above. Beth's face appears. 'Get me out of here!'

I glare up at her. 'Did you know Maria was here?'

'How else would she have come down the lift shaft?' she asks, confused. 'I helped her.'

'She's not a vampire! She can't be here. It's too bloody dangerous.' I point upwards. 'Maria, you are going back in there and crawling your way back to...'

Beth sighs. 'She can't, Bo. There's a long line of vampires behind me. She'll have to wait until everyone's through.' She wiggles her way forward, performing a neat somersault and landing on her feet. Then she tosses her hair like she's in a shampoo advert. She doesn't smile. 'The girl deserves to be here.'

I ball my hands up into fists. 'She could get hurt. Or worse.'

'It's her decision.'

'She's a kid! She doesn't get to make decisions!' I put my hands on my hips and square up to Beth.

She blows her fringe out of the way. 'Has she ever done anything you've told her to?'

'That's not the point!' I turn back to Maria to harangue her but she's wandered off to the far corner. As I watch, she hunkers down and reaches for the wall, her long fingers tracing over something there.

I bite my lip and join her. Suddenly she seems very, very small. 'What is it?'

She points. I look and my heart constricts. Etched into the flaky plaster are the letters M + A, followed by a heart. 'Did you do this?' I ask softly.

Maria shakes her head. 'No,' she whispers. 'Alice must do it after...' She swallows. 'Just after.'

I remind myself to breathe. 'I'm going to get them, Maria. I'm going to make them pay. I promise you that. But you need to stay here. I can't risk you getting hurt.'

She doesn't answer, she just stares at the wall. I jerk my head at Beth. 'Stay with her,' I instruct. 'Don't let her out of your sight.'

She rolls her eyes. 'Who died and made you boss?' Then her face drops. 'Okay. I'll look after her.'

One by one, the others appear in the room. William seems particularly uncomfortable, clawing at his neck after he drops from the vent.

'Claustrophobic,' he grunts. A few seem to be in an even worse condition. The horrid room we're in doesn't help matters. I watch with narrowed eyes. When the last vampire, Chester, pops out, he immediately gets to his feet and stands on his tiptoes to hold the fallen aluminium panel back in place. Above our heads the vent creaks and groans. I edge over to the door. It's not easy to ignore the tiny claw marks round the edges.

'The place is surrounded by police now,' Chester whispers. 'I think they're preparing to storm it.'

'Then they're fools,' I mutter. 'With the lift as their only way in, they're going to be sitting ducks. We need to get moving and stop the bloodbath.'

'Or start one,' someone mutters. I don't disagree.

The door is unlocked because there are no young prisoners to keep trapped inside. I nudge it open with my toe and look through. Outside, the corridor is just as dark but there's a chink of light at the far end. I gesture at William and Billie. 'You two with me,' I say. 'Everyone else keep back until I give the signal.'

'What's the signal?'

'Lots of screaming,' I answer grimly. Then I tiptoe ahead.

If I'd expected a welcoming committee, I'd have been sadly disappointed. I kick open the door to reveal nothing more than the hospital bed where, once upon a time, Maria was strapped down. At least this room is cleaner than the rest of the lair. I stare at the two-way mirror. Is someone behind there now, watching us?

'Now what?' William whispers.

Before I can answer, there's a sudden crackle. William throws himself at me, knocking us both to the ground, and Billie lets out a yell. Unfortunately her reactions are slower and she's struck in the chest by some kind of magic bolt. She collapses and I hear a laugh. Rolling free from William, I spring to my feet.

'Who'd have thought that a Medici vampire would help Bo Blackman?' says a disembodied voice. 'Did you like my little magic display? I've been making friends, too. Hybrid witches are very easy to work up into a rabid frenzy.'

I scan round. The magic attack – and the voice – have to come from somewhere; bolts like that don't materialise out of thin air. I spy a hole in the wall next to the mirror; it looks like some kind of dumb waiter linking this room to the next.

'It's such a shame that you all didn't die when you were supposed to. The bombs were unexpected but a marvellous boon. Why do you think I was so happy to join in with the hybrids when they tried to mop up the mess? You see,' the voice continues, 'vampires live long lives. People don't think it's fair that bloodguzzlers get to experience so much more of the world but most of them don't want to have to drink blood to achieve longer life. We offer a better alternative. *We're* the healthy option. And Tov V'ra kindly rid us of our biggest competition. It's not a bad thing that the police are at our door, you know. It means we can go public. There will be some loud noises and complaints for a while, but when we show that we offer what the vampires could not, the possibilities will be endless.'

'You steal children,' I hiss.

'Children who don't have a future. It's population control. Besides, think how much smarter the world will be when we have three-hundred-year-old minds to draw from. Soon we won't need the children from the streets, we'll grow bodies in test tubes. Clone ourselves then implant our minds into waiting vessels. The public will come around, especially when all the vampires are dead and that option is closed off.'

I snort. 'Hardly anyone becomes a vampire anyway.'

'And hardly anyone wins the lottery but it doesn't stop people trying. Eternal youth for everyone. Don't you want that grizzly old grandfather of yours to live forever?'

I ignore the question. He's very proud of himself; like all psychotic tossers – and I include myself in that group – he believes he's doing good. He likes the sound of his own voice. I want to keep it that way. The more distracted he is, the better.

William kneels down and checks on Billie as I prod further. 'Alice Goldman has a family. She has a future.' I refuse to speak about her in the past tense.

'She was an experiment,' he says. 'She ended up causing more trouble than she was worth.'

'Mm.' I pause. 'Tell me, how did you get hold of enough of her blood to make it appear as if she were dead?'

'Well,' he says, 'that's interesting. You see, I...'

I launch myself at the mirror, aiming smack bang at the centre where the glass will be weakest. It's neither reinforced nor bullet proof – and it's certainly not Bo Blackman proof. I guess that when this place was built they never expected it would be the scene of their final showdown. There's a loud crack as the glass shatters. I ignore the shards and leap through towards three shadowy figures.

I hear a bang and fling myself sideways to avoid the shot. I'm too slow, though, and the bullet grazes my shoulder. I wince in pain and shake myself. It'll take more than that to bring me down. There are whoops and war cries as the other vampires flood through from outside. William abandons Billie in favour of leaping after me.

I straighten up and cast my gaze across the three figures. There's the human man whom I remember from the street confrontation; he is holding the gun. Stephen McIntyre's skinny teenage frame lurks next to him, together with Scarlet, the hybrid witch, who has magic sparking up all around her.

The vampires fan out on the other side of the destroyed mirror, each one ready to spring towards us and help win the day. I'm not sure I've ever felt this powerful before.

'You're outnumbered,' I say, focusing my attention on the fake teen.

He smirks but he can't quite pull it off; he might look like an adolescent but his attitude doesn't match his appearance. I've spent enough time around real teenagers lately to tell the difference. Real puberty is a one-time deal, no matter what age your body might be. Now I know the truth, I wonder how I could have ever believed he was a kid.

'Sure,' he says easily, 'we're outnumbered. But I still have the upper hand.' He raises his hand; clasped in his fingers is a remote control.

Before I can do anything, he presses a button. A shutter begins to rise on the other side of the tiny room. I suck in a breath when I see what it reveals.

It's another two-way mirror. This one looks into a long room filled to the gunnels with pallets wired up to complicated-looking computer monitors. On each pallet a body lies, eyes closed as if asleep. Most are white haired and wrinkled, but not all.

'One hundred and thirty-two ancients,' MacIntyre says. 'The souls have been swapped but we keep the bodies in stasis. It's tidier that way.' He points. 'You see the one nearest us?'

I glance at the sleeping body. It's a gaunt-looking man with pasty cheeks and the pallor of death. 'Let me guess. That's you? The original you?'

McIntyre appears annoyed that I worked it out before he could tell me. 'Yes and...'

I take an educated guess. 'Cancer?'

He scowls. 'You don't know everything,' he spits. He reaches over and raps sharply on the glass. A small figure emerges from the back of the room. She's instantly recognisable, despite the dyed, cropped hair and mature clothing.

'Alice.'

'Well,' he demurs, 'not as *you* know her. We call her Eliza.'

I watch as the freak in Alice's body strolls up to the mirror. A small smile plays around her lips. My body is rigid with rage.

'You see,' McIntyre says quietly, 'you can't win. If you destroy us, then you also destroy Alice. And,' he waves a hand at himself, 'whoever this body belongs to.'

My lip curls. 'You don't know?'

'Why would it matter?'

I want to punch his smug, self-satisfied face but I can't. It's not *his* body that I'd be punching.

'You're angry,' he murmurs. 'You shouldn't be. This body enjoys a better standard of living that its original inhabitant did. We took him off the streets in broad daylight and nobody cared.'

'Aliens?' I ask, trying to buy some time. William throws me a strange look.

McIntyre claps his hands. 'Why, yes! You have been busy, haven't you? We wore masks to cover our faces in case we were spotted but there were some fabulous side effects.' He leans towards me. 'The first person who saw us reported us to the police. They wouldn't even take a statement!' he crows. 'We didn't need to use magic. People are so stupid sometimes.'

From the other side of the mirror, Alice/Eliza's head jerks upwards. I smile. 'You're right. People *are* stupid.'

Michael, O'Shea, Rogu3 and Hope crash down from the ceiling. I wince as Michael seems to hurt himself in the fall but he gets back to his feet quickly enough. In fact, he's the first one to grab hold of Alice's body and hold her fast. I watch O'Shea's lips move as he no doubt makes some daft quip. His stance is ready and his eyes are alert, however.

MacIntyre's jaw drops. 'What's going on?'

It's satisfying to see the first hint of panic in his eyes. I lurch to the side then spin and kick the gun out of the adult male's hands. It clatters to the ground and William scoops it up.

'Hey,' the man says, holding up his hands. 'Now hold on a minute...'

William shoots before I can say a word. In slow motion, the man drops to the floor. William grins and darts over, grabbing hold of him and sinking his fangs into his throat. Scarlet reacts, throwing out magic at both of us. One bolt smacks William on the forehead, making him to drop the man, while the other sears into my arm.

'Uhhhh,' William groans.

I glance at the limp body on the floor. 'You deserved that,' I tell him.

'I'm a vampire!' he protests. 'It's what I do.'

I consider this. 'True.' I leap towards Scarlet.

She goes into a frenzy, magic bursting out of her. I'm forced back several steps and I crash into McIntyre as I move away. The other vampires tense as if they're about to join the fray. I wave to them to keep back for now.

'I'd stop that if I were you, Scarlet,' I gasp. 'There's a witch on the other side of this glass who knows exactly how to suck out all of your magic. Black and white.'

She frowns as if she's confused. Her eyes are glowing but there's still a glimmer of awareness in their depths. 'What...?' she begins, stumbling over words as her head swings from me to Hope. Her magic fizzles out.

MacIntyre curses in disgust. 'You can attack all you want but you can't hurt me. And you can't hurt Eliza.' Despite his brave words, there's a tremor of uncertainty in his voice.

I gesture to the nearest vampires. They come into the observation room; two of them grab Scarlet and two grab MacIntyre. Neither try to struggle.

'You can't reverse the process without me. Unless you let me negotiate my freedom, all those children will be trapped without their own bodies.' He licks his lips. 'Some are already on the point of death as it is.'

I tap on the glass. 'That's a powerful witch out there,' I say casually.

'So?' he sneers. 'We used more than magic to create the transitions.'

'And,' I add with a small smile, 'a very skilled computer expert.'

We watch as Rogu3 and Hope go to a nearby monitor. Rogu3 turns it on and it flickers into life as Alice/Eliza continues to struggle against Michael's grip. Michael might only be a human now but she's in the body of a kid; she doesn't have the strength to fight against him, even in his weakened state.

I take the gun from William and fire four bullets into the glass. Shards fly everywhere. Scarlet shrieks and McIntyre ducks but everyone else ignores it. I kick away the shattered glass as O'Shea peers in.

'Bo,' he says plaintively. 'You do realise you could have just opened the door, right?'

I shrug awkwardly. 'It seemed more dramatic this way.'

McIntyre strains against the vampires who are holding him. 'Stop this!' he yells. 'You can't...'

'Got it,' Rogu3 says, sounding satisfied. He stands up and walks down the room, stopping at one of the beds. 'This is her.'

Eliza/Alice's eyes go wide. 'No, no, no, no, no.'

'Hope?' Rogu3 says. The witch smirks and joins him. She holds her hands over the inert body and murmurs an incantation while Rogu3 attends to the monitor above her head. I forget to breathe.

There's a yelp and Michael jerks. 'Electric shock,' he mutters.

'What?' Alice/Eliza mumbles. 'What's going on?' Her smooth brow furrows and she looks around. 'Where am I? What's going on?'

Michael doesn't release his hold. 'How do we know it worked?' he asked.

'You'll never know,' McIntyre hisses. 'That's why you need me.'

'Tell Beth to bring Maria in here,' I order.

One of the vampires in the far corner nods and vanishes. Moments later, Beth and Maria appear and the crowd of vampires parts as they walk towards us. Maria stares through the two shattered windows at the slight figure in Michael's arms. I grab her arm. 'Don't say anything,' I warn in an undertone. 'Not yet.'

My words are unnecessary. Alice's gaze has already fallen on the tall teenager by my side. 'Maria?' she whispers.

Michael releases his hold and Alice runs forward. I shout out to her to be careful of the glass but she doesn't notice. She jumps over and flings herself at Maria. 'I thought you were dead!' she sobs.

I look back at McIntyre. 'That's good enough for me.'

He begins to shake. 'No! It's temporary,' he babbles. 'She won't stay like that unless I...'

The body in front of Rogu3 and Hope begins to twitch. 'I think she's arresting!' he yells.

'Of course she is!' McIntyre shouts. 'By reversing the transition you're going to kill all these people! Do you want their deaths on your conscience?'

I look at Michael. He raises his eyebrows. 'This one is your call,' he says. 'I have no argument with whatever you do.'

'Me neither,' O'Shea, my daemonic conscience, says.

I nod at them and turn to MacIntyre. 'I'm trying to be a good person,' I say softly. 'But it's hard.' I touch my chest. 'There's a darkness inside me that will always be there, no matter what I do. If rescuing the children means letting the bastards who stole their lives die, then so be it.'

Hope reaches down to Eliza's body, feeling for a pulse. 'She's gone.'

I exhale. Reversing the process means a lot of sudden deaths. I examine my feelings, wondering if my guilt should be heavier. 'So be it.' I point at MacIntyre's original shell. 'Do that one next.'

'No!' he screams. 'You can't!' With a show of sudden strength, no doubt fired by adrenaline, he lunges for me with his hands curved into claws. 'You can't! You can't do this! We did what you bloodguzzlers do! All we wanted was more time. You can't kill us for that!'

'We're not killing anyone,' I say. 'We're rescuing them. Unless you want to tell us how to reverse the process without killing the original souls?'

He stares at me. 'You can't.' His body sags. 'You're a bloody monster.'

I think about this. 'Yeah,' I agree. 'I probably am. But my

heart is in the right place.' For the first time in a long time, I actually believe it is.

~

WE EMERGE into the fresh air, a ragtag band of vampires and human children. The area is surrounded by blue flashing lights.

'You know,' William comments, his arm round a limping Billie, 'that was a lot of fun.'

I raise my eyebrows. 'Fun?'

He shrugs. 'Yeah. And I feel all warm and fuzzy inside too.' He purses his lips as if he's never experienced that kind of emotion before. 'I like it. I think I'm going to do more of this.'

I'm thoroughly confused. 'Attack subterranean laboratories?'

'No. Help people. Humans.' He gestures at some of the children. 'I'll fight crime. Stop any child anywhere from being vulnerable enough to have shit happen to them. That kind of thing.'

I think of the woman I overheard in the witch-owned newsagent's a few days ago. 'Maybe,' I suggest, 'you should find a local community and integrate yourself. Help them out and live amongst them so you really get to know what's going on.'

He nods thoughtfully. 'I like that idea.'

We smile at each other. Maybe there is hope for a vampiric future after all.

Foxworthy approaches from the mêlée of police officers. 'You know I don't approve of vigilantism,' he begins.

I sigh, exasperated. 'Oh come on.'

'You didn't let me finish. I don't approve of it but you did good.' He pats my arm. 'I've been getting reports from MI7. They suddenly have a lot of bewildered teenagers in their custody and that's down to you. I'm proud of you.'

I blink rapidly. I'm not convinced he'll be singing the same tune when he see what we left behind in the lab. 'Er … thank you.' Behind him, Nicholls roll her eyes. I try not to smile. Some things never change.

'Someone's here,' he says.

A woman appears from one of the waiting police cars. She takes a halting step, then another, as if she's not sure whether she's doing the right thing. Her husband, holding baby Hope, gets out as well.

Alice chokes out a sob. 'Mummy?'

That's all it takes. Mrs Goldman starts to run and stretches her arms out wide. Alice's father is right behind her. The second she reaches us, she swoops down, grabs Alice and pulls her into a tight, warm hug which speaks of unfailing and unreserved love. My cheeks feel wet. I blink furiously and clench my teeth. Then Michael makes a strange noise. I glance at him. Okay. It seems that everyone is crying.

'I knew it. I knew you were still alive,' Mrs Goldman gasps. She holds Alice to her as if she's afraid to let her go. As if releasing her will mean that all this is nothing more than a dream.

'Mum, I can't breathe.'

Mrs Goldman blushes and relaxes ever so slightly. 'Sorry, baby.' She looks over her shoulder at me. 'Thank you.' Her voice catches. 'I'm not sure I can ever thank you enough.'

I snatch a look at Maria, who's watching the reunion with a blank, impassive mask. 'Actually,' I say softly, 'I think there is something you can do that would cover it.'

CHAPTER 23
TODAY

'So what feels better?' my grandfather enquires. 'Seeing all those children rescued and returned to their families or re-homed, or seeing Stephen McIntyre and his cronies dead?'

I roll my eyes. He merely shrugs. 'By the way, Maria left you a present when she came back to pick up her things. I took the liberty of putting it in the fridge.'

I frown. 'She shouldn't have done that.'

'It was her choice. Young Alistair took his things as well. I rather think that, now they'll be living on the same street, he'll have less time to spend on his criminal hacking activity. I'm not sure Maria approves of what he does and the pull of young love can be strong.'

'Not just young love,' I murmur. Kimchi comes up and noses at my hand. I stroke his ears. 'Speaking of packing up, we should probably go ourselves.' I look round the warehouse. 'We can't stay here forever.'

'Well...' he demurs.

My eyes narrow. 'Well, what?'

'I might not have told you the entire truth when I said that MI7 didn't know we were here.'

'Excuse me?'

'You're excused.'

I put my hands on my hips. 'Arbuthnot Blackman, you need to explain right now what's going on.'

'They've been monitoring your actions and they're quite impressed. They are prepared to offer you the premises and their contents if you agree to help them out from time to time.'

I glare. 'I thought you said I'd never make a spy.'

He throws back his head and laughs. 'Not as a spy. As a ... consultant. Now that you've shown you can play nicely with all the other little tribers.'

'The other vampires aren't staying. They want to head off and make their own lives. Join other communities.'

'Yes.' He scratches his chin. 'There will be a few problems with that, you know.'

'We'll deal with them if and when they occur.' I feel remarkably serene – until one of the sirens suddenly goes off. Kimchi whines. I whip my round to the camera feed and grit my teeth. It's show time. Bugger.

THREE GULPS of Maria's blood swirls round my body as I go out with O'Shea and Michael flanking me. The Kakos daemon has been outside for half an hour. I'll give her this – she's bloody patient.

'Well,' she says, tapping an immaculately manicured fingernail against her mouth. 'Have you come to a decision, Ms Blackman?'

I smile coldly. 'I don't respond well to ultimatums.'

'You haven't answered my question.'

'The tide has turned,' I respond. 'Maybe you saw the news? We're responsible for rescuing more than a hundred children. The vampires are the heroes of the hour.'

'You know as well as I do that public opinion turns on the toss of a coin. As you said, you're the heroes of the hour but what happens in the next hour? It wouldn't take much for everyone to remember that you're nothing more than a bunch of bloodsucking fiends.' She regards me steadily and switches tactics, apparently desperate to do anything to rile me. 'X pretended to be your friend but he manipulated you. He used you.'

I shrug. 'He didn't enter my mind like you did. He didn't force my own thoughts against me.'

'He didn't enter your mind because he didn't need to. You were only too happy to fall into line.'

'I used him as much as he used me,' I say frankly. I step forward. For the first time, I realise I'm not afraid of her and I'm not afraid of X. 'Tell me, do you consider yourself evil?'

'That's an absurd question.'

I cross my arms and wait. The daemon sighs, as if under a great imposition. 'No,' she answers, sounding bored. 'I do not. The things we have done are necessary.'

'You massacred the Families because you were afraid of them.'

'We massacred the Families because they pinned the blame on us every time they needed an excuse to kill someone.'

I meet her eyes. 'Everyone is afraid of you. We've always known that Kakos daemons were to be feared. If you had simply communicated your displeasure to the Families, they would have stopped.' I flick my finger at an invisible piece of lint. 'But you chose to act first, to kill rather than communicate. I'd call that evil.'

'Please,' she scoffs. 'Evil doesn't exist. Everyone has the

capacity to do bad things, just as everyone has the capacity to do good things.'

'That's bullshit. Evil does exist.' I smile. 'You and I are perfect examples of that.'

She raises an eyebrow. 'You don't really think you're evil.'

'I think I have the capacity for it but I have people on my side who will keep me right.'

'The half-breed.' She scoffs. 'And Michael Montserrat.' There's no denying the sneer in her voice. She doesn't even glance in his direction. 'You do realise why X turned him to a human, don't you?' Her lip curls. 'He was jealous. He still is. He wants you to leave Montserrat. In a way X is right. A vampire mating with a human will never work.'

'Maybe it will and maybe it won't.' I raise my arms nonchalantly. 'You know, X also *saved* Michael. He would be dead otherwise.'

'Am I to take it that you do not wish for X's head?'

'I'd love his head. I'd love to rip it off his shoulders myself.' The daemon smirks and opens her mouth to speak. She doesn't need to read my mind to know I'm telling the truth.

I hold up my index finger. 'I'm not finished. Yes, I want him dead. Maybe I always will. I want you dead, too, and every other Kakos daemon in London. There's part of me that also wants to be human. Part of me that still wants to attack every black witch I see, despite the pact I've made with them. I want to see Magix go bankrupt. I want Vincent Hale to die very, very slowly. I want a lifetime's supply of blue raspberry lollipops. I want to be able to fly. I want unicorns to exist and no child to ever suffer again. I want happiness and sunshine and smiles for the entire world forever.' I toss my hair. 'But it's not about what I want. Reality isn't always perfect, in fact sometimes it's sodding terrible. But we manage. We get through it. We live to fight another day.'

She rolls her eyes. 'Spare me the philosophical sermonising.'

'Fine. This is the deal. I will not leave London. The vampires will not leave London. You got what you wanted and the Families are dead and buried. It's a new age now. You will no longer find yourself blamed for a trail of corpses. But if you or X or any other Kakos daemon ever lifts a finger to harm us or manipulate us again, then Magix will receive a vial of Romany blood and instructions about what to do with it.'

'You think that's a win for your kind?' she sneers. 'It's not much of a happy ending.'

'This is about survival, not vengeance. Nobody needs more blood on the streets. There's been enough already.' I pause. 'Consider the vampires as peacekeepers rather than warmongers. That makes us better than you. We have the method to destroy you and we choose not to use it.' I smile again. 'Unless you force us to.'

'That doesn't make you better, it makes you weak,' she spits.

I gaze into the distance. 'Aggression is so unbecoming, don't you think?' I smile. 'Now scat.'

She stares at me. I can almost feel the ice emanating from her. 'Fine. We'll leave you alone. There are hardly any vampires left anyway.'

'There'll be more some day soon,' I respond calmly. 'By removing the Families, you've removed centuries of irksome tradition. We're no longer above human law but we no longer have to abide by our ancient strictures either. I wonder what will happen when we start recruiting Romany people as vampires,' I muse.

'You wouldn't dare.'

I shrug and smile. The daemon throws me one more glare, then spins round on her heel and stalks away.

O'Shea moves up beside me. 'Man, I'm still shaking.'

Michael walks up to my other side. 'Well done.'

I bite my lip. 'I hope I've done the right thing. In truth they all deserve far, far worse and we all know it.'

'It's harder to stop a fight than to start one. We're safe. And every vampire has a new beginning. They don't have to spend the rest of their lives looking over their shoulders.'

I slip my hand into Michael's and he squeezes it. We watch the Kakos daemon as she reaches her car and gets into the back. Someone else steps out and I draw in a shocked breath as I realise it's X. Perhaps he's being punished after all. He raises a hand, whether in gratitude or acknowledgment or flippancy, I don't know. Then he returns to the vehicle.

As the three of us watch them drive into the city dusk, lights begin to spring up across the skyline, illuminating London. I smile. She might be a bitch sometimes but she's my bitch. I love this damned place.

My phone rings, breaking the temporary peace. I glance at the caller ID and answer. 'What's up, D'Argneau?'

Michael stiffens.

'The lengths I go to for you, Bo Blackman! It's taken me days of digging but I think I finally have something. It turns out that Streets of Fire is involved in some serious illegal activity. I don't know about Kakos daemons but this could bring them down. They're breaking just about every rule in the book. In fact...'

'Don't tell me,' I interrupt.

There's a moment of silence. 'Excuse me?'

'Put it in a file and sit on it. It's information that might come in useful in the future but I don't want it right now.'

'Do you have any idea how many hours I put into this?' His voice is rising.

'Feel free to bill me.'

'You bet your sweet arse I will, darling.'

Michael leans across. 'Call her darling again,' he growls into the phone, 'and you'll live to regret it.'

'Who's that?' D'Argneau asks suspiciously. 'It sounded like Michael Montserrat.'

'Mm. Thank you so much for everything, Harry,' I say warmly. 'You've been fabulous and I'll make sure all the other vampires know in case they wish to procure your services for themselves.'

D'Argneau manages an impressive volte-face. 'All the vampires? I know there's not very many left but *all* of them?'

'You could be the sole vampire representative if you play your cards right,' I purr. 'They're no longer above the law so you might find yourself very busy indeed.'

Appeased by thoughts of legal grandeur, D'Argneau hangs up. I lean my head against Michael's shoulder, pretending not to notice that O'Shea does the same on his other side.

I'm a vampire, a creature of the night with occasional psychotic tendencies. Surprisingly, I think I'm alright with that. Maybe the world needs people like me, at least for now.

I have no idea what tomorrow will bring, whether it will be good or bad or simply ambivalent. I'm not convinced any more that tomorrow matters. Today is what counts and today I have the man I love by my side while the people who matter to me are hale and hearty. Sure, tomorrow's another day. But today is pretty sodding good – and that's all any of us can ask for.

ABOUT THE AUTHOR

After teaching English literature in the UK, Japan and Malaysia, Helen Harper left behind the world of education following the worldwide success of her Blood Destiny series of books. She is a professional member of the Alliance of Independent Authors and writes full time, thanking her lucky stars every day that's she lucky enough to do so!

Helen has always been a book lover, devouring science fiction and fantasy tales when she was a child growing up in Scotland.

She currently lives in Edinburgh in the UK with far too many cats – not to mention the dragons, fairies, demons, wizards and vampires that seem to keep appearing from nowhere.